JINX

MELISSA K. MAGNER

STARTED BY PATRICIA M. KASPAR

Maoliosa Press

ISBN-13: PB: 978-1-7322506-0-4
EBOOK: 978-1-7322506-2-8

Library of Congress Control Number: 2018908262

Summary: At the start of summer vacation in 1972, two girls find a box in the ocean with cursed contents and are thrown into an intricate web of lies and deception, forcing them to make choices that affect the safety of themselves and their small town.

Content Warning: *Jinx* is a dark fantasy/mystery novel intended for teens and young adults. It contains depictions of the following: cursing, delusions, addictions, suicide, torture, murder, violence, gore, stalking, kidnapping, guns, explosives, and trauma.

Front cover design by Bespoke Book Covers.

Illustrations by Viktoriia Davydova.

Printing edition 2018, United States of America.

FOR MY GRANDMOTHER, PATRICIA KASPAR

Who constructively encouraged my love of writing
And who created Jan and Shelley before I was born

1932-2012

ACKNOWLEDGMENTS

I would like to start out by thanking my grandmother, Patricia Kaspar, because if she never started the original *Jinx* decades ago, this book would not be a reality. It is because of her years of writing and dedication to her work that I was motivated to continue and re-create this story for the both of us. I love and miss you infinitely, Grandma; thank you so much for inspiring everything I do.

Thank you to my parents, Heidi and John Magner, who were the first to read *Jinx* and who provided endless support throughout this process. Thank you to my younger sister, Jaclyn, for helping me choose cover designs and for listening to me read aloud as I edited my drafts.

Thank you to my friends and family who read early drafts and gave me constructive and valuable feedback. You are all amazing and I cannot thank you enough. And, of course, thank you to my friend since childhood, Jessica Angell, for being the Shelley to my Jan and for accompanying me on all our adventures (many of which inspired—albeit loosely—some scenes in this book).

Also, a special thank you to Peter and Caroline from Bespoke Book Covers for creating this beautiful cover for *Jinx*, as well as my editors, Sasha and Angie, and my illustrator, Viktoriia Davydova.

In The Beginning

SHE MADE THE BOX IN HER IMAGE, DURING A TIME when time was not recorded and in a world that was at its genesis. When the Earth was nothing but ocean—when there were no mountains and no land—she took the emerald from the sea and the silver from the sky. Inside the little box, she placed her treasure, and within her treasure, she placed something else entirely. And then, she waited.

Chapter 1
THE BLUE BOMB

JAN JENKINS, OR "JINX" AS HER FRIENDS CALLED her, rounded the corner in top gear and eased her car into the gentle slope leading down to Shelley's house. Her aging, bright blue automobile bumped against the pavement and threatened to stall as usual, but Jan knew the car and the corner too well to be intimidated. She turned the car off and waited as she coasted toward the driveway at the bottom of the dip.

Judging the moment carefully, she flipped it back on, smiling with satisfaction as the car responded with one of the loudest backfires it had ever produced.

She screeched into the driveway, which angled up steeply from the street to a quaint two-level cottage above. The car, which she had lovingly named "the Blue Bomb," rebelled at the angle, gave out a reproachful wheeze, and stalled obstinately. Jan pulled the emergency brake and piled out, pulling her sleeping bag and suitcase behind her.

"Hey, Shelley, I'm here!" she called out as she banged the car door closed. When it creaked open, Jan slammed it closed again, trying to make it catch.

"I see you are, Jan," came a deep-voiced reply from the workshop beside the house. The voice belonged to a wiry, slightly graying man of about fifty who stood, hands on his hips, observing her flamboyant arrival.

"Hi, Mr. W." Jan rolled out the "W" for Mr. Waldbauer's benefit. It never ceased to rattle him. "I hope you don't mind if I park in your driveway while I get my things out," she said as the car door slowly swung open again. Finding both of her hands to be full, she gave it a mighty push with her foot. This time, it remained shut. Jan grinned. "Is Shelley home?"

"Up here, Jinx!"

Looking up, she saw Shelley leaning on the porch railing. She was shaking her head, silently warning her friend to ease off a bit.

Everyone seemed to be intimidated by Mr. Waldbauer. He was the Captain of the police department after all, and he had a reputation to maintain. In a town as small as Aledale where every other person knew your name, someone as proud as Mr. Waldbauer prided himself in his social standing. But he had never intimidated Jan. In fact, not much intimidated her, save the occasional roller coaster and heights.

"I'll be right down," Shelley called, quickly disappearing from view.

"It's sure nice of you to let me spend the summer here, Mr. W.," Jan said, turning back to Shelley's dad and smiling brightly. She had known Shelley and her dad for five years now, shortly after Mrs. Waldbauer had passed away. "My folks were worried about me staying alone while they're out of the country."

"Yes," Mr. Waldbauer responded. He gave her a strained smile. "Scotland, was it?"

"Visiting the homeland," Jan said, tucking her long red hair behind her ear. Though she'd been born in Scotland, her family had moved to the states when she was less than a year old. "I usually go with them, but they wanted to stay until September. I'm afraid I'd be missing too much school if I went along."

"Quite understandable. Well, there are a few things we have to discuss before you and Michelle make too many plans." His Austrian accent gave the impression of a well-running machine—sharp and precise. "I'll be up after you've settled," he continued, "and we will go over the rules." Having said that, he went back into his workshop and began sawing, somewhat more vigorously than before.

"What took you so long, Jinx?" Shelley asked, taking the wooden stairs down to the driveway two steps at a time. "I've been waiting for you all morning." She took Jan's sleeping bag out of her hands to help lighten the load.

"Oh, first I saw my folks off, then I had to go down and pick up my traffic school certificate. They always make you wait there, which takes forever. Anyway, I'm finally done. Just think of it: four Saturday mornings shot because of two lousy tickets."

Shelley grinned and rolled her eyes. "That'll teach you not to go speeding around in the Blue Bomb. I told you it was too conspicuous. I have no idea how you even make it go that fast."

Jan shrugged, following Shelley as they climbed the steps back up to the little house perched on top of the small garage and workshop. The stairs, bright white with a fresh coat of paint, were offset by the neat blue trim of the banister. A light breeze rustled the lace-like leaves of the gnarled pepper tree that framed the balcony, bringing along the fresh smell of salt from the bay.

"Let's put your things in my room," Shelley said as she pushed open the screen door at the top of the stairs. "Dad doesn't like it scattered all over the place."

As they headed through the kitchen, Jan noticed that Shelley's skin had already started to tan from the summer sun—something Jan always wished hers would do. Shelley loved lying outside and sunbathing. Although Jan usually joined her, she hated having to quarantine herself to the shade when she didn't have sunscreen with her.

Whenever Jan got burned, her dad would always joke that it was simply one of the pitfalls of being a redhead. Jan didn't think it was funny, though, especially when more than fifteen minutes outside without sunscreen left behind scaly red patches that stuck around for weeks.

The girls weaved through the living room and out onto the porch. Shelley's bedroom had been fashioned out of half of a small balcony with swing-out windows facing the sea. Mr. Waldbauer had built the room himself, which he proudly pointed out to anyone who would listen.

The only problem for Shelley was that she had to pass through all the rooms to get out. That way, he would always know what she was up to.

Shelley tossed Jan's sleeping bag and suitcase toward the corner of the bedroom and plopped down on her bed, which occupied the bulk of the space. A small desk, dresser, and closet took up the rest of the room, leaving a small spot on the floor for Jan's sleeping bag. The rest of Shelley's bedroom was covered in clothes and jewelry that she never found the time to hang up. In fact, the only organized part of Shelley's room was her walls, and that was only because Mr. Waldbauer didn't let her hang pictures or posters. According to Shelley, he was worried it would ruin the paint job.

The one picture he did allow her to hang, however, was of her and her mother. Jan guessed it was taken when Shelley was around four years old.

The resemblance was breathtaking. Just like her mother, Shelley kept her dark hair cut just above her shoulders and never left home without pinning it back. She was petite like her mother as well, and had the same small, upturned nose, warm eyes, and olive-brown skin.

Sometimes, Jan thought that was why Mr. Waldbauer was so protective of Shelley. She looked so much like her mother that Jan wondered if, deep down, Mr. Waldbauer was scared of losing her as well. She never said anything about it though; she was worried she would come across as presumptuous.

"I know you hate it messy," Shelley said, giving Jan a half-apologetic, half-teasing smile, "but not everyone can have a bedroom as organized as *yours*."

"It looks like a tornado destroyed your room," Jan said, flashing back a grin. "Doesn't your dad complain?"

Shelley laughed. "He certainly does."

"Well, since I'm to be sleeping amongst your closet," Jan said, crinkling her nose playfully, "I'll toss ya' for the bed."

Shelley snorted. "We'll trade off. I know you and your two-headed dimes."

"I don't have a two-headed dime."

"Well, you sure can call them right. Makes me wonder." She kicked off her shoes, hurling them across her room into a pile of clothes. "Look at this," she continued, brightening. She pointed to a little pot on her desk that housed a cactus, its crown adorned with a halo of pink flowers. "My dad brought it home for me the other day. I forget what it's called, but it's adorable, isn't it?"

"Mammillaria," Jan said, giggling when Shelley shot her a grin.

"I thought you'd know that," Shelley said. "Your mom's love of botany really rubs off on you, doesn't it?"

Jan shrugged. "Not really. I just pick up on her plant-lingo from time to time. A Mammillaria's a great little plant, though. It doesn't need much water, so it'll be perfect for you and your forgetfulness."

Shelley fake-scoffed before squealing out in delight. "I can't believe this, Jinx! We've got the whole summer ahead of us. There's no school, my dad will be at work ninety percent of the time, and the water is great. What more could you ask for? I hope you brought your bathing suit."

Jan nodded as she returned to her suitcase and knelt beside it. "I did. And I got something for you."

"For me? What is it?" Shelley's eyes widened as she scooted to the edge of her bed, craning her neck to see.

"You mean, what are *they*," Jan corrected her, reaching into her suitcase and proudly producing two red and blue strings of firecrackers. "Not one, but *two* strings of firecrackers for the Fourth. See?"

"Are you serious? That's sick! Where'd you get them?"

"Some kid at a theater camp a few summers ago sold them to me. I bought like ten packs. Figured you'd never know when you may need one."

"My God, that is such a *you* thing to do." Shelley's grin quickly faded. "We can't light them here though. My dad would have a fit."

"We'll find a place where they won't be wasted."

Shelley nodded in agreement. "Maybe until then, we should put them in the back of the Blue Bomb. That way, he won't come across them accidentally."

"That's probably a good idea," Jan said through a chuckle. Mr. Waldbauer certainly wouldn't react well if he found Shelley in possession of firecrackers.

"It's only been two weeks of summer vacation and he's already watching me like a hawk," Shelley said irritably. "I never say anything because I don't want to piss him off, but my god, I'm going to go insane."

"What does he think you're going to do?"

"I don't know," Shelley replied, shaking her head. "I don't even know if he knows. I think he just feels better when I'm home, but there's no way I'm going to spend my entire summer vacation indoors." Shaking her head again, this time violently, she repeated, "There's no way."

"Maybe you'll be able to get some air now that *I'm* here," Jan suggested, even though she knew it wasn't true. If anything, Mr. Waldbauer would keep a stricter eye on them now. He liked Jan, but it was obvious that he thought she was reckless.

Shelley had once told Jan that although Mr. Waldbauer was impressed that she was an honor student, he thought she was far too confident and brash. Though he hadn't meant it as a compliment, Jan took it as one. What was so bad about being a little bold from time to time?

The sound of footsteps on the stairs and the banging screen door brought Shelley to her feet.

"Come on. Dad said he wanted to talk to us," she said.

Shelley led Jan back to the kitchen where Mr. Waldbauer was pouring himself a cup of coffee as they arrived. He looked the two over with a frown.

"Pull your pants up, Michelle, before they fall off," he ordered firmly. "And you too," he continued, turning to Jan.

Hip-huggers, T-shirts, and tennis shoes weren't exactly his idea of appropriate dressing, but he was always one to carefully monitor the appearance of both himself and his daughter.

"You can't pull them up," Shelley said as she draped herself over a chair. "They're made like that."

"That's the fashion, Mr. W," Jan chimed in.

"Mr. *Waldbauer*," he emphasized, shooting Jan an icy glare as he poured a cup for her.

Jan could always count on lively discussions with him over a cup of coffee, whether it was about the world's situation, stock market fluctuations, or the behavior of teenagers. That was one of the reasons Mr. Waldbauer enjoyed having Jan over, despite the fact that she sometimes irritated him. Shelley hated those discussions, and Jan was the only person who would entertain his ramblings about national politics.

Unlike Jan, Shelley was laidback and reticent. She couldn't stand coffee, and she certainly didn't like to talk about weighty subjects. She was the type who would rather be out sailing in the bay with the high school Mariners Club.

Mr. Waldbauer sat down beside Shelley at the small kitchen table. "First of all, Jan," he said, "I want you to remove that 'vehicle' from my driveway and park it on the street. I don't want it to leak oil on the cement, and I'm afraid it might roll there by itself if you don't do it."

"I'll move it," Jan replied, grimacing at the intense heat of her first sip.

"Personally, I don't think sixteen-year-olds have enough experience to be out driving around," he stated flatly.

"How are we supposed to get experience if we don't drive around? That's illogical, Mr. W," Jan said. Upon noticing his reddening face, she decided it would be best to withhold the information about her traffic tickets.

Mr. Waldbauer leaned back in his chair, ignoring her remark. "I want you both to let me know where you're going this summer. You must be back when I tell you to. This is honor code, ladies. You know very well how long my work hours can be. Don't take advantage of them."

"We won't," Shelley said. "Is that all?"

Mr. Waldbauer nodded curtly.

Once Jan finished her coffee, Shelley quickly pulled her back to her bedroom.

"Another inheritance scandal," Jan heard Mr. Waldbauer mutter as they left. The sound of crinkling newspaper echoed from the kitchen. "People have too much money these days."

"I've got an idea," said Shelley as soon as she closed her bedroom door. "I know a lady down at the Fun Zone who runs a small gift shop. She's always looking for driftwood and shells. We could make a deal with her or something."

"Fun Zone?" Jan asked. She paused, a sly grin appearing on her face. "I have a feeling the only reason you want to go there is because you know Gabriel is working this summer."

Shelley giggled, but she didn't protest. Gabriel Parri was a year older than them and about to enter his senior year. Shelley had been infatuated with him since the ninth grade. His father ran a food stand at the Fun Zone, which Gabriel had been helping out with since he was fourteen. Three years later, Shelley still insisted on dragging Jan along to see him whenever possible. She had promised Jan that this would finally be the summer she mustered the courage to ask him out, but Jan took her promise with a grain of salt. Shelley had made the same promise last year.

"That's true," Shelley confessed, shrugging. "But I've got another reason too. We could make extra money. If we check the tide table for low tide and hit up the beach when we can collect the most shells, we can take them and whatever else we find to Ms. Johnson. She's the lady who runs the gift shop."

Jan smiled and fell back onto Shelley's bed. "Sounds fun. And extra money is a big plus."

"Yeah, I knew you wouldn't say no to that," Shelley said. "Hang on, I'll get the newspaper." She left, jumping over the obstacles in her bedroom to reach the door, only to return a few moments later with the weather section. The girls hastily spread it out on Shelley's bed and flipped to the tide table.

"It says here low tide for Thursday morning is at 6:34 a.m.," Jan said through a groan. "Crap, Shelley, that's way too early."

"You'll have all summer to sleep in, drama queen. Azuline Cove would be the best bet for collecting. There are lots of starfish and shells in the rocks, and the sandy part is alive with sand dollars." When Jan didn't respond, Shelley nudged her playfully. "C'mon, where's your usual sense of adventure?"

"It shows itself when I'm not dying of sleep deprivation," Jan said as she slid off Shelley's bed and onto the carpet. She rested a hand on her forehead and let out a long sigh.

Shelley bit down on her lip to keep from laughing, and Jan responded with a theatrical smile. Then, after a moment of due consideration, she concurred.

"Fine. Azuline Cove it is," she said, accepting her early-morning fate.

Chapter 2
VOICES ON THE WATER

THE BLUE BOMB ROLLED INTO THE DESERTED parking lot at Azuline Cove half past six the next morning. The doors of the car flew open as it lurched up against the cement curbs. Jan reached down to turn the car key, but the engine was quicker; it had already died.

"Boy, I've got her trained," Jan said.

Shelley climbed out and squinted into the gray-white mist.

"It's foggy," she said, zipping up her jacket and shuddering at the lonesome sound of the foghorn in the distance. "You can't even see across to the Fun Zone. I guess I'll just have to keep my eye on your hair to guide me."

Jan responded with a teasing glare in Shelley's direction.

Even in the thick fog, Jan's hair was visible. She was easy to spot regardless, but her long and wavy red hair, which was always tangled no matter how many times she brushed it, was the staple of her look. It stood out sharply against her pasty skin, the way a cardinal stands out in the snow. Her bright blue eyes, nearly invisible freckles, and aquiline nose topped it off; Jan didn't usually go unnoticed. The one thing that gave her away without fail, however, was the ring she wore on her left index finger. Her dad had brought it home from Switzerland three years ago, and Jan hadn't taken it off since. The ring itself was just the size of a nickel, with a thick silver band and a yellow gemstone on top. It was a citrine stone, her father had told her—her birthstone.

Her dad always brought home the best souvenirs. This summer, he promised to bring her a special gift from Scotland.

Using her thumb to fiddle with the gem, Jan observed the fog in the cove, which hung silently over the water.

"I don't like it when it's so quiet," Shelley said, jolting Jan out of her thoughts.

"Well, who'd you expect to be crazy enough to come to the beach at this time of morning except us?" Jan said as she reached under the dashboard to deposit the key.

"You're not leaving the key in the car, are you?"

"Nobody will be able to find it under the dash."

"But didn't you put the firecrackers in the trunk? What if someone finds them? We'll get in trouble."

"Shelley, look at this place," Jan said, gesturing to the empty cove. "It's deserted. Nobody's going to be here this early, and if they are, I highly doubt they'll decide to look inside my car. Besides, I don't want to bring my keys to the cove and risk losing them."

"But..."

"Honestly, Shelley, chill out. It's 1972—everyone either wants a Thunderbird or a Galaxie 500. Do you really think they'd risk trying to steal this old thing?"

Shelley shrugged and grinned wryly. "Well, nobody but you could drive this car anyway," she said. "It'd either stall, catch fire, scare 'em with the shimmy, or the hood would fly up."

"It's only caught fire twice," Jan protested, "and it only shimmies over thirty-five." She slipped off her tennis shoes and stuck them in the back seat. "I've got some bags for the shells."

The two girls started off toward the lapping sound coming quietly from the edge of the water. Seagulls cried out as they ascended from their sand crab breakfasts, disturbed by the young and eager invaders.

"I've never seen the tide this low," Shelley said as they reached the water. "I'll bet the rocks where we usually dive are sticking out. We could stand on top of them."

"We've got an hour or so until the tide turns," Jan said. "Let's split up and work fast, then we can go diving. Maybe the fog will lift in the meantime."

"Good idea. I'll head near the point, you go toward the island."

"Back here in twenty minutes?"

Shelley responded with a nod and took one of the bags from Jan. After walking a few yards away, she disappeared into the fog.

Jan kicked her toes into the sand, watching the grains fly out ahead of her feet in small landslides, where shells of all sizes, broken and whole, lay white against the wet sand. Jan looked them over, her head bent toward the ground as she walked along the shore.

Some looked like little gas station signs, others were just ugly bits of broken clams and mussels intertwined with brown clumps of seaweed. Jan searched carefully for the tiny cone-shaped shells that could be used for making necklaces.

After she found a few good ones, she stopped for a moment and stood close to the water. She watched a small wave retreat, then dug deep into the cold sand with her toes where a tiny air bubble marked a sand crab. A flock of gulls somewhere out on the point squawked noisily and flapped away. She listened and squinted to see, but the fog refused to yield its secrets.

Azuline Cove was a tiny bay within a bay formed by a curved spit of land and rocks. The rocks from the ocean swells, which surged in past the lighthouse on the breakwater tip, sheltered the cove. Though the lighthouse still functioned properly, complete with its bright lights and foghorn, it was close to being abandoned.

Now, at low tide, the waves were silent as they lapped against the shore. In fact, barring the occasional blare of the foghorn, the beach was eerily quiet. The silence, as stifling as it was, made the mellow chug of a boat and the sound of voices drifting over the water all the more noticeable.

Jan perked up and strained to hear. Considering the direction of the sound, the boat seemed to be dangerously close to the rocks. The fog still covered the point like thick gray cotton candy.

Who would be stupid enough to go near the point with the tide so low?

A deep, firm voice cut through the fog. "Here, I said here!"

"How do you know we'll ever find it again?" questioned another in a raspy whisper.

"Nolan, just *drop it*," demanded the first.

The order was followed by a quiet splash. The motor chugged faster and the sound became softer as the boat moved slowly away from the cove.

"Any luck?"

Jan gasped and swung around. Shelley stepped back and put her hands up, startled by Jan's reaction.

"You okay?" she asked.

"Yeah," Jan replied through an exhale. She put her hand to her heart. "I just didn't see you."

Shelley giggled. "Sorry. Were you able to find anything?"

"A couple of things here and there. Lots of necklace shells

and some ashtray types. How about you?"

"I got a couple of really nice sand dollars, but not much else."

Jan turned and looked back out at the water. "Shelley," she whispered, "did you hear anything?"

Shelley tilted her head. "A couple of cars and a boat, I think. Why?"

"Have any idea what kind of boat it was?"

"Why?"

"Just think, Shelley. You're the mariner. What'd it sound like?"

"Something like one of those rental motorboats, I think. It couldn't have been much larger by the sound of the engine. But *why?*"

"That boat came almost up to the point, which is either very dumb considering the tide or very suspicious."

Shelley only shrugged as she took out one of her loose pins and fixed it back in her hair.

"I heard two voices on the water," Jan continued. "One man told another to drop something into the ocean. It sounded like they were in a hurry. Maybe they're crooks?"

Shelley let out a loud laugh. "Stop being so melodramatic. They're probably fishermen dropping their bait tanks. Besides, judging by the sound of the boat, I'm pretty sure they were headed back to the marina. That sounds normal to me."

Jan sighed. She had expected Shelley to be more curious.

"Hey, look! The sun's starting to break through the fog," Shelley pointed out, changing the topic. "It'll burn off in about half an hour. Let's put the bags in the car and go diving."

"Sure. I want to dive near the point..." Jan stopped halfway through her sentence as Shelley raised an eyebrow at her. "Just for fun, you know?" she said innocently.

"Well, you won't find anything but sand dollars and starfish out there, but since that's what we're after, I guess that's the spot to look."

They walked back to the parking lot, estimating their future fortunes on the way. Jan set the worth of their findings twice that of Shelley's, undaunted by her friend's reasons why her price was outrageous.

"You're just not a good business-woman," Jan said as she tossed her bag into the car's back seat.

"And you're too confident," Shelley retorted. "What you mean is that I'm not a wheeler-dealer like you."

"Perish the thought, my dear friend," Jan said, taking off her jacket and shorts before adjusting the straps of her bathing suit. "When we get to the Fun Zone, let *me* do the talking."

"Fine," Shelley said, tossing her shorts and jacket into the car, "but pardon me if I hide while you peddle our wares. Race you to the water?"

"You're on," Jan said. They took off across the sand and

plunged headlong into the bay.

"*I win,*" Jan cried out in a singsong voice.

"Only because you have longer legs."

Jan stood in the waist-deep water, shivering. "I'll be glad when it gets warmer."

"Landlubber," teased Shelley, splashing Jan playfully. "You're always cold. Good thing you're not a mariner."

"I guess that's true," Jan said, grinning. "C'mon, let's swim out to the point."

Shelley didn't need any coaxing. Anything athletic was straight up her alley. The girls paced each other, swimming evenly through the small swells as they made their way to the point.

In a matter of moments, they reached the outermost rocks and carefully worked their way toward one they could climb onto. The swells began to come in larger as the tide started to change.

"Watch out for the barnacles," Shelley warned as she tried to climb up on one of the rocks. "They may cut your feet."

"Try this one over here. It's the flattest." Jan carefully raised herself onto the rough outcropping, panting for breath when she finally sat down.

"What's the matter, Jinx? Winded already?" teased Shelley as she pulled herself up beside Jan. The remark cost her an elbow to the ribs.

"This *has* to be where they were."

"Where who was?"

"The men in the boat."

Shelley scoffed. "Oh, them again?"

"They had to be inside the cove, or else they would've been lifted onto the rocks by the waves. See, it figures: they came around here where the water was quiet so they could dump something."

"Jinx, your imagination is running wild. I suppose you think it was a body?"

"It was too small a splash for that."

"You're serious, aren't you?"

"Of course I'm serious. Let's look around. It's pretty shallow now compared to what it usually is, and the sun is coming out. We can probably see the bottom really well."

"Okay, but if we actually find a body, I'm getting the hell out of here," said Shelley, laughing nervously.

After waiting for a wave, they dove out and away from the sharp rocks. They floated for a moment to catch their breath, then did a jackknife dive and slid smoothly below the surface of the water.

Blinking against the burn of the salty water and wishing she'd brought a mask, Jan worked her way out from the rocks and scanned her surroundings. Gray-brown sand dollars lay flat on the glimmering yellow sands of the seabed, which she collected as she forged ahead. Though it took effort against the growing force of the tide, she dove closer to the main bank of rocks that formed the curve of the cove and pulled herself along them hand over hand.

For a fleeting moment, she thought she saw something reflecting in the sunlight, nestled in the rocks just ahead. As she tried to swim forward, she could feel the strength of the swells increasing, tearing her away from the rocks one moment, then hurling her mercilessly toward their razor-sharp edges the next. Finally, lungs aching for air, Jan pushed hard on the bottom with her feet and shot up, gasping as she reached the top.

"Hey, Jinx," Shelley called out from a few yards away. "We have to move away from the rocks. We're going to get cut up if we don't."

"I'm just going to do one more dive. You take what we've got and swim over to the closest beach."

"You can't go near those rocks now until the tide is in. This half-way surf is tricky."

Jan pretended not to hear but took careful bearings in case she had to leave before she found what she was after. The swells were now rising over the flat rock where they had previously rested. She filled her lungs with air and dove deep under a white-frothy wave. The movement of the tide began to stir up the sand, making the water murky.

It has to be close, she thought as she pulled herself nearer to the rocks.

A searing pain stung her leg, and Jan felt the flesh on her calf rip as she caught her skin on a cluster of barnacles. Her lungs already ached from lack of air, now this—she knew she had to surface soon.

Before she shot up again, however, a blurry emerald reflection caught her eye. Jan struggled to get close, fighting against the current that pulled her back again. Reaching out frantically, she grabbed the shining object and pushed hard on the sand, catapulting toward the surface.

She floated there limply on her back, breathing in great gulps of air. As she turned to swim to the shore, she realized that she was clutching something in her hand. Though the salty water stung her leg, she ignored it; her curiosity and excitement were far more pressing.

Shelley was waiting for her when she reached the shore.

"Christ, Jinx, you were under for a long time," she said. "I was beginning to...holy shit! What happened to you?" She pointed to the blood trickling down Jan's leg. "And what's that?" she asked, this time pointing to the object in Jan's hand.

Jan plopped down next to Shelley. Although she had felt the larger cut, only now did she notice the smaller ones beginning to form around her knees and shins. Still, she ignored the sting of her legs and stared at the object before her.

"This is it, Shelley. This must be what those men threw

overboard."

She held out a small silver box, large enough to fit a pair of baby's shoes. The strange green eyes of a mermaid, faintly but carefully carved onto its metal lid, stared back at her.

Chapter 3
THE MERMAID BOX

LIGHT GLINTING FROM THE BOX MADE JAN BLINK and rub her eyes. She leaned unsteadily on one arm and took a shaky breath.

"You okay?" Shelley asked.

"Yeah. Guess I stayed down a little too long," Jan replied, keeping her eyes on the box.

She turned it over, observing the fine lines etched on the sides. A small padlock tightly guarded the mysterious contents. Other than the mermaid carved on its lid, there were no markings to indicate ownership.

"This is heavy for such a little box," she said, tossing it carefully in her hands.

"Jinx, if those men really did throw this overboard, don't you think they're going to come back for it?"

Jan shrugged. "Finders, keepers."

Shelley bit her lip nervously but scooted closer to Jan nonetheless. "What do you think is inside of it?"

"I'm not sure. I may be able to open it if I have a hairclip, though. Do you have one on you?"

Shelley nodded, then pulled out her clip and handed it to Jan, who began picking at the lock intently. After a few seconds and a slight twist of the clip, the lock sprung open.

"Sometimes I worry about the things you know how to do," Shelley said.

Jan grinned and took off the lock. "Don't give me all the credit. My dad is the one who taught me. Besides, this one isn't too complicated."

"I'm worried it'll explode," Shelley muttered.

"Now look whose imagination is running wild," Jan teased. Still, she handled the box more cautiously now that the thought had been planted in her mind. Once she had slipped the lock out of its hook, she slowly opened the lid.

"Rocks," Shelley said, disappointed. "Seriously? That's it? Who would put a bunch of rocks in a box like this? That's so stupid."

"Wait," Jan said. "Maybe it's not."

She turned the box over and dumped the rocks onto the sand. A small shiny object clinked out on top of the last one.

"It's just jewelry," Shelley said, picking up a copper-golden necklace. She held it out in front of her to get a better look. Jan studied the oval locket at the end of the chain as Shelley snapped it open and shrugged. "Nothing. No pictures or anything. Maybe it's worth a lot?"

Jan observed the blackening bits of the chain. "Probably not," she said. "It looks ancient."

"I doubt Ms. Johnson would take it anyway. She has a thing for making her own necklaces."

Jan held the box back up and peered inside. Loose grains of sand stuck to the bottom. Wiping them to the side with her fingers, she reached over and tapped Shelley on the shoulder.

"Shelley, look. There's writing at the bottom."

"Like a note?"

"No...it looks like it was carved there."

Shelley craned her neck to look into the box. Both girls squinted to decipher the small letters, which had tarnished over the years.

Oval to oval, golden to green.

Jan stifled a laugh and put the box down. "Is that supposed to mean something?"

Shelley shrugged. "Maybe someone thought engraving words on the box would make it look fancier."

"It's a pretty bad poem," Jan said. She took the locket from Shelley and held it out in front of her.

Shelley narrowed her eyebrows as they stood. "That's not a poem. Poems can't be two lines."

"Yes, they can. It's called a couplet when two successive lines form a verse. This one just doesn't rhyme, but I don't think it needs to. But it does have the same meter..."

"Jinx, please shut up," Shelley said. "Save your stupid school nonsense for when we have to go back in September."

Jan snorted and looked back at the locket. "Oval to oval," she said. "The locket's oval."

Shelley shrugged. "You should wear it. Copper and gold look good on you. They match your hair."

Jan held her hair up and let Shelley clasp the locket behind her neck.

"How do I look?" she asked, striking a dramatic pose.

"Like a princess, but don't go acting anymore royal than you already do."

Jan grinned and opened her mouth to respond, but was cut short by what felt like a punch to the stomach. She staggered backward, gasping for air.

"Oh my gosh, Jinx, are you okay?" Shelley asked, putting her hands out to steady Jan.

Jan blinked back her shock as a metallic smell stung her nostrils. It reminded her of the taste of blood.

"I'm fine," she said as she regained her breath.

"What happened?"

"I...I have no clue."

"It must've been lack of oxygen from your dive," Shelley

said. "You were under for a really long time."

"I feel fine now, though." Shaking the lingering feeling off, Jan gestured for Shelley to follow her back to the parking lot.

By the time they got back to the car, their bathing suits were almost dry. A fine white crust of salt from the ocean water tugged at the little hairs on their skin. They brushed themselves off, put on their shorts and sweatshirts, and hopped into the car.

"You're feeling well enough to drive, right?" Shelley asked, furrowing her brows when Jan slid into the driver's seat.

"I'm fine. Honestly. I think I just pushed myself a little too hard."

The sun was higher now, and the fog had retreated from the cove and most of the bay. Across the water, the Ferris wheel and roller coaster of the amusement park stood out sharply against the skyline.

Jan maneuvered the car out onto the slow lane of the main highway, pushing it up to the thirty-five mile-an-hour mark.

"You should take the side road over the island," Shelley suggested, holding on as the shimmy turned into a real shudder. "I don't trust this car on the freeway."

"Don't let her hear you talk like that," Jan teased. "She'll get even." Still, she took Shelley's advice and turned off at the first exit.

The Blue Bomb nosed onto a bridge that angled up sharply to let the masts of boats pass under safely. Just as the girls reached the apex, the bridge disappeared in a flash of blue as the hood caught a gust of wind and flew up.

"Guess you were right," Shelley said, gritting her teeth. "She does get even."

"I told you." Jan brought the car to a standstill in the middle of the bridge, then climbed out and slammed the hood closed. "Quick, Shelley, hand me the old pair of jeans from the trunk."

Shelley crawled into the back of the car. She reached into the trunk through a hole in the back seat and moved her hand around blindly, only to pull out a clear hose.

"Does that look like jeans to you?" Jan asked sarcastically.

"Why do you have a hose in your trunk?"

Jan shrugged. "My dad taught me how to siphon gas a year ago. I guess he had an extra hose for the Blue Bomb. There's a smaller one back there too, I think."

"Your dad taught you to siphon gas? Lucky you. My dad never teaches me anything like that."

"He always says you never know when you might be in an emergency."

"Your dad is so cool," Shelley muttered, stuffing the hose back through the hole and feeling around with her hand until she pulled out a pair of ragged pants.

"If you ever need your spare tire, you're screwed," Shelley said. "It's too big to fit through that hole."

"Just hold down the hood."

Shelley got out and pushed down on the hood while Jan struggled to tie one pant leg to the bumper and the other around the nose of the hood. Horns began honking as traffic lined up on the highway exit of the bridge.

"You can pick a lock and siphon gas, but you can't tie for shit," Shelley said. "Move over. I'll do it."

Shelley had the hood secured in a minute, and the girls piled back into the car. Jan heaved out a shaky breath as she gestured an apology to the drivers behind her.

"Now, watch what you say, kid," she warned Shelley as she slowly started over the crest of the bridge. Jan could have sworn that the car had a rather self-satisfied hum.

The island's narrow streets were lined with shops and snack bars. A solitary movie theater stood guard over the main crossing, its marquee promising an evening of excitement and romance. A few shops were beginning to lure in their first lotion-covered vacationers of the day to buy their wares.

The Blue Bomb and its two silent occupants crossed the tiny island in a matter of minutes, arriving at the main sand spit forming the harbor. They passed the marina boat dock and pulled into the parking lot of the Fun Zone.

Jan got out and looked around at the sky. "I guess we can remove the jeans for the time being," she said.

"Until the next wind comes up?" asked Shelley with a

nervous grin on her face. "I don't know about you, but I don't feel like stopping on the bridge again."

"It'll be fine," Jan said. She tossed the jeans into the back seat, then pulled out the sacks of shells and sand dollars and handed them to Shelley. She scooped the mermaid box up for herself, which was heavier now that it had been filled with shells.

"Here we go, Jinx," Shelley said. Her eyes sparkled as she examined the bags. "We're off to a new start—the start of a business venture."

Jan laughed and followed her friend through the entrance of the Fun Zone, all the while fiddling with the little locket around her neck.

Chapter 4
THE FUN ZONE

"MS. JOHNSON HAS A LOT OF CUTE SOUVENIRS," Shelley said, pointing to a shop sandwiched between the House of Mirrors and the Sea Witch's Castle. "I can't believe you've never been in this shop before. You know, when we get enough money, we should get a set of friendship rings. She has some really nice ones."

Ms. Johnson was turning over the sign in her window to show the side that read "OPEN" when the girls arrived.

"Hello, Shelley," she said, smoothing the starch apron she always wore. "Hello, Shelley's friend. I don't think I've seen you around before."

She had a delicate, musical voice that sounded like tinkling glass. The sound ignited a warmth so deep within Jan that she almost felt guilty about her plan to overprice the shells.

"I'm Jan. Nice to meet you," she said, shaking hands with

Ms. Johnson.

"Come on in you two. Aren't you a little early today? The rides don't start until noon."

"I know," Shelley said. "We actually came to talk business."

"Business?" When Ms. Johnson smiled, little lines appeared beside her eyes. "Please, come into my office."

She ushered them past the tables of souvenirs to a room at the back. Her office wasn't much more than a tiny room with a desk, one chair, and a burner where some water was heating, but much like Ms. Johnson, it was warm and inviting.

"Would you like some tea?" Ms. Johnson asked.

Both girls nodded.

"So what kind of business did you have in mind?" Ms. Johnson inquired as she poured three cups.

Shelley glanced over at Jan.

"Well," Jan said in her most salesperson-like voice, "Shelley and I specialize in collecting the finest specimens the sea has to offer. In this little silver box right here, we have a sample of exquisite shells from the Pacific." Jan placed the mermaid box down on the desk and opened it up.

Ms. Johnson took a look at the box first, then at the shells, then back at the box. "What an interesting little box you have there," she said, closing its lid to look at the design.

"Jan found it," Shelley said. "We use it to carry our shells."

"I think I've seen a design like this once before, but I can't remember when or where," Ms. Johnson said as she ran a hand through her graying hair.

Before she could continue, Shelley placed another bag on her desk. "We also have starfish, sand dollars, and driftwood," she said proudly.

Ms. Johnson picked up one of the starfish. "This is beautiful, girls. The sand dollars are in great shape." She put on her glasses and looked into the box again. "I'll have to set a price on each piece of driftwood, but what about these shells? Does five cents a dozen sound okay?"

"Shells like these are hard to find," Jan said slowly, "but we could probably keep you supplied for...let's say, ten cents a dozen. What do you say, Shelley?"

Shelley choked on her sip of tea.

"She agrees, Ms. Johnson," Jan continued. "Ten cents a dozen for the shells, ten cents apiece for the starfish, and five cents each for the sand dollars. Agreed?" She smiled, looking at Ms. Johnson as though they had already made a deal.

Ms. Johnson chuckled. "Agreed. Count what you brought, then set the starfish and the sand dollars out in the back to dry. When you finish, I'll get your money for you." She got up and left the two girls alone.

"You robber!" Shelley hissed. "That poor lady doesn't have enough to live on as it is. Look at her shop...it needs painting."

Jan shrugged. "Think of it this way," she said, laying out

the starfish. "We're helping her keep her business running."

Shelley groaned, shook her head, and began counting. In a short while, they came up with a list of forty-one cone-shaped shells, eighteen sand dollars, and five starfish.

While Ms. Johnson busied herself tending to a customer, the girls admired the sequin and glitter jewelry boxes, colored shells, imported corals, and shiny rings.

When Ms. Johnson came over to them, she gave the girls a friendly smile. "Looking at the rings again, Shelley? They are nice, aren't they?"

"They really are," Shelley replied. "But we can't afford them. Jan's spending the summer with me, and my dad says I have to buy trinkets with my own money. That's why we're collecting the shells. Jan has a really nice one, though."

"It's a citrine stone," Jan said, showing Ms. Johnson her ring. "For my birth month."

"Well, look at that! My birthday is in November too." Ms. Johnson smiled again, then turned back to Shelley. "How much do I owe you for the shells? That should help you get some cash so you can buy those rings."

"Three dollars and ten cents," answered Shelley, "not counting whichever driftwood you want."

"What if I make it an even five dollars?"

"Are you sure, Ms. Johnson?" Jan asked, puzzled. Ten cents a dozen for shells was already a good bargain.

Ms. Johnson nodded. The girls brightened up, side-eyeing each other giddily as she reached into her pocket and produced the money. "I'll throw in a little something for that cut too," she added, handing Jan a Band-Aid.

Jan glanced down at her legs. The barnacles had done more damage than she'd thought.

"Thanks, Ms. Johnson," she said. She placed the Band-Aid and the money in the box, then tucked it under her arm and nodded affirmatively. "We'll be back in a day or so."

As soon as the girls stepped out into the fresh air of the amusement park, Shelley poked Jan eagerly. "How about a chili dog?" she asked, grinning.

Jan rolled her eyes and laughed through her nose. "Are you really going for the chili dog? Or do you want to see Gabriel?"

"How about both? Besides, his shop is next to the Fun House. We can go there after."

As always, Gabriel leaned against the counter of his father's chili dog stand, watching the passersby with a laid-back air. When he saw the girls, he brightened. It was with amusement that Jan realized most of his attention was directed toward Shelley.

"My two favorite customers!" he greeted as they reached the counter.

Jan couldn't help but glance at Shelley, who stared intently at the young man standing in front of them. Although she often teased Shelley for her obsession with him, she had to admit: with his bronze skin and dark, curly hair, Gabriel certainly wasn't hard on the eyes.

Jan could have sworn she saw Shelley nearly swoon.

"Nice to see you again, Gabriel," Shelley chirped, giving him her sweetest smile.

"Two specials?" he asked, flashing one back. Shelley giggled and Jan caught herself before she audibly groaned.

As Gabriel hustled off to the back of the stand, Jan turned to Shelley. "I wonder if Gabriel knows something about those guys on the boat," she said. "He always seems to hear interesting stuff."

It was true—the Fun Zone was a magnet for gossip, and after having worked there every summer for three years, Gabriel had developed a knack for knowing everything concerning the amusement park, as well as the whereabouts of nearly everyone in Aledale. Still, he always insisted that he didn't like to gossip, but that was just Gabriel being Gabriel. Shelley said it was because he had a strong sense of morals, to which Jan would reply that anyone could be corrupted given the right persuasion.

"Oh, Jinx, come on," Shelley groaned. "Doesn't anything embarrass you? He'll think we're crazy."

Jan shrugged as Gabriel returned with two large hot dogs dripping with chili sauce and grated cheese. She handed him the money and, as usual, he filled two large coke glasses—one with ice for Jan and one without for Shelley.

"Do you know everyone's order by heart?" Jan asked him as Shelley sipped her coke.

"Not *everyone's*," he said. "But I have a decent memory."

Jan grinned and side-eyed Shelley before she continued. "Say, Gabriel," she ventured, "would you happen to have any idea why two men would take a small boat over to Azuline Cove early in the morning and dump something overboard?"

Shelley flushed and glared at her.

"Which morning?" Gabriel asked.

"This morning. Know anything about it?"

He glanced at the box, then at the locket hanging around Jan's neck. "Is this a riddle?" he asked through a teasing smile.

"Nope," Jan said. "It's an honest question."

Shelley put down her half-eaten chili dog and turned away, stifling a cough.

Gabriel shrugged as he placed the money in the register. "I can't say I do. But maybe I'll hear something today. I'll keep my ears open for you two and let you know when I see you next, okay?"

"Right-o," Jan said. "Sounds like a plan. Thanks, Gabriel." She grabbed Shelley by the elbow and dragged her away.

"Screw you," Shelley said when they were far enough away. "Now he definitely thinks we're weird."

"He said he'd keep his ears open for us!"

"Only because he's so nice," Shelley said, picking at the tip of her straw with her fingernails.

Jan gave her a playful nudge on the shoulder. "Get over yourself. If little things like that embarrass you, then you'll never be able to ask him out."

"Have *you* ever asked anyone out?"

Both of them knew it was a rhetorical question. Jan had never been flirtatious, and she had never taken up much of an interest in romance, despite Shelley's many quips.

"You know I don't like that stuff," she said, shaking her head and quickly changing the subject. "Let's go down to the docks and look over the boats. Maybe we'll find something interesting."

"Jinx, I know what you mean by 'something.' This whole mystery thing of yours is going too far. It's just a stupid box. Your curiosity is going to lead you to nothing. Besides, what if we run into those two guys there?"

"They don't know us, but I might recognize their voices."

Shelley groaned. "Fine. But we're just going to look, not conduct an entire investigation, okay? And you'd better not go all Sherlock Holmes on me and try to solve whatever this is." She gestured at the box tucked beneath Jan's arm.

"Oh, my dear Watson," Jan said, smiling as Shelley sighed and laughed in spite of herself, "this is only the beginning."

Chapter 5
MYSTERY HUNT

A CHIPPED AND SUN-FADED SIGN THAT READ "Boat Rentals, $2.50 per hour," stood at the entrance to a small dock a hundred yards or so away from the Fun Zone. Perched precariously on its end was a wooden shack, one wall of which supported a tilted chair and its occupant. Under the chair lay a small, snoozing dog, one ear perked toward the girls' voices.

"We'll just stroll on down to the end and ask a few questions about renting boats, okay?" Jan said.

"Yeah, okay." Shelley gave Jan a defeated grin before adding sarcastically, "We can also throw in a few about crooks and their stolen treasures."

Soft tapping noises came from the boats bumping gently against each other and the dock. Small sailboats and outboard motorboats competed for space along the aging wharf, lifting and lowering one after the other with each swell of water.

"Good morning," Shelley said as they approached an older man, who only opened one eye upon their arrival.

The man, still leaning back lazily in his chair, pulled out an antique pocket watch. "Good afternoon, now," he corrected her.

"You must be the man in charge here," said Shelley as she perched on top of a piling. "I'm Shelley. This is Jan. I recognize your boats. You're Mr. Brown, right?"

He straightened and peered at her, both eyes open now that his interest had been piqued. "You a sailor?"

"I belong to the high school's Mariners Club," she answered proudly. "We do most of our sailing here in the bay. Yours are the cleanest boats around. I'd know them anywhere."

"You've got a keen eye," he remarked proudly, glowing from beneath his leather-brown skin. "Where's your club get its boats from?"

"Our leader has a friend who lives beyond the cove and gives us a discount," Shelley said. "Just out of curiosity, what time do you usually open?"

"Five a.m.," he answered plainly. After his reply, a long silence ensued.

"Mr. Brown," Jan ventured finally, "did you happen to rent out a boat this morning?"

"Rented out a couple," came a second short reply. "You a sailor too?"

Jan shook her head. "Did you rent out any, say, around seven or so in the morning?"

Mr. Brown poked at the tobacco in his pipe with a nail he kept in his shirt pocket, then said, "Two young men did take a boat out this morning. I don't remember them carrying any poles, though, so I don't think they were fishermen. I didn't make 'em sign in or out because I figured I'd remember 'em. One looked pretty familiar to me, actually, but I can't quite place his face in my mind." He frowned at his pipe.

Jan and Shelley exchanged a quick glance.

"What did he look like?" Jan asked, eagerness pricking at her fingertips. Shelley nudged her gently, quietly begging her to stop asking questions.

Mr. Brown shrugged. "Tall, young, dark hair. Mid-twenties, if I had to guess. Came with a blond fella around the same age."

"Do they come here often?" Jan pressed on, avoiding eye contact with Shelley.

"Nope. Never seen 'em here before. They didn't even use up their full hour. I reckon they didn't like the fog. It's understandable, though. People think they're up for sailing in that weather 'til they actually do it." He chuckled, stood up, and looked at the girls. The little dog stood up as well. "You two fixin' to go for a sail today?"

"Not today," Shelley answered. "We just wanted to know how much we have to save up to rent one."

"Two dollars and fifty cents per hour with a five-dollar deposit. You're welcome to stop by anytime." Mr. Brown smiled and cleared his throat. "Well, if you ladies will excuse me, Schätzli and I got work to do. You're welcome to take a look at the boats." He tipped a non-existent hat to them and walked away, Schätzli padding along behind him.

"You oughta be a reporter or something," Shelley said. "You ask questions like it's the only thing you know how to do."

Jan rolled her eyes, but couldn't help the small smile that tugged at her lips.

"Well, what do you think?" Shelley asked. "Were those the two men you heard out by the rocks this morning?"

"They had to be. I highly doubt two other guys *also* decided to take a sail at seven in the morning."

"Yeah, you're probably right," Shelley said. "Well, if that's over and done with, what do you say we pay the Fun House a short visit? It won't be too crowded this time of day."

Jan glanced back at the boat dock.

"C'mon, Jinx, we'll do our mystery hunt later," Shelley said, getting to her feet. "Besides, where else can you find anything as fun as the Alpine Slide and the Bamboo Shoot for just fifty cents? Just ten minutes, okay?"

"I'm not going on the Bamboo Shoot."

"Chicken," Shelley teased.

"Maybe, but I'm still not going on it."

The two girls linked arms as they headed away from the dock and toward the amusement park. Jan looked once more at the rows of boats floating on the sparkling water, more desperate than ever for information that would quench her growing curiosity.

Chapter 6
EPISODES

"FIVE DOLLARS FOR A DAY'S WORK SHOULD GIVE us enough to get along," said Shelley as she stirred up the spaghetti sauce that evening. After a few hours at the Fun Zone and Jan insisting they tidy up the Blue Bomb once they arrived home, the girls were famished.

"And we still have two bucks left from today," Shelley continued, grinning.

Jan set out the dishes on the small kitchen table, then went to the refrigerator to grab some lettuce.

"One day, Jinx, I'm going to get you to go on the Bamboo Shoot."

"I may be adventurous, but I don't have a death wish. That thing twists around while it drops straight down. Everybody comes out with friction burns."

"You're supposed to stay on the gunny sack. That way you

don't get burned."

"That's not my idea of fun."

"I know," Shelley replied sarcastically, pulling out a string of spaghetti from the pot. "Fun to you is chasing crooks. All very mild."

"Milder than your Bamboo Shoot!"

Just then, the door swung open and Mr. Waldbauer was greeted by a piece of flying spaghetti.

"What is this?" Though he maintained his composure, Jan could tell it was strained.

"We were just having a discussion," said Shelley, turning her face away from him to hide her laughter. The piece of spaghetti that Shelley meant to throw at Jan dangled limply from his shoulder.

"I see that you've started making dinner," he said, finally managing a smile. "Thanks, girls."

"It'll be on the table in about five minutes," said Jan. "How was your day?"

"Busy, as usual," he responded, picking the spaghetti off his shirt and putting it in the sink. "But I got off early, just in time for dinner, which is nice for a change."

He sat down and stared silently at the table for a moment before looking back up at the girls. "What did you do today? You were gone even before I left."

"We had an idea about how we could make some money,"

said Shelley. "We collected shells and driftwood. Then we sold them to Ms. Johnson, who runs the gift shop at the Fun Zone. She paid us five dollars."

"Five dollars? That's very good. What have you done with your money?"

Shelley dished up the spaghetti and let Jan speak.

"Food and Fun Zone, mostly," Jan said.

Mr. Waldbauer eyed the Band-Aid on her leg. "Hopefully you didn't go too crazy at the Fun Zone."

Jan felt her face flush. She set down her plate of spaghetti, feigning casualness. Even if he didn't know they had been swimming in the cove that early in the morning, which he surely wouldn't approve of, she had a feeling he knew her scratched legs weren't because of the Fun Zone.

She gave him a sweet smile and shrugged. "Sometimes I get a little ahead of myself."

"She's clumsy," Shelley added a bit too eagerly.

Mr. Waldbauer must have chosen not to argue—either that or he was too tired to care—because the conversation swiftly drifted away from the girls' day and back to his work at the station.

"This was a big year for the department," he said proudly. "I don't think we've ever had a Chief of Police in Aledale younger than forty, but I suppose times are changing."

"Oh, yeah," Shelley said between bites of spaghetti. "Isn't

it Aiden Aimsworth?"

Mr. Waldbauer nodded. "Thirty-two years old and already the Chief of Police. There are quite a few guys down at the station who'd kill to have his job."

If any family was well known in their little town, it was the Aimsworth family. Jan had heard that Mr. Aimsworth owned oil plantations in the East, which still accumulated wealth for his family, even though he'd passed away years ago. His widow, Eliza Aimsworth, and her two sons lived in their mansion at the northernmost part of Aledale.

Though the family mostly kept to themselves, it wasn't until recently that the oldest son, Aiden, proved himself at the police department. Even Mr. Waldbauer complimented his talent, and he did not compliment generously.

"You know, at first I thought he'd moved up in the ranks so fast because of his family's status," Mr. Waldbauer confessed. "But I'll give it to the guy: he's worked hard and he's a good Chief. Much better than some of the older ones we've had, actually."

Jan took a sip of water. "I've always thought that working at a police station when I'm older would be really cool. I love reading those crime novels, and I—"

Before she could finish, her breath caught in her throat and something within her convulsed. It sent her back into her chair so forcefully that Jan thought she might tip over.

"Jan! Are you okay?" Mr. Waldbauer exclaimed, his voice wrought with concern. He reached an arm out to stop her from falling off her chair, but Jan put up her hand.

"I'm fine," she said, her voice trembling as she inhaled sporadically. The terrible, dizzying feeling was so strong that she began to worry she wouldn't be able to shake it. She clutched the side of the table as the familiar metallic sensation coursed through her body in currents.

"Are you sure?" Shelley asked, her eyes wide. "Didn't the same thing happen to you after you dove this morning?"

Jan shot Shelley a glare between breaths, but judging by the regret on her face, Jan knew Shelley had checked herself.

"Diving?" Mr. Waldbauer asked.

Shelley clamped her lips shut and let Jan flounder in the explanation.

"I just went for a swim in the cove this morning," Jan said, still struggling for air. She glared at Shelley again. "But I stayed close to the shore, I promise."

"The tide is dangerous at that time, Jan," Mr. Waldbauer said. "I'm not comfortable with you two in the water so early, especially when nobody else is around to help you if something happens."

I'm a perfectly good swimmer, Jan thought, but she kept her mouth shut.

"And I assume that swimming out there is how you got

your legs cut up?" he continued.

Jan nodded. There was no use arguing with him.

Mr. Waldbauer sucked in a breath. "I'm fine with you going to the beach, girls. But swimming out there that early isn't safe, and I'm not just talking to you, Michelle. I'm responsible for you too, Jan, and I'm going to treat you like my own daughter while you're here."

"I'm sorry, Mr. Waldbauer," Jan said. The apology felt dry in her mouth. "I was just trying to find shells. I didn't think the tide would be that bad. I swear I didn't swim out too far. I'm not going to go in again if we go to the beach to collect shells."

Mr. Waldbauer's expression softened. "I'll believe you both," he said, "because I think it's important for you two to have your freedom this summer. But you need to understand that there's a stipulated time for going in the water, and it's not when the tide is dangerous and when you two are the only ones on the beach."

"I understand," Jan said. "I learned my lesson after getting so cut up today." It was a blatant lie, but Mr. Waldbauer seemed to believe it.

After dinner was cleaned up and Mr. Waldbauer returned to his workroom downstairs, Shelley apologized for her slip-up.

"I don't know how you worked that, Jinx. I really thought we were in for it."

"Well, I had to say something, didn't I? You went all silent on me."

"You're better at lying than I am," Shelley said, shutting the dishwasher. "I would've blown it even more."

"Well, do me a favor and *don't* blow it again. I want to dive this summer."

Shelley sighed. "I do too. I wouldn't have normally blown it, but I wasn't thinking, especially after those two episodes you've had." She paused for a moment, then sat back down at the table with Jan. "What do you think those are?" The concern in her eyes mirrored the concern in Mr. Waldbauer's.

"I don't know," Jan admitted, picking at the tablecloth.

"Maybe it's a heart palpitation? I remember my dad's friend used to have them and he said he felt short of breath and dizzy."

"Do I *look* fifty?" Jan said, giving her friend a sarcastic smile. "It's not heart palpitations."

"Well, I don't know. Asthma, maybe?"

"I don't have asthma. It's the weirdest thing. It's like all the air has been punched out of me, and then I'll feel this weird metallic sensation. It's like a taste and smell, but it goes beyond that. My entire body is affected by it."

"That's not normal," Shelley said. "We should tell my dad."

"Honestly, I feel fine. If it keeps happening, I'll tell him, but I feel great now. I promise." She finished with a reassuring nod, directed more to herself than Shelley.

Although some of the worry left Shelley's face, Jan couldn't help but feel uncertain. Though her breath had returned to her quickly, the metallic sensation lingered. Fiddling with the locket around her neck, she let out a shaky exhale.

It was probably nothing.

Chapter 7
THE MERMAID'S FACE

THAT NIGHT, JAN TOOK THE BED. ON ANY OTHER night, Shelley would have argued with her for it, but after what Jan experienced at dinner, Shelley offered it up. Jan gladly accepted the opportunity to get a good night's sleep, especially since Shelley was dead set on leaving early in the morning to catch low tide again.

Shelley cleared the floor to make room for Jan's sleeping bag by chucking pieces of clothing over by her desk. After creating a massive pile of shirts, jeans, and dresses, she curled up by her closet and fell asleep within minutes.

Jan, however, had never been able to fall asleep quickly, and this night proved to be exceedingly difficult.

Shelley had placed the mermaid box on her desk, and the moonlight creeping in through the blinds cast narrow beams of silver light across the room, illuminating the green eyes of the mermaid. Jan found herself, quite to her discontent, unable to look away from its glare. An uneasy part of her imagined that the eyes were blinking in the moonlight. After nearly an hour, she got up and turned the box upside down.

Though she fell asleep soon after, Jan woke up the next morning feeling as though she hadn't gotten much rest at all.

Low tide at the cove came a little later that morning, but since Shelley insisted they be there early to take advantage of it, Jan found herself up and ready by six-thirty.

Despite her sleepiness, the morning went by quickly. By nine o'clock, they had finished their beachcombing and began diving near the rocks at the point.

A cool breeze kept the fog away from the open ocean beyond the breakwater. Bright sunlight sparkled on the tiny mountains of water that stood up everywhere like peaks of frosting on a cake.

"These rocks are like a fairyland," Jan said, surfacing for the hundredth time that morning. "The place where I found the box is really nice too. Take a deep breath and I'll show you."

Shelley inhaled and the two dove down toward the golden floor where sand dollars lived and swam smoothly into the tiny hollows of the rocks. As long as their lungs would let them, the girls remained underwater to enjoy the unexplored world that lay before them. Then, with a gasp, they broke the surface.

"I wish I had gills," Shelley said between gulps of air. "I'd stay down there forever."

"Me too," Jan said, grinning. "Imagine how much fun we'd have if we were mermaids."

"That'd be so cool," Shelley said. She opened her mouth to say something else, but closed it just as promptly.

The hollow chug of a motor echoed through the water.

"Jinx," Shelley whispered frantically. "Look."

She pointed toward a small boat approaching slowly from the marina. Though they couldn't make out exactly who was on board, Jan noticed its two occupants were both men.

"C'mon Shelley," she breathed, uneasiness forming in her stomach. "Let's swim back."

Just as they started for the shore, a hoarse voice called out, "Hey, you two! Wait a minute."

As soon as he spoke, Jan knew to whom the voice belonged. Her muscles stiffened and she held her breath, treading beside Shelley as the boat idled its engine and pulled up beside them.

Two men, neatly dressed in expensive-looking jackets, watched them closely. The first man—the one who did the talking—was a thin, bird-looking fellow with blond hair and gray-green eyes that burned in their sockets as he stared at them.

"You girls swim here often?" he rasped out.

Jan clamped her lips shut and observed the second man. He was tall, noticeably handsome, and dressed even nicer than

his companion. His dark hair bordered even darker amber eyes, and he tapped a silver watch on his right wrist patiently. These were the same men Mr. Brown had described to them—the ones who'd taken a boat out onto the water at an unnervingly early hour.

Mr. Brown had certainly been right about the second man, Jan noticed. He *did* look oddly familiar.

"I asked you a question," the first man repeated.

Nolan, Jan remembered. The other man—the familiar one—must have been the one who ordered Nolan to drop the box into the water.

"Sometimes," Jan said, straining to appear calm. When she noticed the second man's eyes drift to her neck, she dipped slightly underwater to hide the necklace. Though she hoped her attempt would draw the attention away from her, the man only eyed her suspiciously. Something in his dark eyes glinted, and Jan felt the overwhelming urge to sink to the bottom of the ocean. Whether out of fear or instinct, she reached for Shelley, clutching the fabric of her bathing suit and preparing to bolt if the man mentioned the locket.

"Stay clear of those rocks," the second man said after a few moments of unsettling silence, taking his eyes off of Jan's neck. His voice was smoother than his friend's, and he managed a soft but stiff smile. "They're dangerous. Swim nearer to the shore where it's safe."

"Thanks for the advice," Jan said quickly. "Come on, Shelley. It's time to get out now."

Without waiting for the men to respond, they both dunked underwater and swam away from the small boat before the men could advise them further.

Scrambling up to the shore, Shelley let out a relieved breath.

"What on *Earth*?" she breathed as they dropped down on the warm sand. "Do you suppose...?"

"I'm sure of it," said Jan, panting. "I'd recognize the first guy's voice anywhere."

"That's one of Mr. Brown's boats too. I saw it at the dock yesterday. Maybe you were right, Jinx. I don't like those guys. They gave off a weird vibe."

"I bet we can find out who they are from Mr. Brown."

"I don't know," Shelley murmured, picking at her nails nervously. "I don't feel like this is any of our business." After pausing for a moment, she added, "Did you see the way he was eyeing your neck? Maybe you should take that necklace off. If he figures out we stole it..."

"Why would anyone go through all this trouble to hide a stupid locket?" Jan said, hardly minding Shelley's remark. She watched the boat as it left the cove. "Let's take our shells to Ms. Johnson. Then we'll check our leads."

Though Jan could tell that Shelley wasn't overly fond of the idea, she didn't argue.

Once Jan began to pilot the shaking Blue Bomb toward the Fun Zone, Shelley pulled out the mysterious little box, which was now filled with the shells they had collected earlier.

"I think the blond guy's name is Nolan," Jan said, veering out of the small dirt parking lot by the beach. "That's what I heard the other man call him yesterday. So if two guys—one by the name of Nolan—rented out that boat, then we've got our box owners."

"And locket owners," Shelley added.

"Well, technically the locket is ours now, if you think about it," Jan said, tapping impatiently on the steering wheel and feeling a tinge of possessiveness course through her. "We were the ones who found it."

Shelley held up the box toward the light, giving Jan no more than a distant nod.

"Why so quiet, Shelley?" Jan glanced over at her friend, then took a hard second look. "Don't tell me you're getting car sick," she teased. "Stop looking at that box. It wouldn't do to have the story get out that a mariner gets sick on land."

Shelley fake-laughed. "Funny. I'm not car sick. Did you ever take a close look at the mermaid on the lid of the box?"

"No," Jan said. "Why?"

"There's something weird about her. I'm not quite sure what." Shelley squinted at the box. "If this car wasn't shaking so much, I could probably tell."

"Don't insult her. Remember what happened last time?"

A bump on the road caused a small bang under the chassis.

"See?"

Shelley ignored Jan's comment. "This isn't a real mermaid."

"What do you mean?" Jan asked. She tried to stay focused on the road, but the curiosity bubbling within her urged her to steal glances at the little box.

"Well, the hair and the tail are, but the face…" Shelley held the box nearer to get a closer look. "Holy shit," she said through a surprised exhale. "The face is a skull."

The car shuddered as if it had heard her. Even Jan felt a chill go up her back.

"How did we not see that yesterday?" she asked.

"It's small," Shelley said. "We probably just missed it. Besides, it blends in with the box so well."

"You're right, it really does." Jan took another quick glance at the box. "The details are intricate too."

Even the tiny scales on the mermaid's tale looked as though they had been carved by hand, each one almost as small as the tip of a needle. Jan studied the mermaid while she drove. The skull looked less like a skull and more like an oddly shaped egg, but the little teeth and cheekbones indicated otherwise. Save her beady emerald eyes, the mermaid's face looked like the make-shift skeleton decorations that filled the Halloween stores every

October.

"You're right," Shelley said, admiring the tiny emerald dots that gleamed back at her. "That's sick. Hey, Jinx! Watch where you're driving!"

Jan jerked the car back to their side of the road.

"Maybe we shouldn't go diving at the point anymore," Shelley said, chewing her lip nervously. "This entire situation is getting weird. The box, the locket, those men..."

"It's not their cove," Jan argued. "They don't have a monopoly on it. Besides, there's nowhere else we can collect shells that easily."

Shelley raised an eyebrow. "Do you really care about the shells?"

Although Jan could sense the annoyance in Shelley's voice, she ignored her question. "You'll feel better after Ms. Johnson pays us," she said. "Cash always has weird supernatural healing powers."

She grinned at Shelley, who rolled her eyes, and pulled into the Fun Zone parking lot.

Chapter 8
A FAMILIAR STORY

AS SHELLEY PLACED THEIR DAY'S EARNINGS INTO the mermaid box, Jan turned to Ms. Johnson, who sat at her desk admiring the sand dollars and cone-shaped shells.

"Ms. Johnson," she ventured, "do you remember yesterday you said something about our box?"

Ms. Johnson looked up, her eyes twinkling. "Of course I do. Could I see it closely, if you don't mind?"

Shelley handed her the box, and Ms. Johnson lifted her glasses up closer to her eyes to get a better look.

"A mermaid and a skull," she said, more to herself than the girls. "That strikes quite the chord. Come to think of it, it reminds me of a very familiar story. My father used to tell it to me. He was a sailor back in the day, you know. So naturally, he knew all the legends of the sea."

"Do you remember what the story was about?" Jan asked.

"Not entirely," Ms. Johnson admitted. "It's something about a treasure, I think." Her glasses dropped to a dangle on the string that held them around her neck. "Where did you get this box?"

"We found it underwater near the rocks at Azuline Cove," Jan answered, shortening the real story by quite a few facts.

"Was there anything in it?"

"Just this necklace and a bunch of rocks." Jan pulled the chain slightly, holding out the locket so Ms. Johnson could see it. "There's a little poem engraved at the bottom too."

"It's not a poem," Shelley interjected.

"Yes, it is. Like I said, it's a..."

Shelley put her hand up to stop Jan. "Right. It's a *couplet*."

"Interesting," Ms. Johnson said, opening the box. Her eyes scanned over the words at the bottom. "Oval to oval, golden to green." She paused for a moment and looked back up at the girls. "I do suppose that, at one point, the necklace might've had a nice golden hue to it," she said. "Though I don't doubt that the years have taken their toll on the little thing. I'm sure exposure hasn't helped either."

"Exposure to what?" Shelley asked.

"All sorts of things. I assume it's very old and that's why there's discoloring. Tarnishing usually occurs on lower karat golds since they're mixed with other types of metals, so this necklace probably isn't pure gold at all. That doesn't mean it's worthless, though. And it's still a pretty color."

Jan held the necklace out from her chest to study it. Time had certainly worn it down, leaving the little locket more pinchbeck brown than gold.

"I don't think it would be worth trying to sell unless you got someone to clean it up," Ms. Johnson added.

"We're not selling it," Jan said hastily.

Ms. Johnson chuckled. "Do you suppose someone lost it?" she asked, taking her eyes off the necklace and looking back up at the girls.

Shelley opened her mouth, but Jan gently kicked her shin. If Ms. Johnson knew the entire story involving the two men, she would tell the girls to leave the box and the locket to avoid any trouble. And that was the one thing Jan did *not* want to do. Although she could do without the trouble, her curiosity urged her—beseeched her—to continue her hunt for the meaning behind all of this.

"Do you remember anything else about the legend? Even small details?" Jan inquired, ignoring Ms. Johnson's question.

"Unfortunately, I don't," she said. The spark of hope in Jan faded. "But, come to think of it, if anyone here knows old sailor legends, it would be Mr. Brown. He sells rental boats down at the docks."

"We know him," Shelley said. She smiled, looking quite proud of herself.

"I'd say he's your best bet," Ms. Johnson said as she handed the box back to Jan.

"Thank you, Ms. Johnson!" Jan said. She tugged at Shelley, who smiled in defeat.

"Guess we're off to Mr. Brown's," Shelley said, giving Ms. Johnson a weak shrug.

Ms. Johnson laughed and handed them the money for the shells. "You girls have fun. And thank you for these. They're absolutely lovely."

Chapter 9
A SAILOR'S LEGEND

ALMOST AS QUICKLY AS THEY LEFT THE SHOP, THE girls ran down the boardwalk to reach the docks where Mr. Brown sat. As always, Schätzli lay under his chair.

At the sound of their footsteps, the little dog perked up, his small white tale thumping against the hollow wood.

"You two again?" Mr. Brown gave the girls a warm smile. "What brings you girls back?"

"A couple of questions, actually," Jan said.

Mr. Brown squinted at them from his chair, using his hand to shield his wrinkled eyes from the sun's glare. "Let's hear 'em."

"The first question is about this box," Jan said, handing him the box to look at. "Ms. Johnson, the lady who sells those shell necklaces at the Fun Zone, said she recognized the mermaid carved on the lid from a sailor's legend. But she didn't remember what the legend was about. She said you might know about it."

Mr. Brown took the box and shifted it in his grimy hands, bringing it closer to his eyes and then farther away again to get a good look at it.

"Oh, wow," he mumbled under his breath, blinking rapidly in surprise. "Haven't seen this image in years. But yeah, I remember the legend."

"Really?" Jan asked. The excitement in her chest surged to a crescendo.

"What was it about?" Shelley added.

Handing Jan the box, Mr. Brown leaned back in his chair and looked up at the two eager girls. "It was one of them lesser known stories we used to tell when we were out sailing. But you could always tell a real sailor apart from an amateur by those who knew it." Patting Schätzli's head softly, he took another long look at the box in Jan's hand. "She's not really a mermaid," he continued. "She's supposed to be a sea witch. I think it's a Celtic-Irish legend of some sort, but I can't be sure." He turned to Jan. "Aren't you Irish?" he asked, tilting his head and pointing at her hair.

"I was born in Scotland."

Mr. Brown shrugged. "Same thing, isn't it?"

Jan opened her mouth to correct him, but Mr. Brown didn't heed her.

"From what I remember of the story," he said, "this sea

witch in particular was known for her power of destruction." Mr. Brown exhaled through the side of his mouth and scratched his chin. "If I'm bein' honest, I don't know the entire story by heart, but I got a good idea about it. It's got somethin' to do with the fact that she guards a treasure within some box of hers. They say if someone manages to destroy her treasure, she'll grant that person her own power as a reward, allowin' them to cause all kinds of chaos and destruction."

He snorted. "Not exactly a great power to get, I suppose, unless you're a bit screwed up in the head. But I guess most folklore has the tendency to be a bit odd." He leaned back in his chair again, forcing Schätzli to scoot aside as the chair's legs tilted backward. "The story claims that her power attracts anyone who finds her treasure, but only the really malicious are capable of wieldin' it."

Mr. Brown smiled to himself as though he had heard a slightly amusing, slightly morbid joke. "A bunch of sailors used to joke about what they'd do if they got ahold of something like that—how they'd bring justice to everyone who'd wronged 'em," he said. "Lots of sailors hold grudges, at least in my experience. Though, now that I'm thinkin' of it, maybe it was just the guys I knew. One of my closest mates swore he'd use the power to get back at his old girlfriend for—"

"Wait," Shelley interrupted. "By destruction, do you mean like...death?"

Mr. Brown shrugged. "Revenge, death, ruin...I guess it's all up to the individual who gets it, right?" Shaking his head, he added, "Plenty of variations of the story say that the sea witch's power makes most people go insane. After all, no magic is completely foolproof. I reckon it'd have some nasty effects on the owner. But it's said that the very spiteful and wicked few are well-suited for it. Like I said, the legend is a bit messed up."

Jan and Shelley stared at Mr. Brown in disbelief.

He chuckled and crossed his arms. "Don't look so surprised, girls. It's just a sailor's legend. A lot of hocus-pocus. Sailors have a pretty notorious reputation for makin' up strange stories."

"We found a locket in the box," Shelley said, pointing to Jan's neck.

"Guess that's her treasure, then," Mr. Brown said, his eyes twinkling. "In all honesty, I'm sure someone just used that box as a keepsake holder of some sort. Either that or some devoted fan of the legend wanted to replicate the story for the fun of it. Where'd you find it?"

"At the bottom of the cove," Jan said.

"Maybe it's worth a lot," Mr. Brown suggested, shrugging. "Maybe someone figured they'd hide it there and keep it for later." Chuckling again, this time more to himself, he smiled at the girls. "It's a pretty locket. Might as well keep it. It matches your hair...Jean, was it?"

"Jan," Jan clarified. "And thanks. We had one more question, Mr. Brown." She paused for a moment, then added, "If you don't mind."

"Go right ahead. Business is slow this time of day."

"Actually, business was what we wanted to ask you about," Jan said. "Did you rent out boats to anyone both this morning and yesterday morning?"

"I did, actually. Any particular reason for your interest? You asked me if I'd rented out any boats yesterday too."

Jan gave her best casual shrug. "Just curious, that's all. The same boat was out in the cove yesterday and today. Shelley was thinking that maybe it was someone in the Mariners Club."

"Yeah, exactly," Shelley chimed in, a bit too eagerly.

"To be honest, it's a bit odd to me when people rent that early in the morning, especially two days in a row." He laughed again, finishing with a cough. "But what people do is their business. Seein' as I don't view boat rentals as a confidential thing, I don't see why you can't know."

"Who was it?" Jan asked.

"Someone by the name of Nolan Tillet, and that young man Owen Aimsworth, the son of that dowager lady...Eliza Aimsworth," he said, snapping his fingers when he thought of the name. "Remember how I said one of the men looked familiar? When I made 'em sign in today, I realized it was Owen. I knew I'd seen that fella somewhere."

"Owen Aimsworth?" Shelley asked, confusion rushing to her face. "Isn't he the Chief of Police's younger brother?"

"Believe so," Mr. Brown said, finishing with a nod.

"I don't know anything about him," Shelley admitted. "I wonder why he was out on the water so early in the morning, especially when the tide was low."

And more importantly, Jan thought, *what is his connection to the box and the locket?*

"He doesn't seem like a sailor to me," Mr. Brown said. "Wears too nice of clothes. Regardless, though, young men his age seem to be prone to recklessness. They don't quite give a damn about how safe anything is. I bet he and his friend just wanted to face a challenge on a crappy tide."

Owen Aimsworth. Nolan Tillet. Jan stared down at the dock, trying to piece everything together. Owen Aimsworth and whoever this Nolan man was had specifically gone out to the cove—much closer to the rocks than sensibly safe—to drop the box with the locket into the water.

Something was certainly amiss. The mysteriousness of the situation made an excited trill rise in Jan's chest.

"Well, thank you, Mr. Brown," she said. "Guess it wasn't anyone from the Mariners Club."

Mr. Brown smiled softly, doing his best to hold back his amusement. "I think we both know that you two weren't askin' about anyone from the Mariners Club."

Shelley glanced nervously at Jan. After a few seconds of uncomfortable silence, she said, "Okay, you got us, Mr. Brown. Jan thought it was Owen Aimsworth, and she wanted to know for sure because she thinks he's cute and thought if she knew his schedule she could—"

Jan smacked Shelley's arm.

Laughing, Mr. Brown put his hands up. "It's fine. I don't need to get involved. As long as you two are safe and not getting into trouble, your adventures can continue."

Relieved, the girls thanked Mr. Brown and quickly headed up the pier.

"Thanks a lot," Jan hissed when they were far enough away. "You totally embarrassed me."

"You're the one getting us into all of this."

"Oh, please. You were asking just as many questions as I was, so don't go saying you're not as interested as I am."

"I *am* interested! Not as much as you maybe, but still. Besides, would you rather have me say, 'Mr. Brown, we actually think those two men—one being Owen Aimsworth, who's probably like a *trillionaire* or something—brought that box to the cove and dumped it in the water, and we decided: hey! Let's just go grab it and keep it for ourselves!'?"

"Okay, I get it," Jan said. "Also, he's not a trillionaire."

Shelley shrugged. "I dunno. Whatever the word is for people who are super rich."

Jan laughed and shook her head. "Nice lie, by the way."

"Thanks." Shelley grinned. "I learned from the best."

75

Chapter 10
RUMORS

"IT KIND OF MAKES YOU DIZZY TO LOOK AT," Shelley pointed out as they made their way into the Fun Zone.

"It's like it's watching you wherever you move," Jan added, shifting the box from side to side. A shiver coursed through her when she remembered how real the eyes had looked in the moonlight.

"Imagine if that legend was real," Shelley said, taking the box from Jan. "Then, if we destroyed the locket, we'd have a ton of power and Gabriel would *have* to marry me."

Jan burst into laughter. "Dream on, idiot," she teased as they entered the House of Mirrors. "If that's the only thing you'd go after with all that power, maybe I should have it for myself."

"Like I'd let that happen," Shelley said. She gave Jan a playful push, the momentum of which forced her forward as well. As if in response to their movements, one of the tall, wavy mirrors stationed at the edge of the little room tipped over ever so slightly, then fell with a crash where Jan had been standing.

The girls froze in their tracks, gaping at the mess.

Jan took a defensive step back. "I didn't touch that."

"Neither did I," Shelley added quickly, her eyes filled with panic. "Crap, how are we going to convince the staff that it wasn't our fault?"

Before Jan could reply, a short, shiny-headed man dashed out of the ticket office, waving his arms around and shouting in a high voice, "What've you two done? Look at that! You've broken my mirror. What have you got to say? Well?" He wrung his hands violently and paced back and forth near the shards of glass. "This is the first time I've lost a mirror!" he continued, his beady eyes narrowed. "I barely get paid as it is. Not to mention that this brings seven years of bad luck! Seven years!" He smoothed his hairless head and went back to wringing his hands.

"You've got to be kidding," Jan muttered.

"We didn't touch it, I swear," Shelley said.

"Yeah, right. It just fell by itself, did it?" The man gestured to the pieces of broken glass. "They've never fallen before! And now you've jinxed this place!"

Shelley snorted despite the situation. "Well, that's actually kind of funny because my friend's nickname is—"

Jan stopped Shelley with an icy look. "There's a first time

for everything, right?" she interjected. When the ticket man shot her a glare, she smiled sweetly. "I'm so sorry, sir, maybe it was just the—"

Before she could finish, Jan's knees buckled. She stumbled back, winded, as the terrible metallic tinge returned. It was so bad that Jan would've hit the ground if it weren't for Shelley.

"Holy shit! Are you okay?" Shelley gasped, reaching out for Jan to hold her steady.

Even the ticket man stopped his ranting, though he sounded more annoyed than concerned when he asked, "What's wrong with her?"

"She's been having weird episodes," Shelley said. "Jinx, I really think you should go to the doctor. These are getting scary. What if they're seizures?"

"I...just need to sit down," Jan managed between breaths.

Shelley nervously looked up at the ticket man.

"Go, go," he scoffed, waving them off.

Helping her to the nearest bench outside the House of Mirrors, Shelley sat beside Jan and placed a hand on her shoulder.

This had been the worst one yet. The reeling sensation that coursed through Jan's body left her emotions in a whirlwind, rendering her disillusioned and somewhere in the middle of angry and terrified.

"Maybe you were right about seeing a doctor," she said

after she finally regained her breath. "I've never had anything like this happen to me. I'm feeling better now, but these episodes come on so quickly."

"I can drive us home if you're still not feeling well."

Although it was a sincere offer, Jan could tell that the idea of driving the Blue Bomb made Shelley nervous.

"It's okay, I'll drive us home in a bit. Maybe I just need to eat something."

"Right. Good idea. We can stop by Gabriel's and grab something. It's close."

Jan nodded. Though her head had stilled and she could see clearly again, the metallic sensation lingered.

By the time they came within ten feet of Gabriel, who stood resting against the counter waiting for customers, the metallic feeling had all but subsided. Jan's stomach churned as she struggled to pinpoint the cause of her episodes. The unknown didn't usually bother her, but this was different.

Jan shifted her focus from her thoughts to the menu, hoping a distraction would ease her nausea. Only four items were listed there, but it was as good a diversion as any.

"What was that crash?" Gabriel asked.

"It was one of those big mirrors back there," Shelley answered. "Gads, that was really close. The ticket guy thought we broke it."

Gabriel raised an eyebrow. For a moment, despite knowing

it hadn't been her fault, Jan felt guilty.

"Why would he think that?" he asked.

"Probably because it fell right behind me," Jan said. "It does look suspicious, I'll give him that. But I swear, neither one of us touched it."

"Anyway, Jan got us out of there," Shelley said.

Gabriel laughed. "How'd you manage that? They're pretty stingy about their stuff."

"I think I almost fainted," Jan said as she leaned against the front of the counter.

Amusement turned to concern in Gabriel's eyes. "Are you okay?"

"Yeah, I'm fine." She did her best to sound casual, praying for a change of topic.

"She's been having these weird episodes," Shelley said, staring keenly at Gabriel, who shifted his worried gaze between the two girls. "They happen out of nowhere. She'll be totally fine one minute, and then all of the sudden, one will hit and she'll almost faint. It's the weirdest thing. It's been happening only since yesterday, though, when we went diving at the cove. I'm thinking maybe it has something to do with diving too far down in the water and not getting enough air."

"You might want to see a doctor," Gabriel said.

"Yeah, Shelley keeps saying that too," Jan replied curtly. Realizing her tone, she softened. "It's probably a good idea."

"Did you hear anything about those men we mentioned yesterday?" Shelley inquired, eyeing Jan. It was clear she hoped her question would improve the mood.

Gabriel gave her a crooked smile. "Not yet," he answered plainly.

Seeing Shelley's eyes drop in defeat, Jan tried to put forth a cheerier demeanor.

"Come on, Gabriel," she insisted. "You know everything that goes on around here."

Gabriel laughed. "Nobody knows everything."

Shelley let out an obnoxious giggle, and Jan tried to stifle her own laughter.

"What about the Aimsworth family?" Jan asked. "How much do you know about them?"

"As much as anyone, I think," Gabriel said.

Jan shrugged. "I don't know much about them at all."

"Well, the oldest son, Aiden, is Chief of Police," Gabriel said, drumming his fingers against the counter. "The youngest one, Owen, isn't talked about much, though. He's kind of the outcast of the family."

His voice lowered, and he leaned closer to Jan and Shelley. "According to some gossip I've heard," he said, barely above a whisper, "Owen went to college for a year or so but came back because he was too much of a bum."

"Oof, what a lousy reputation to have," Jan said.

"This one takes her schooling *very* seriously," Shelley joked, patting Jan's head playfully.

Gabriel chuckled. "A buddy of mine has an older brother who went to school with him. Said he was always kind of lazy and didn't really care that much about his future. I don't know..." he trailed off, then shrugged. "Maybe he just figured he had enough money already and didn't need college."

"Or maybe he has some valuable stuff saved up for himself," Jan thought out loud.

Gabriel narrowed his eyebrows. "What do you mean?"

Jan glanced at Shelley, who gave her a reassuring look.

"When Shelley and I went to the beach yesterday, we heard a boat out by the rocky area in the cove. When we went diving, we found this box. Inside it was this necklace right here, which I'm wearing," Jan explained, pointing to the locket that hung around her neck. "I guess the box and the necklace were part of an old sailor's legend about a sea witch who hid some kind of treasure inside of a mysterious box."

"Her treasure is supposed to contain a bunch of dangerous power or some mumbo-jumbo like that," Shelley said. She held up the box so Gabriel could get a good look at it.

"Anyway, we figured out that Mr. Brown had rented out a boat to Owen Aimsworth and his friend around the same time that morning," Jan said. "I think the necklace is worth a lot of money. He must've stolen it, and now he's trying to hide it so he can sell it later." She instinctively reached for the little oval-shaped locket that rested on her chest.

"Well, if you're right and that's the case," Gabriel said, "you should probably put it back, or at least get rid of it. If it's worth a lot of cash and he realizes it's missing, he'll come after it. That's just unnecessary trouble."

"He'd have to swim to the bottom of the cove to realize it's missing," Shelley said.

"Or see it on me," Jan whispered, remembering how Owen had glanced at her neck when he approached them on the boat.

"It looks like any other locket you could buy at the mall," Shelley said. "And plenty of people swim in that cove."

Not near the rocks, Jan thought, but she didn't say anything.

Gabriel shrugged. "It's probably best not to get involved in other people's business, especially if that business is sketchy and involves something valuable. I wouldn't want you two getting into something you couldn't get out of. Besides, I've heard some weird things about him."

"Owen?" Jan tilted her head.

Gabriel nodded. "Between us, I don't think he left college because he was too lazy to hack it. He's clearly a trust fund baby, but..." Gabriel bit his lip nervously before continuing. "I think something else happened."

"What do you mean?" Shelley asked.

Gabriel shrugged awkwardly. "I don't usually like to spread

Chili Dog
Chili Dog Chili Dog

rumors, and I don't even know if this story is true, but my friend—the one with the older brother who knew Owen—told me that there are a few people who say he got kicked out of college because he tried to hurt his roommate."

Silence lingered between the three of them.

"He tried to *hurt* his roommate?" Jan finally asked in disbelief. "How?"

"I don't know. People were saying Mrs. Aimsworth paid the school a ton of money to cover up the incident, but I can't say for certain if it's true." He wavered for a moment. "Just don't repeat that, okay? I really don't want to be spreading false information."

"We won't," Shelley said. "Geez, I sure hope it's just a rumor. That's really scary."

"It probably is," Gabriel said. "I've never actually met Owen, but from the few pictures I've seen of him in the paper, he looks pretty damn normal. Still, I can't help but wonder."

"Well, keep your ears peeled for us, okay?" Shelley asked.

"I think you mean eyes, Shell," Jan whispered.

"Right. Eyes. Keep your *eyes* peeled," Shelley said quickly.

Gabriel laughed and grinned endearingly at Shelley. "Will do. Until then, can I get you ladies anything to eat?"

Realizing how red Shelley's face was after her blunder, Jan smiled at Gabriel. "We're fine for now. Thanks," she said, pulling Shelley away from the counter.

"You're welcome. And Jan?"

"Yeah?"

"Take that necklace off, okay? Throw it back in the water or something," Gabriel said.

Jan smiled at him and nodded as she walked away, though she wasn't so sure she would take his advice.

"Any longer and I would've made an even bigger fool of myself," Shelley said as they approached the parking lot. The dismay was obvious in her voice as she covered her face with her hands.

"I dunno, Shell. Something tells me he thinks you're cute."

Shelley laughed dryly. "I doubt it."

Jan shrugged and linked arms with her friend. "C'mon, let's go back home. I feel a bit better now. We can come back later."

Chapter 11
METAL

IN THE EVENING, AFTER A LONG SHOWER, JAN stood in front of the mirror in the Waldbauer's cramped bathroom. The steam from the shower swathed around her body and clouded her reflection, making it hard to see anything but the occasional glint of the locket.

Rubbing the condensation away with her towel, Jan rested her elbows on the porcelain sink. The longer she studied the necklace, the more attached she felt to it—as though each breath drew the two closer. And yet, after her encounter with Owen in the morning, Jan couldn't help but wonder if she was putting herself and Shelley in undue danger by keeping it on. Though she desperately longed to know why the locket was so important to him and why he had hidden it, even Jan knew that wearing it around would stir up unwanted trouble.

The way Owen had eyed her neck sent a shudder through Jan's body. She'd tried to cover the locket with her hair and the water, but she knew he was suspicious.

It would be foolish to keep it on, especially somewhere so noticeable. Slowly, she ran her hand along the chain, hesitating at the clasp.

Keep it on. The metallic smell, like that of an old rusted teapot, returned. Though she didn't feel breathless, the smell was unmistakable. It was the same smell that overcame her whenever she had her episodes—the smell she noticed the first time she put the necklace on.

What if...? No, that's stupid. Shaking her head to herself, Jan pulled on her jeans and a hoodie. She dried her hair quickly, all the while trying to rid herself of the terribly disconcerting smell of metal, then slipped out of the bathroom and headed back to Shelley's room.

"Weird question," she said, trying to sound casual as she began folding up her clothes and swimsuit.

"Hmm?" Shelley mumbled, her eyes glued to the glossy pages of a summer magazine.

"What do you think magic feels like?"

Shelley looked up. "What?"

"If magic had a *feel*, what do you think it would be like?"

Shelley shrugged. "Maybe a tingling sensation? Why?"

"Just wondering." Jan shrugged as well, trying to mirror her friend's casual movements. "Do you think magic has a smell...or maybe even a taste?"

Shelley stifled a laugh. "You can't taste or smell magic. It's not tangible."

"Well, technically *smells* aren't tangible," Jan said, arranging the clothes she had brought with her into a neat pile beside her suitcase.

"You know what I mean, smart-ass." Shelley rolled her eyes and returned to her magazine, where she observed a picture of a model flaunting a bikini. "That's a cute swimsuit," she said absent-mindedly. "I bet my dad would never let me buy it."

"I wonder if anyone has ever tried to study magic," Jan continued, "like way back when. Or maybe there are still people who study it, even though most of us don't believe in it. And if they *have* studied magic, I wonder if they've ever come across any evidence that proves it has a smell and a taste, or at least a very apparent feeling—"

"Jinx," Shelley interrupted, "you're organizing my clothes."

Jan looked down at her hands, realizing that she had begun folding Shelley's messily strewn T-shirts and sorting them into separate piles.

"We both know that you organize when you're nervous," Shelley said through a giggle. She smiled gently, then put down her magazine and sat up on her bed. "What's up? Are you okay?"

"Yeah," Jan replied, putting down one of Shelley's shirts. "I'm fine. Just wondering about some stuff."

Shelley eyed her inquisitively but only shrugged and closed

her magazine.

"What do you say we go back to the Fun Zone tonight?" she asked. "We can go on some rides and maybe even go back to the House of Mirrors if that ticket man doesn't kill us."

"That would be fun," Jan said, praying that a distraction of some kind would ease her anxiety. Although the metallic tinge in her mouth and nose had begun to fade, a knot in her stomach took its place.

"Sweet. I'll change into something warmer."

While Shelley dug through a pile of jackets lying on her carpet, Jan fiddled with the locket. Something within her felt more comfortable—safer, even—to have it on. She had never felt like this about anything.

Honestly, Jan, a necklace can't make you feel sick, she thought, chastising herself for being so illogical.

Nevertheless, the knot in her stomach remained.

This wasn't normal. Jan began to feel even worse. Was something wrong with *her*? How could one necklace possibly be causing all of these irrational thoughts?

For a moment, she desperately wished her father were there to console her and explain that everything was okay—that things like magic and dangerous powers created by sea witches didn't exist.

"Ready?" Shelley asked, pulling up her tattered jeans.

"Ready," Jan smiled at her friend through her nerves. She

would take the necklace off later.

While passing through the living room, Shelley informed Mr. Waldbauer where they were going. After a curt nod, which was followed by a "Be back by eleven," the girls were out of the door.

Sliding into the Blue Bomb, Shelley looked over at Jan, curiosity in her eyes.

"Jinx?" she ventured as Jan turned the engine on. "What do *you* think magic feels like?"

Jan pulled out of the driveway and turned onto the gravel road. Keeping her eyes on the street and her thoughts on the necklace, she took a deep breath.

"Metal," she whispered.

Chapter 12
THE BIRDLIKE MAN

NIGHT TRANSFORMED THE FUN ZONE INTO AN entirely different world from that of the colorless, fog-filled day. Bright lights blinked and circled as the Ferris wheel rolled on its endless journey. Tinny music chimed out of the slowly turning carousel, its painted horses gliding up and down smoothly, forever chasing each other, while turning, spinning, and plunging machines flung out the delighted screams of their riders.

Even Jan was affected by the magic of the park. Something about the colors, music, and crowds that the Fun Zone attracted at night distracted her from her thoughts about the necklace, which felt unusually heavy around her neck. Still, the nagging voice within her urged her to keep it on, and Jan obeyed. Though she knew it was irrational, she couldn't help but view the necklace as a security blanket, clad in the childish fantasy that she'd be safer with it on.

"How about we get our picture taken?" Jan suggested as they entered the park. "There's a photo booth in here." She pointed at the penny arcade. "Only fifty cents."

The girls crowded onto the tiny bench inside the booth and pulled the curtain. A few moments later, the lights flashed and a card dropped into the slot beneath the machine.

"These are always such ugly pictures," Shelley remarked, laughing.

"Yeah, they are," Jan said as she stuffed it into her pocket. "Whatever, it's not like we're going to show it to anyone."

"Think we dare pass the mirrors again?" Shelley mused. "I'd like to see you go right up to one and *not* break it."

That was a dare Jan couldn't pass up.

"Observe, my dear friend." She marched up to one of the mirrors showing her distorted reflection. "I'm facing the thing head-on. No cracks or chips have appeared. Step right up and see this wonder of wonders for yourself." She gave a grand gesture toward the mirror and grinned. Despite her theatrical confidence, part of her expected the mirror to come crashing down again. When it didn't, she exhaled in relief.

"Well," she continued, giving Shelley a melodramatic smile, "who will be the next to witness this amazing feat?"

Taking the bait, Shelley walked up and stood next to Jan.

"Actually, Shell," Jan said, poking Shelley playfully, "you

might want to step back. I heard mirrors break when something hideous comes in front of them."

"Hey!" Shelley laughed and pushed Jan to the side.

They doubled up in overdone hilarity, greatly relieved that the glass hadn't actually shattered upon their appearance.

As they straightened up to point again at their warped forms, their laughter quickly faded. Over their shoulders, staring at them in the mirror was the thin, birdlike man from the boat. The colors swirling in the Fun Zone glinted onto his blond hair, changing it from yellow to green, red, blue, and pink every time a light outside the House of Mirrors flashed.

Shelley glanced at Jan, her eyes wide. In a flash of impulse, Jan grabbed her by the arm and began walking away from the man.

"Try to look unconcerned," she instructed. "Just keep a normal pace. We'll see if he follows us."

The steady tapping sound of his advancing steps did not die down; instead, they quickened as he pursued them like a hungry vulture closing in on its prey. Jan rounded a corner abruptly and whisked Shelley into a small hamburger joint.

Two cokes and thirty minutes later, the two stealthily emerged from their hiding place and looked about.

"I don't see him," Shelley whispered.

"I don't either, but keep alert. Let's go."

They started off, glancing over their shoulders every now

and then for the stranger with gray-green eyes.

"Maybe it wasn't Nolan," Jan said finally.

"Right," Shelley whispered. "Maybe that was just someone who looks like him. We're probably freaking out unnecessarily. Just because he saw us once in the cove doesn't mean he knows we've got anything to do with the box."

"I guess so." Jan wavered for a moment, biting her lip before whispering, "But I'm not so sure about his friend. I think Owen noticed the necklace on me."

"Maybe. But lots of people wear necklaces. I don't think he'd suppose it's anything out of the ordinary."

"He would if he knew it was *his* necklace."

Shelley groaned. "I don't know, Jinx. Either take it off or forget about it. We're not going to have any fun if we carry on like this."

Jan didn't respond. Perhaps Shelley was right. If Nolan noticed she wasn't wearing the necklace, he would have less reason to follow them. It was with a tinge of unease, however, that she realized she would rather Nolan follow them than take the necklace off.

I'll keep it on...just for now, she told herself. At that very moment, the metallic feeling returned, as though it agreed with her decision.

"Want to go on the roller coaster?" she asked Shelley, yearning for another distraction.

Shelley raised a lone eyebrow and smirked. "Are you sure you're up for it? Don't you dislike roller coasters?"

"Only the super high ones."

Shelley brightened. "Okay! Let's look backward this time," she suggested gleefully as they approached the short queue before the line. Looking back at Jan, she teased, "Unless you're too scared."

"Anything you can do, I can do," came Jan's uncertain answer, and they climbed aboard.

~

Wobbling and gasping after a harrowing ride, the girls got off and leaned against the railing that hovered over the rocky shore.

"Want to go again?" Shelley asked, grinning.

"It'd be better if we save our money for other things."

"I knew you'd say that. You're such a chicken." Shelley dodged a poke she knew was coming.

"How about we go to the Fun House? That sounds like a safer alternative."

Shelley rolled her eyes, but she nodded in agreement nonetheless. "Fine. I guess that means I can try to get you to go on the Bamboo Shoot."

"Not a chance."

The Fun House was far more cramped and noisy than the

rest of the Fun Zone, which made it a safe place to be. How could anyone find anyone else in there?

Two hours passed before the girls noticed how much time they had spent. It wasn't until groups of people began to leave that Shelley glanced up at the wall clock to check the time. Realizing how late it was, she roughly grabbed ahold of Jan's arm.

"It's eleven-thirty!" she hissed. "We need to get home. Shit, my dad is going to kill us."

Jan wriggled free from Shelley's grasp. "One more ride on the Alpine Slide," she said. "I promise it won't take long."

Shelley looked at the clock again, then back at Jan and sighed irritably. "Fine. But *hurry*."

They grabbed a gunny sack from the trough at the bottom of the slide and started up the stairs to the top. Just as they were about to begin their descent on the thirty-foot-long undulating slide, Shelley looked back.

"Jinx," she whispered, smacking Jan's shoulder to get her attention. "There he is again!"

Jan whirled around. As hard as Nolan tried to conceal himself amongst the remaining crowd, the lank, grim-faced man lying in wait at the bottom of the platform was hard to miss.

What made him even more noticeable, however, was that he was staring right at her.

Chapter 13
THE BAMBOO SHOOT

JAN CURSED UNDER HER BREATH AND GRABBED Shelley's arm.

"Quick, Shelley, let's go. When we get to the bottom, we'll run for it."

"Run where?"

"Christ, I don't know! Just *run*."

Plunging headfirst, they pushed off. The first drop, the steepest one, leveled out slightly on a short plateau that cut their speed. By the time they reached the second plateau, Nolan had started his descent from the top. They glanced back up the slide when they reached the bottom.

"Are you kidding?" Jan gaped at Shelley. "He's following us on the damn slide? He needs to work on his subtlety."

"Just *move*, you idiot," Shelley said, pulling Jan up.

They chucked their sacks into the bin and started running.

Shelley stopped at the bottom of a foot-wide ladder and pushed Jan up ahead of her. They scaled the ladder in front of them two rungs at a time.

On reaching the platform at the top, Jan stopped dead in her tracks, staring into the gaping hole before her.

"Shelley, you clod!" she gasped. "This is the Bamboo Shoot! Why'd you choose this? You know I hate things this high!"

"It's not much higher than the Alpine Slide," Shelley persisted, pushing Jan closer to the hole.

"No, no, no," Jan stammered, backing up. "It's one hundred feet down. The Alpine Slide was only thirty, and you know how long it took me to mentally prepare myself before I went down it!"

"But you ended up doing it, remember? You bragged all of last summer about how you finally got over your fear. I promise the Bamboo Shoot isn't much different."

"It's *totally* different!"

"You can't back down now. Look at all the people behind you. Just go!"

"I'll get killed and it'll be all your fault!"

"Stop being a drama queen and *go*. Nolan isn't going to come up here and wait patiently for us to go down, so just grow a pair and get it over with."

"How do you know he won't be waiting for us at the

bottom?" Jan argued, desperately trying to stall her jump.

"Because he's about ten people behind us," Shelley said coolly, crossing her arms.

Jan swung around. Her stomach dropped when she realized that Shelley was right. Standing impatiently behind a dozen people was the blond-haired, dull green-eyed young man. But where was Owen?

Regardless, seeing Nolan was enough for Jan. She wrapped herself tightly in one of the sacks that was lying on the platform and squeezed her eyes shut. She was trying to wriggle into the slide feet first when Shelley gave her a shove. Down she went, headfirst, eyes clenched shut, disappearing from view at the first turn of the funnel-like slide.

Once Shelley hit the bottom, Jan warned her in a trembling voice, "Don't *ever* do that to me again. You hear me?"

Shelley ignored her. "We might've just lost him," she said. "Let's book it to the Blue Bomb."

The run to the parking lot left both girls breathless. They quickly reached the Blue Bomb and slid into the front seats. Neither of them said a word until they finally rounded the corner to Shelley's house.

"I don't think we were followed," Jan whispered, glancing at the rearview mirror.

"Thank God." Shelley rested a trembling hand on her chest. "I can't believe he tried to follow us. Isn't that illegal? I'm almost one hundred percent sure that's illegal. Maybe we should tell the police about this. Or maybe that's a bad idea...we don't want to blow this out of proportion. Besides, if my dad finds out, he'll make the situation even *more* stressful." Shelley opened her mouth to say something else but clamped it shut when she noticed that the necklace was still clasped around Jan's neck.

"Jinx, you really oughta take that off," she said after a moment of uncomfortable silence. "It's obvious they want it back. Wearing it around constantly is only going to piss them off and put us in way too much danger."

"I know, I know. I will." Even saying it sent a shiver of reluctance through her. It wasn't until now that she realized she really did not want to take the necklace off.

Why? Jan scolded herself. *It's just a stupid necklace that's far more trouble than it's worth. Why am I so against taking it off?*

The entire matter made Jan upset. She felt her face growing red and had to bite down hard on her lip to distract herself from her brimming tears. How could she possibly explain what she was feeling to Shelley when even she didn't understand it?

Shelley shifted nervously in her seat. "We need to be quiet now. I don't want to wake up my dad, especially since we're already way past curfew."

Jan nodded in agreement. She turned off the lights and the motor to avoid attracting attention and coasted down the hill, coming to an abrupt stop.

Bam! A minor explosion rocked the Blue Bomb. With a couple of apologetic wheezes, the car settled down for the night.

"Thanks a lot, Jinx." Shelley winced as a light flicked on in the living room.

"Are you kidding? Do you seriously think *I* made it do that?"

Not surprisingly, the girls were greeted at the door by Mr. Waldbauer, silent and tight-lipped. Instead of lecturing them, he simply said, "I've had an incredibly long day. I'm far too tired to argue right now. We'll talk in the morning."

With that, he turned on his heel and stalked away to bed.

"Maybe we should tell him about Nolan," Jan said after he had left the room.

"No way! With this curfew-breaking shit, we're going to be in trouble as it is. I don't want my dad watching us a thousand times more closely than he already does, especially because of some twenty-something-year-old creep."

"Fine," Jan said. She put her hands up in surrender. "All we can do right now is try to sleep and see what mood he's in later."

Shelley clenched her jaw and gave a terse nod. "You're right," she said, her voice low. "I guess we'll just have to see what tomorrow brings."

Chapter 14
FOR SANITY'S SAKE

BREAKFAST WAS TOUCHY THE NEXT MORNING. Since it was Saturday and rotations at the department allowed Mr. Waldbauer the day off, he was up early working in his shop. When he came in for breakfast, it was clear he hadn't gotten over what had happened.

"Michelle and Jan," he said as he sat down at the table. "I'll tell you this once more. I make the rules here. If you cannot follow them, you lose your privileges. I hate making idle threats, but I also don't want to ground you. Just respect your curfew timing. That's all I ask. You were an hour late."

"We were only at the Fun Zone," Shelley said.

"I don't care where you were," he said through a sigh. "Weird people hang out all over the place at night, and two young, pretty girls are the perfect target. I put a curfew in place for a reason. You're allowed to be out all day as long as you're home by eleven."

"I know," Shelley murmured, her eyes flitting to the laced edge of the tablecloth. "I'm sorry."

"Me too," Jan lied.

Even with the apologies and the girls promising that they would adhere to their curfew timing, breakfast ended curtly that day, with nothing more than uncomfortable small talk. Jan decided not to bring up the Nolan incident, especially since she knew Shelley didn't want to.

After Mr. Waldbauer returned to his workshop, Shelley turned to Jan and scoffed.

"You still haven't taken off that damn necklace, have you?" she said icily.

Jan only shrugged in response, then said, "I was thinking about something last night."

Shelley shot her a chiding look, but Jan ignored it.

"You know how the county library keeps archives of old newspapers?" she asked.

Shelley furrowed her brows and shook her head.

"Oh, come on, haven't you ever done a school project where you needed to look at current events or something?"

"I usually just grab some random newspaper off the neighbor's lawn before I go to school and find something there," Shelley said, shrugging and grinning lazily.

"My goodness, you're impossible," Jan teased. She shook

her head, but smiled anyway. "Well, they do, and I know I've seen a couple articles throughout the years that mention the Aimsworth family. I bet if we went through some of those archives, we could find some interesting stuff."

Shelley sighed through her nose. "And what exactly would we look for?"

"I dunno. I was thinking we could just look, you know? There's no harm in that. We could pop in this afternoon and see what we find. Worst case, if we don't find anything, who cares? I'm just curious."

"Are you sure it's a good idea to dive even deeper into this thing? After what happened last night with Nolan, maybe we should leave it be."

"What? No, we can't!" Jan persisted. "Besides, nobody will know what we're doing, so it's not like it'll cause any trouble."

"Just listen to yourself," Shelley said softly. "I don't want last night to repeat itself. This whole necklace thing clearly means a lot more to Owen and Nolan than we expected. You should just take it off so we can move on with our summer and not get into trouble again."

Jan scowled. "What's taking it off going to do?" she argued. "They already suspect us."

When Shelley didn't respond, Jan gave her a dramatic puppy-dog look. "Please," she said. "Do me a solid and come with me. I'm really curious about what we may find."

"Your curiosity is going to kill us," Shelley muttered.

"Maybe we'll find a clue about why the necklace is so important to that family." Jan poked Shelley encouragingly.

Shelley sucked in a deep breath. "You're not going to give this up until we look there," she said, more to herself than Jan.

"No, I'm not. I promise it won't take long. I just want to see if we find anything. For sanity's sake, if not anything else."

"You mean for *your* sanity."

"Who knows," Jan shrugged. "Maybe we'll find something super interesting."

Shelley crinkled her nose. "I sure hope not," she said. "For *my* sanity's sake."

Chapter 15

TANYA DAY

THE LIBRARY WAS NEARLY DESOLATE DURING THE summer. Only a few people sat scattered around large tables, each one engrossed in their reading. The librarian, a pinch-lipped lady with bright blue cat-eye glasses, hardly acknowledged Shelley and Jan as they entered.

"We can find the archives at the back," Jan said.

Shelley followed her reluctantly. After about five minutes of sifting through old papers, the girls had accumulated a stack dating all the way back to 1962.

"This should be a good range," Jan said. They plopped the bulky pile down onto an isolated table at the corner of the main reading room.

"Ten years?" Shelley let out an exaggerated sigh.

"They're all small papers, Shell. Aledale never has anything to report on."

Shelley blew a wisp of hair out of her face. "What exactly are we trying to look for?"

"Just skim through the papers and see if any articles mentioning the Aimsworths pop up."

For a while, the two girls sat next to each other, quietly flipping through the crisp, aging pages. There was something pleasant about the redolence of paper and ink that made the uneasiness in Jan's mind go away, even if only for a bit.

"Holy crap!" Shelley exclaimed suddenly, staring down at the page of a 1967 issue.

"What?" Jan asked, curious excitement rushing through her. "Did you find something?"

"Aledale's Mariners Club went undefeated at our school for the *entire* year in 1967! Dammit, why did I have to be in sixth grade?"

Jan shifted in her seat, stiffening as her eagerness deserted her. She drummed her fingers on the table, loud enough so Shelley would notice her impatience.

"We're supposed to be looking for stuff about the Aimsworth family," she said.

"You have your obsessions, I have mine," Shelley replied curtly, her eyes still glued to the page.

"It isn't..." Jan caught herself. She pursed her lips and softened, careful to mind her tone. "Maybe you can try junior and senior year," she said. "We both know you're going to end up being the captain."

Shelley sighed wishfully, but she didn't respond. Jan stared blankly at the page before her, struggling to define the lingering silence. Though she hoped it wasn't strained, she knew Shelley well enough to tell when she was annoyed.

It isn't an obsession.

She opened her mouth to justify herself, but promptly closed it when Shelley turned the page, returning to her search for information about the Aimsworth family. Losing a sigh, Jan followed suit.

Page after page revealed nothing but run-of-the-mill articles. Although a few papers here and there included snippets about the Aimsworths, they only briefly mentioned family donations and Aiden Aimsworth's appointment as Chief of Police.

A short article published in the December 1963 issue described Mr. Aimsworth's death and funeral preparations. Another brief article outlined his contributions to Aledale, accompanied by pictures of the family. Jan looked at the picture of Owen, who was probably only a year older than her at the time. She studied his face, thinking about what Gabriel had told her and Shelley. Whether or not the rumors were true, Jan felt a cold shiver run down her spine.

Dozens of articles later and still no mention of the necklace or the box, Jan leaned back in her seat, discouraged.

Shelley yawned, unfolding a July 1966 issue. She clicked her tongue as she flipped through the pages, growing louder with every passing moment until, abruptly, she clamped her lips shut.

"Hey, take a look at this." She slid the paper sideways to Jan and pointed at a brief article published on the corner of one of the back pages.

A photo of a smiling young woman with large eyes and bobbed hair was centered between the writing. Following Shelley's finger to the print, she read the text closely:

Aledale County mourns the death of twenty-year-old Tanya Day. Day was admitted to Sapphire Waters Community Hospital in May 1966 as a result of various episodes that were believed to be a threat to her safety. She stayed for two months before committing suicide last week. Though Day was said to have been a close and longtime friend of the Aimsworth family, they have declined to comment.

"Wow," Jan said through a heavy sigh.

"Man, if I were this Tanya chick, I definitely wouldn't want my death to be broadcasted like that," Shelley said.

"It's the media. They publish whatever information they can."

"I guess so. But gosh, Jinx. She was twenty when she died. That's only four years older than us."

Jan cringed as she turned her attention to Tanya's picture. She ran her finger over the page, let out a frustrated sigh, and muttered, "This tells us *nothing* about the Aimsworth family."

"I don't know what you were expecting," Shelley said. She tapped her foot impatiently against the leg of her chair.

Jan skimmed the paragraph again, stopping where it read *"...as a result of various episodes that were believed to be a threat to her safety."*

"Do you see this part?" she asked.

Shelley nodded. "What do you think it means?"

Jan's stomach sank, but she played off her discomfort by overturning the newspaper and giving Shelley a casual shrug. "I guess we're not going to find much here. Every article that mentions the Aimsworth family is either about money or dead people."

"That's pretty depressing," Shelley said. "Almost as depressing as the fact that we're spending our summer break in a library."

"We've been here less than an hour," Jan said, rolling her eyes. "Whatever. It looks like we hit a dead end anyway."

"Does that mean you'll finally stop trying to dig up buried information about the Aimsworth family? You have to admit that it's a little creepy. Not many people decide to look through ten years of newspaper archives."

"It is *not* creepy," Jan argued. When Shelley grinned and raised an eyebrow at her, she resigned. "Okay, maybe it's a little weird. But it's not like we found anything useful."

"Just a lot of upsetting articles."

After a moment of silence, Shelley folded up the newspaper and said, "You know, I've been thinking: this whole necklace business is getting a little out of hand. Maybe we should just rent a boat, sail out to the point, drop it back into the water with the box, and voila! We know nothing about it. That way, we get ourselves out of the shit we're in, and if those creeps come asking about the necklace and the box, we just say we know nothing. We'll even drop it close to the place they left it so they can find it again. Owen and Nolan will have their stupid locket and box back, and more importantly, we'll get our summer back. See? Everyone'll be happy."

Jan hesitated and glanced back at the newspaper. A small, unrestrained part of her desperately wanted to dig up more information. If only she could discover more history about the Aimsworth family, then maybe things would finally start to make sense.

When she looked back at Shelley, however, she realized that the search would be fruitless. On top of that, after what had happened at the Fun Zone, she had to admit that Shelley had a point.

"Fine," she said. "I guess that's our best bet if we want to avoid unnecessary trouble."

"And intervention. If my dad figures out some dude was following us..." Shelley trailed off. "God, he'd have a fit. I bet he'd never let me out of the house again."

"You're right. I have a feeling he would overreact *just* a bit." Jan shot Shelley a teasing smile, but her friend remained serious.

"We can go straight to Mr. Brown's after this," Shelley said. "He'll just think we're going out for a sail. I know he won't suspect anything. It shouldn't take long."

Jan forced a smile. "Yeah. Good idea."

Though she tried to sound optimistic, something in her voice must have signaled her reluctance. Shelley's determined expression softened, and she placed a tender hand on Jan's shoulder.

"The necklace looks pretty on you," she said, "and it might be worth a lot of money. But it's not worth all the trouble."

Jan looked down at the locket.

Keep it on, that small, galling part of her begged.

"I don't want it because it's pretty or valuable," she said.

"Then why haven't you taken it off yet?"

Jan only shrugged in response, reluctant to admit that she didn't know the answer.

Chapter 16
BOAT CHASE

MR. BROWN WAS LEANING BACK IN HIS CHAIR when the girls arrived. Jan noticed that it had been kept in the same spot for so long that it had formed a little niche. Hearing them approach, he looked up. He didn't seem surprised at all to see them. Schätzli eyed them for a moment as well, then dozed off to sleep again.

"Finally decide to go for a sail?" he asked, his tiny eyes twinkling underneath his bushy eyebrows. "Or do you have more questions for your *investigation*?"

Shelley laughed, but all Jan could manage was a strained chuckle.

"We'll take a sail this time, Mr. Brown," Shelley said. "Good day for it, isn't it? How about this one over here?" She pointed to a smaller boat, its paint worn off on the sides. "I've sailed one like her before, so I think it should be easy."

"We'll just take it out for an hour, maybe less," Jan added. She held the mermaid box in place under her arm as she pulled crumpled money out of her pocket. "Two fifty, right?"

"Two fifty, plus a five-dollar deposit," Mr. Brown clarified.

"Five-dollar deposit?" Jan said. "Oh crap, Shelley! We don't have five dollars." Though she tried to sound upset, the growing part of her that dreaded giving up the necklace was overcome with relief. Even though Shelley had told her to put it in the box, Jan had ignored her.

It'd probably be best to wait until we reach the cove before taking it off, she'd decided. After all, she didn't want to risk accidentally losing it.

"Well, Mr. Brown," Shelley said, "I'm a mariner myself and I'm pretty good with boats. Maybe we could give you your deposit later? I promise we will. From one sailor's honor to another."

Mr. Brown chuckled, scratched his head, and sucked on his pipe for a moment. "Seein' as how you're with a club and all, I guess I could let it fly this once. No deposit necessary."

Jan felt her heart sink but forced a smile upon observing Shelley's brightened expression.

"Wow, really?" Shelley said, grinning. "Thanks a ton, Mr. Brown!"

"But mind you, next time, bring your deposit along. Now get in. I'll push you away from the edge."

Shelley eagerly climbed into the boat. Jan followed reluctantly, feeling her tiny ray of hope shrivel up and die. Once they were clear of the dock, Shelley turned back and waved to the old man smiling on the wharf.

"Know where to go?" Jan asked through gritted teeth, terribly sick of the chipper attitude she was forcing.

Shelley nodded affirmatively. "We'll have to head out toward the breakwater. It's upwind, so it'll take a bit. I sure hope we can make it over to the cove before our hour runs out."

I don't, Jan thought to herself. Still, she nodded and said, "As long as you tell me when to duck under that sail, we'll be okay."

The small boat headed out slowly into the rougher and more open water near the mouth of the bay. On and on it bobbed, bucking both the wind and the incoming tide.

"Coming about," Shelley called for the umpteenth time. She swung the boom around to catch the wind for another tack. It had only been about twenty minutes since they had left the wharf, and Jan could already see the rocks of the cove in the distance.

When they were a couple yards away from the rocks where they had found the necklace and the box, Shelley brought the boat to a standstill.

"We got here earlier than I expected," she said, beaming. "Not too shabby, huh?"

Jan said nothing but laughed at Shelley's rhetorical remark nonetheless. She couldn't let Shelley know that she was still hesitant to give up the necklace.

"Okay," Shelley continued, "now I'll just—"

"Excuse me!" shouted a distinct voice from afar.

Jan's breath caught in her throat. Following steadily behind them, far enough to obscure the identities of the figures aboard, was another small boat. Jan didn't need to see the men to realize who they were—the gravelly voice was unmistakable.

"Owen and Nolan?" Shelley said between gasps.

"What the hell?" Jan cried out.

"Jinx, *shut up*. They can hear you."

"Are you kidding? They must've been following us and boarded right after we did!"

"Why would Mr. Brown let them if he knows—"

"He has no idea they're after us, Shelley!" Jan snapped, louder and harsher than she had intended. "They probably just came up and casually asked for a boat, and he thought nothing of it because *you* made up that lie that we were trying to find Owen because I thought he was cute or some bullshit like that. So of course Mr. Brown thinks it's all some stupid teenage game!"

"Jesus! Calm down," Shelley said. "Why don't we just wait for them to approach us so that we can give them the necklace and the box? We'll say it's all been a huge misunderstanding like we should've done in the first place."

Although Jan knew Shelley was right, she didn't respond. The thought of giving the necklace up made a terrible knot form in her stomach—one so large that she thought she may vomit.

She couldn't give it up. Not now. It was *hers*.

"No," she said finally, looking straight at Shelley.

"No?" Shelley narrowed her eyebrows. "What do you mean 'no'?"

"I mean...it's mine," Jan asserted firmly, feeling her grasp tighten around the mermaid box. She hardly knew what she was saying. It was like someone else—someone completely devoid of logic and intent on keeping both the necklace and the box close—was speaking on her behalf.

"You've got to be kidding me, Jan. Are you serious? For a stupid necklace? If you want one that much, I'll go to the mall and buy you one. Just give them back what we took. It isn't ours."

"No," Jan declared, much louder than before. "I found it, which means it's mine." Although she realized how irrational she sounded, the urge to keep the necklace on blocked out any remaining sensible thoughts.

"Yeah, that's them," she heard Nolan say. "The redhead and the brunette. Just like in the picture."

Jan and Shelley exchanged glances in horror.

"What picture?" Shelley asked, her eyes wide.

Jan fervently stuffed her hand inside her back pocket. Feeling nothing in there, she tried her front ones. The photo from the penny arcade was gone.

"The one we took last night," she said. "I must've lost it when we were running from Nolan."

"Hey!" yelled the smoother voice—Owen's voice.

Jan's body seized up.

"Shelley, they kept our *picture*," she said hurriedly. "If we're going to get rid of the necklace, then I don't want to give it to them. I want to take it to the police or something. I don't trust them."

"But..."

"Remember what your dad said about creepy people who hang out at the Fun Zone at night and target girls like us? *They* are those people!" Jan continued, pointing at the approaching motorboat.

"Okay, okay, we'll get out of here. But we go to the police immediately after and give them the necklace. We'll tell them everything, right?"

"Yes, of course," Jan agreed, hardly thinking. She would take any reason to keep the necklace on a little longer. "Now go!"

Shelley fought to catch what wind there was while the little boat struggled away from the cove, moving toward the open channel of the bay, its sail full out against the wind.

"Do you think we can go around them and reach the dock?" Jan asked.

"If we can stay in front of the wind, we might," Shelley answered, her hands shaking. Looking down at her own fingers, which clutched the mermaid box tenaciously, Jan realized that she was trembling as well.

"Problem is," Shelley continued, nodding her head toward the motorboat, "it doesn't look like they'll let us."

The motorboat began closing in on them, cutting them off until the two small boats were headed straight toward each other, far too quickly to be safe.

"Shelley!" Jan shrieked.

"Shut up, Jinx, let me think!"

Shelley held the rope of the sail in one hand and the tiller tight in the other. She fixed her eyes on the oncoming boat as it came closer and closer to their own.

Intent as the two men seemed to be on reaching them, it was obvious that they didn't want to die in the process.

Owen shouted something unintelligible. With a great spray of salty water, the men turned abruptly away from the sailboat, sending the rough waves of their wake crashing into its bow.

"Duck!" yelled Shelley. She pulled the boom around and took a sharp turn away from the motorboat.

As they sped away from each other, Jan sucked in a deep breath and looked over to see Owen gesturing wildly in their direction. Within seconds, the boat was trailing behind them.

"It's not going to work, Jinx. I've got to head out toward the breakwater. They're too fast. I can keep tacking when they're closer, but I can't fool them forever."

The increasing swells of the incoming tide between the breakwater and the coastline made tacking all the more difficult. Luckily, the motorboat was facing problems of its own; it was being roughly buffeted about by the waves.

"I need one more tack," Shelley said to herself. "I've got to get away from the kelp." She swung around again in an attempt to distance the boat from the greenish-brown seaweed and headed out toward the central channel once more.

"Look out, Shelley!" Jan shouted. Her heart thumped against her chest, threatening to break free.

The motorboat came up fast, seemingly out of nowhere. Shelley made a quick tack to avoid them and caught a giant swell from the side. The little boat lurched and rolled helplessly as Shelley struggled to catch the wind again. As hard as she tried, the sail only flapped uselessly on the mast.

"What's wrong?" Jan asked. The boat rocked violently. She held the mermaid box tight to her chest, determined to keep it and the necklace with her at all costs. "What's happening?"

"I...I can't seem to steer it," Shelley answered, her face wrought with distress. She jerked the rudder from side to side, but in vain. The shoreline and the offshore barrier of the rocks inched closer. Each successive swell threatened to upturn the little boat on its side, emptying its occupants into the water. Soaked by the cold ocean spray, the girls' clothing and hair clung to them like wet Saran Wrap.

"Okay, we just need to calm down," Jan said, heaving a shaky breath. "I think they've backed off a little. I'll tell you if I see them the next time we get to the top of a swell."

As the boat dipped and then rose on the water, Jan gripped its sides, looking about for their pursuers while Shelley battled with the rudder.

"They're farther away now. We can relax a little," Jan said, finally regaining some control over her trembling voice. Shelley, however, didn't seem relieved.

"They're farther away because they're smart," she snapped.

"What's that supposed to mean?"

"It means we're being carried toward the rocks. I can't catch the wind if I can't steer. The rudder is caught on the kelp."

Jan's stomach dropped. "What do we do?"

"Stay with the boat."

"What? We're not *that* far gone, are we?"

Shelley didn't answer. She simply pointed to the rocks boiling beneath the surface of the water a few yards away. Each wave lifted the tiny boat high in the air before dropping it like a stone as the trough of the wave followed the rise.

"My God, Shelley! We'll be smashed to bits on the rocks!"

Jan shouted. "We should jump off!"

"No chance. We're better off with the boat between us and those rocks. Sit still, hold on tight, and pray to God we get lucky."

Shelley's voice sounded impressively calm despite the situation. Her eyes stayed focused on the rocks ahead and her hands had surprisingly stopped shaking. Jan, however, felt as though a hummingbird had replaced her heart, and her stomach churned with every wave.

The tide was coming in fast now, relentlessly carrying them toward the shore. Jan watched in horror as they dropped closer and closer to the monstrous dark forms beneath the surface with each passing wave. Gray-blue water swirled white froth as it rushed over the rocks' jagged tips.

"Hold on, Jinx!" Shelley yelled. *"Hold on!"*

Jan clutched even tighter onto the slippery sides of the boat and gritted her teeth. As the churning mass rose up beneath them, the bottom of the sailboat crashed down on the first of the rocks with a crunching sound. The water on the boat's deck covered their shoes, but it was impossible to tell whether it came from the waves or was flowing through a hole in the boat.

"Another one!" Jan yelled, bracing herself.

The next wave lifted them off their perch, flinging them onto the next rock in the mass with another grinding blow.

"We're going to lose the entire bottom!" Jan shouted over

the thundering roar of the surf.

"We haven't tipped over yet," Shelley responded. "Maybe we can ride this out."

Curious sunbathers on the beach who had seen the boat floundering began to gather, watching the girls nervously. A bright orange rescue truck from the nearby lifeguard station raced down the beach toward a break in the rocks—its color a bright and welcome contrast against the brown of the beach.

Six more giant swells and subsequent blows on the rocks brought the little boat over the rock outcropping into the safer waters near the beach. On reaching the shore, the dripping and shivering girls looked at each other with relief. Advancing toward them were two sleek surfboards guided expertly by sun-bronzed lifeguards from the truck.

"Hang on," one said with a cheery smile. "We'll have you out in a minute."

They paddled up beside the boat and grabbed on, guiding them through the breakers of the narrow channel to the beach.

The moment they touched the sand, the crowd on the beach erupted in loud cheers and ran down to help the lifeguards pull the boat up onto the shore.

"Give you a hand, miss?" asked one of the lifeguards, extending his hand to Jan. Shelley had already hopped out and was talking to the other one.

Jan nodded numbly. She took his hand, clutching the

mermaid box tightly in the other. When she tried to stand up, her legs threatened to drop her back onto the boat.

"You okay?" the lifeguard asked.

"I'm...I'm fine."

"Do you need us to call anyone for you?"

"No...no, I'm okay."

"At least let us give you two a ride back to your car."

Jan nodded again and looked down at her arms and legs. Although she had gained a few scratches here and there, it wasn't half as bad as she had anticipated.

After helping her out, the lifeguard diverted his attention back to his truck. Jan nearly asked him not to leave. She couldn't face Shelley—not yet. It was with a rush of shame that she realized nearly getting skewered by rocks scared her less than facing her friend.

Forcing as much confidence as she could, Jan approached Shelley, who stood—arms crossed and eyes on her feet—a few yards away from the wooden remains of the boat. Jan opened her mouth, but the words didn't come out.

"Why couldn't you have just given them the necklace and the box so we could be done with this whole thing?" Shelley whispered.

"I..." Jan's voice trailed off. She took a breath as she tried to sort out what to say. "I don't know. I can't explain it. It's like...it's like the necklace doesn't want me to take it off."

"Do you hear yourself, Jan?"

"I know it sounds silly, but—"

"It sounds a little more than silly," Shelley said through a mirthless laugh. "You know what I think? I think you just wanted to keep it on because you care more about yourself than our safety. I think you just wanted to go on this stupid, childish adventure, and you didn't think for once that there could be actual consequences."

Jan gave Shelley a flabbergasted look. "Really, Shell?"

"Don't call me that."

"Christ, Shelley, I'm sorry. I know I should've just taken it off and given it to them. But maybe it really will help if we take it to the police...maybe it's better if they know about all this."

"Maybe," Shelley said coldly. "But if we'd gotten seriously hurt out there, that wouldn't have been worth it, would it?"

"No, but..." Jan felt the anger rising in her voice.

"But you didn't think about that, did you?"

"Don't act like I'm at fault for all of this," Jan snapped. "You were just as interested as I was. Don't act like you didn't ask about the box to Mr. Brown and Ms. Johnson, or like you didn't want to find out who the necklace belonged to."

"Not like this!" Shelley said, fighting hard to keep her chin from trembling. "I was curious, but I didn't view it as some sort of game like you did. I didn't go around pretending to be Sherlock Holmes, trying to find out who it belonged to, pursuing bullshit legends and stories. But you pushed on, just like you always do, because everything has to go your way, doesn't it? I didn't want to ask Mr. Brown about the rentals, but I went anyway because I knew if I didn't, you wouldn't shut up about it. I didn't think this was any of our business in the first place. I told you to take off that stupid necklace. But like always, you did what *you* wanted to do." She blinked rapidly, struggling to clear the tears in her eyes. "And because you refused to take it off and made me steer back," she continued, "we nearly got ourselves badly hurt...maybe even killed. But screw everyone else, right? As long as *you* get to live out your little fantasies."

The comment stung. Tears pricked her eyes, and Jan bit down hard on her lip. "You act like you're some victim who was forced to follow me around," she said. "Like you can't make your own decisions."

"That's not what I mean."

The silence that lingered between the girls felt colder than their wet clothes.

"I'm done," Shelley finally said. The ferocity in her voice made Jan's stomach drop. "I'm done with this stupid mystery hunt. I'm done wasting my summer to appease your need for adventure. I'm done putting my safety on the line because you're too stubborn to know when to stop." With a quick, rage-fueled movement, she snatched the mermaid box from Jan. "And I'm *done* with this box, and this locket, and this goddamn legend."

Jan had no time to take the box back from Shelley. With all the strength Shelley could muster, she chucked it into a pile of sand-covered rocks only a few feet away. She had always had a strong arm, and the box hit the rocks with a resounding clank. The sound made Jan's heart skip a beat. Stifling, protective fear coursed through her.

"What the hell is wrong with you?" she yelled, rushing over to the pile of rocks and scooping up the box. She felt like a mother protecting her child as she cradled it in her hands, desperately praying that nothing had happened to it.

It had to be broken. Or scratched. Or dented. There was no way anything as small and delicate as the mermaid box could emerge from a situation like this unscathed.

I'm never speaking to her again. She's broken it...she's ruined everything.

Jan rotated the box in her hand. There wasn't a single scratch on it. The box looked exactly as it had the day she found it in the water. The hinges still held together, and the mermaid carved on the lid glowered back at her with unremitting green eyes.

That's not possible.

Only, it was. Jan looked over its surface obsessively, each time sure she would find a small part of it that Shelley had ruined. But she never did. Relief rushed through her as she hugged the box close to her chest.

"You could've broken it," she snapped, finally daring to face Shelley again.

"You really need to get over this," Shelley said icily. "You act like that box and your precious necklace are worth more to you than our friendship." When Jan didn't respond, Shelley exhaled and pursed her lips. "Maybe they are."

Whether out of anger or stubbornness, Jan didn't respond.

"I get to say what happens next," Shelley continued. "We're going to let the lifeguards take us back to where we parked your car, then we'll go straight home and tell my dad everything that happened. He'll take us to the police, we'll give them the mermaid box and the necklace, and we'll tell them absolutely everything."

Jan stared at the grains of sand that stuck to her wet shoes, urging herself not to burst into tears. She pressed her tongue hard against the roof of her mouth and nodded.

"Fine," she said after a few moments of agonizing silence.

Neither of them spoke on the ride home.

Chapter 17
THE CHIEF OF POLICE

MR. WALDBAUER WAS STILL OUTSIDE WORKING when Jan pulled into the driveway. Without a word, Shelley got out and slammed the car door behind her.

Jan turned off the Blue Bomb and tossed the keys under the dashboard, then slipped out of the front seat. She eased her grip on the mermaid box, which she had been holding the entire way back to Shelley's house. Her fingers were sore from grasping it so tightly.

"Christ, what happened to you two?" Mr. Waldbauer exclaimed, rushing toward them when he noticed their wet clothes and the cuts across their faces.

As soon as he asked, Shelley began to sob. Between tears, the entire story came flooding out of her: how they had gone diving at the cove, how they had found the box with the necklace, how Owen and Nolan had followed them to get it back, the boat chase...everything.

Secretly, Jan was glad that Shelley managed to tell Mr. Waldbauer the whole story. She knew that if she had tried to, she would have started crying as well.

When Shelley finished the story, Mr. Waldbauer stood dead silent in front of them. After a prolonged moment of thought, he ran his hands through his hair and let out a slow breath.

"Thank you for telling me," he said.

The calmness in his voice took Jan by surprise. She had expected him to set out and track down Owen and Nolan to slit their throats himself. Instead, he remained unsettlingly still and composed.

"I'm going to take you two to the police station," he continued. "I'll talk to Aiden personally since his brother is involved. Bring both the locket and the box, okay? We'll sort it all out there. I promise."

This was the nicest side to Mr. Waldbauer Jan had ever seen. Something in his eyes—fear, sympathy, or maybe both— kept him grounded and collected.

Shelley was still sniffling as the girls went inside to change their clothes. Five minutes later, they climbed into the back of the Waldbauers' car.

The ride to the station was worse than the incident itself. Mr. Waldbauer remained disconcertingly calm, while Shelley stared down at her shoes and made it a point to avoid eye contact with Jan. By the time they arrived, all Jan could focus on was the heat in her face and the ringing in her ears.

Inside the station smelled like coffee and cigarettes. Jan pressed the locket to her chest while the girls followed Mr. Waldbauer past the front desk and into the main room. From there, they weaved throughout the cluttered desks and stacks of cardboard boxes, which led down a hallway to a foggy glass door with "Chief of Police" painted on the glass.

"I'll do the talking first," Mr. Waldbauer instructed before they entered.

The girls nodded in unison, and Mr. Waldbauer pulled open the door.

"Hey, Earl!" the man sitting at the large desk called out, flashing Mr. Waldbauer a smile. His voice was full of conviction and poise. "Always a pleasure to see you here on a Saturday. Anything I can do for you?"

Jan read the gold nameplate on his desk: *Aiden Aimsworth, Chief of Police.*

She then turned her attention to Aiden himself. As soon as she did, she realized how similar he looked to his younger brother. He had the same dark hair as Owen, but his eyes were lighter and softer, like wet sand on a beach. His face was a configuration of high cheekbones and an angular jaw that moved slightly to the right when he spoke. When he stood to greet them, Jan blinked back her shock at his austere posture, which was even better than Mr. Waldbauer's.

Usually, whenever Shelley and Jan came across a good-looking guy, they would give each other the same wide-eyed, giddy look. But since Shelley refused to acknowledge Jan's presence at the moment, it was only by glancing sideways at her friend that Jan realized she was thinking the same thing. Both girls remained silent, wavering between intimidation and awe.

"Unfortunately, yes," Mr. Waldbauer responded, snapping Jan out of her thoughts.

Pulling a chair from the corner of the room closer to Aiden's desk, Mr. Waldbauer sat down and gestured for Shelley and Jan to do the same. Obediently, the girls sat down on the two wooden chairs already in front of Aiden's desk.

"I want to run something by you," Mr. Waldbauer started slowly, "because I feel that in this situation, you'd be the best one to handle it. My daughter, Shelley, and her best friend, Jan, have had quite the encounter with your younger brother."

"I see," Aiden said, turning to the girls. Although he maintained his composure, it was strained. "I'm sorry I had to meet you two on an occasion such as this. Would you mind telling me what happened?"

"Shelley?" Mr. Waldbauer asked calmly. "Could you tell Aiden what happened, just like you told me? I want to make sure everything is explained correctly."

"I think Jinx would be the best one to tell the story," she

replied, her voice sharp. "She plays a bigger part in it than I do."

Though it didn't sound like an insult, Jan knew that was what Shelley had intended.

"Jinx?" Aiden asked. A slight smile appeared on his lips.

"Jan's nickname," Mr. Waldbauer explained.

"Ah." Aiden nodded. "Well, Jinx, are you comfortable telling me what happened?"

Fighting the urge to glare at Shelley, Jan pursed her lips and drew in a long breath.

"Well, Mr. Aimsworth," she began, "I've been staying at Mr. Waldbauer's house this summer because my parents are in Scotland visiting family. Shelley and I had the idea to go to Azuline Cove and collect shells so we could sell them to Ms. Johnson, who makes jewelry for her shop at the Fun Zone."

Fact by fact, happening by happening, the story poured out of Jan. Though she constructed it in a more coherent manner than the sobbing Shelley had earlier, she found it particularly difficult to describe how Owen and Nolan had followed them to retrieve the necklace. Although Aiden's face remained calm, his eyes intently focused on Jan, she felt odd describing the perpetrator to his own brother.

When she finished the story, Aiden leaned back in his chair.

"I see," he said again. "Do you have the locket and the box with you?"

Jan impulsively reached for the necklace, as if to hide the

fact that she was still wearing it.

"Jan," Mr. Waldbauer said softly, "why didn't you take off the necklace when you realized they were after it?"

Because it didn't want me to, she thought. She decided not to say that bit out loud.

"Well, we didn't know they were after us until Nolan followed us last night at the Fun Zone," she half-lied, "and after they cornered us out by the cove, I thought that maybe it would be better to go to the police instead. So Shelley turned the boat around, and..." Jan inhaled sharply to ease her heavy chest, then lowered her voice to a whisper. "And that was when everything else happened."

Jan could have sworn she heard Shelley scoff.

"Could I see the necklace?" Aiden asked gently.

"I..." Jan hesitated.

Keep it on, the familiar, nagging part of her urged.

"Maybe...maybe it's better if I keep it on," she mumbled unintelligibly.

"I'm sorry, what was that, Jan?" Aiden asked.

Shelley snapped her head toward Jan. "She won't take it off," she blurted out. "Even on the boat, when we realized they were following us, I told her to just give it to them. But she wouldn't. She's the reason why we're in this mess."

Jan opened her mouth to respond, but Shelley was quicker. With a swift lunge in Jan's direction, Shelley extended her hand, grasped the locket, and tugged.

As soon as the chain came undone and the necklace left her body, Jan felt a cold tremor rush through her—no metallic smell or taste, no shortness of breath. The chill swept over her body like ocean waves, ending at her fingertips and dissipating in smaller swells.

And then, nothing.

Shelley dropped the necklace on Aiden's desk and crossed her arms. Jan sat back in her chair, flabbergasted. When the shock passed, she turned her attention to Aiden, who had picked the necklace up and was studying the locket with an unreadable expression.

Why on Earth had she wanted to keep it on so badly? It was tiny—pathetic, even—dangling from Aiden's hand. It looked like something that could have been hidden away in an old attic.

Slowly, but not reluctantly, Jan placed the mermaid box on Aiden's desk.

"Just as I'd thought," Aiden said, holding the locket between his thumb and index finger while eyeing the box. "Jan and Shelley, my sincerest apologies on behalf of my brother. In cases like these, I'd advise taking the suspects in for questioning, but I believe I already have the answers to this mystery. As for my brother, I will deal with him personally. This doesn't need to be blown out of proportion within the department."

"Answers?" Jan asked quietly.

"This locket and the box you two found belong to my family—my mother, to be more precise," Aiden said. "They're heirlooms that have been passed down for generations on her side of the family, and even though they look old, they're actually worth quite a lot of money—the necklace especially."

He paused as he put the necklace back into the box.

"My mother is extraordinarily sentimental. She's always placed great importance on family valuables. Needless to say, she's been in absolute distress the past couple of days after figuring out it was stolen. Called me up and everything." He frowned and licked his lips before continuing. "It's clear now that Owen stole the necklace from her. That way, he could make money selling it later. He probably figured the best place to hide it was in the cove where nobody would look for it. Nobody but you two, of course."

Aiden gave Mr. Waldbauer an apologetic look. "I'm not sure if my brother planned to pretend that he found it and coerce my mother into giving him money as compensation or if he intended to sell it to someone else. Regardless of what the case may be, I'm so sorry for what you two have had to endure. This should absolutely not be a situation that two young girls find themselves in. I feel personally responsible that my family lies at the heart of all this trouble."

"It's not your fault, Aiden," Mr. Waldbauer reassured.

"Everyone's okay, I just figured if anyone here can take proper action regarding what's happened, it would be you."

"Of course," Aiden said. "I'll get this sorted out. For now, you can all relax." He turned to Shelley and Jan. "Thank you for bringing this to me. I'm sure my mother will be extremely grateful that she has her necklace back, and more importantly, I don't want you two to worry about this—or Owen—anymore. Go have a fun summer."

Although they left the police station on a fairly good note, tension lingered in the air. Shelley still refused to speak to Jan, and worse was the fact that the questions in Jan's head swarmed at a thousand miles per minute, louder and more demanding than they had ever been.

If the legend was nothing more than a superstition—nothing more than a trivial story told by sailors—why had she felt so attached to the necklace?

Even more confusing was the fact that the metallic feeling, which had loitered relentlessly within Jan for the past two days, had completely disappeared.

Chapter 18
A DISMAL MOOD

LATER THAT EVENING, MR. WALDBAUER SAT THE girls down for a long talk about responsibility and safety. Although he promised them they weren't in trouble and that he would personally take care of repaying Mr. Brown for the damages sustained by his boat, Jan left the conversation feeling worse than she had before.

Since it was seven o'clock in the evening when they got home from the station, which was after midnight in Scotland, Mr. Waldbauer decided to call Jan's parents the following morning to tell them what had happened.

By Sunday morning, nothing had changed. Shelley was still in a foul mood, and Jan had spent the entire night feeling sick.

Mr. Waldbauer called Mr. and Mrs. Jenkins to inform them about what had happened as soon as he woke up. He reassured them dozens of times that Jan was okay, that nobody had gotten hurt, and that everyone was safe. After Mr. and Mrs. Jenkins offered to pitch in for the damaged boat and lectured Jan about her choices, the morning drudged on slowly.

To make things worse, Mr. Waldbauer left home around nine o'clock that morning to speak with Mr. Brown about payment, leaving the house with only the girls' tension to fill the air.

Despite how well Mr. Waldbauer had reacted to everything, Jan didn't feel any better. Part of her wished he was angrier with them for the mess they'd created. But that wasn't the case; in fact, minus Shelley's mood, things quickly went back to normal. For Jan, that was the worst part. The situation *wasn't* normal. The necklace and the box *weren't* normal.

Desperately trying to lighten things between her and Shelley, Jan suggested they go to the Fun Zone. All she got in response was a curt shake of the head.

Since the last thing Jan wanted to do was sit in Shelley's room all day, she decided to go alone. Though she hoped time apart would help ease the friction, Shelley's uncharacteristically icy demeanor left her pessimistic.

To add to her perturbed mood, the weather at the Fun Zone was as dismal as Jan felt. Cold fog drifted silently across the deserted walkways of the pier and hovered above the water like gray ghosts. Jan stuck her hands into her pockets and hunched herself against the chill, following the aging slates and listening to the quiet creaks as she put her weight on each one.

The part of her chest where the locket used to be felt bare and vulnerable, but Jan shook the feeling away, staring out blankly at the calm water while leaning against the metal railing that bordered the Fun Zone.

Magic, legends, and stories—it was all so stupid and caused far too much trouble. Since there was no one at the Fun Zone to hear, Jan let out a long and frustrated sigh, then listened to it echo across the water. She clenched her fists, her nails digging into her palms. Why did she have to find that stupid box? Why couldn't she have just left the necklace where it was? And once she'd put the necklace on, why in the world had she been so unable to take it off?

Keep it on. The familiar, unwelcome thought echoed within Jan's subconscious.

She knew about addictions—about the insatiable cravings people struggled with. That was how it had felt when she wore the necklace: like an addiction, a compulsion to keep it close, a need to wear it at all times. But addictions didn't happen with necklaces. So why had she felt so attached to it?

Perhaps it wasn't the locket she was addicted to, but instead whatever was inside of it—whatever produced that metallic, blood-like stir. Perhaps it *was* the magic from the legend.

No, Jan admonished herself. *What a stupid thing to think. For God's sake, you're not a child.*

She unclenched her fists and ran her fingers over the little marks on her palms. Her attempt at distraction had proved futile; the eerie, forsaken feeling that enveloped the Fun Zone had done nothing to ease her mind. All she could do was sit with the growing knot in her stomach, desperately praying for it to go away.

Throat tight and eyes stinging from the salt of brimming tears, Jan slipped away from the railing and turned back toward the parking lot. She kept her head down and sheathed herself under her hoodie, wishing she could disappear. The Blue Bomb waited patiently for her in a forlorn parking space.

"At least I have you, girl," she said, giving the door a sentimental pat.

Lost in thought, Jan pulled the keys out from under the dashboard and started the car up, grinding the starter until it caught. Acting out of habit, she glanced at the rearview mirror before backing out.

And immediately, she gasped out loud. In the backseat, looking at her over the barrel of a gun, was Nolan Tillet.

Chapter 19
CABIN CRUISER

"FACE FORWARD," NOLAN COMMANDED IN A LOW voice. "Drive. Don't turn around."

He lowered the pistol to keep it out of public view, even though nobody else was in the parking lot to see it. The blood drained from Jan's face so quickly that she could feel her skin grow cold.

Slowly, so as not to aggravate him further, she placed her hands on the steering wheel and pulled out of the parking lot, arriving at a juncture leading straight to a huge pile of rocks that signaled the start of the rugged and desolate breakwater. A left turn led to the mainland.

"Go left," Nolan instructed. He masked his shaking voice with a smirk. "Keep in mind who has the leverage here."

Although he sounded scared as well, it didn't make Jan feel any better. Her arms and legs shook violently, and every brake

jolted the car forward. She swallowed hard as she headed out toward the mainland, her ears ringing with fear.

Idiot, she thought. *I'm such an idiot. Shelley was right. Why do I never listen to her?*

Hot tears pricked the corners of Jan's eyes, the presence of which surprised her. As much as tears made sense given the situation, it was with discomfort that Jan realized they weren't because of the pointed gun or the man in her backseat who reeked of cigarette smoke. They were because of Shelley— because Jan had ignored the one person she shouldn't have, and because her obstinacy had ruined everything.

"Can't this thing move any faster?" Nolan snarled after a few exasperating blocks. "Step on it, kid."

"She's not used to backseat drivers," Jan said. To her surprise, her voice stayed steady.

"Funny. Step on the gas."

Jan inhaled shakily and pressed hard on the accelerator. The Blue Bomb shuddered and blasted out two quick backfires.

"What was that?" Nolan demanded, forcing the barrel into Jan's shoulder.

"It's an old car," Jan said quickly. "I promise I'm not going to pull anything. Please get the gun away from me."

Nolan ignored her. "Out onto the main highway," he ordered. "Then take the Yacht Harbor exit. I'll tell you when to stop."

They pulled up to the curb about two blocks away from the wharf. Nolan reached over Jan and grabbed the keys with a trembling hand.

"This way." He nodded his head toward the little pier, his right hand lurking inside his pocket where he had hidden the gun.

The wharf moored a cabin cruiser with the word "Spoiler" printed on its side. It was fancier than any of the boats Mr. Brown owned, but since Jan assumed it belonged to Owen Aimsworth, she wasn't surprised.

Nolan walked closely behind Jan, watching her intently. He nudged her down into the boat's cabin and shut the door behind him.

It was small, yet pleasant inside, despite the atmosphere. A table and a couple of chairs sat at the center of the room, and a small shelf with a framed picture on it hung above two bunks that took up most of the side space. On the bottom bunk sat none other than Owen Aimsworth. He smiled lazily at Jan and hopped down off the bunk.

Unlike his brother, whose presence was warm and inviting, Owen's aura was far more difficult to decipher. His movements were slow and catlike. He walked on quiet feet over to Jan, all the while observing her with his dark eyes.

"Jan Jenkins," he said, tapping his silver watch. "Pleasure to finally meet you on land. I really do hate forced invitations like this one, but as I'm sure you understand, desperate times call for desperate measures."

"How the hell do you know my name?"

Owen replied with a patronizing smile. Tense silence descended upon the cabin before he said, "You don't really think I'd just pull some random girl off the street without having done at least a little research, do you? I may be desperate, but I'm not stupid." He pursed his lips, then gestured to the table at the center of the room. "Why don't you sit down? We clearly have a few things to discuss."

It was more of a command than an offer, and after being forcefully shoved by Nolan into one of the chairs, the two men sat down across from Jan.

It felt like something out of a crime movie. The way they looked, stuffed around the small table together, reminded Jan of gangsters sitting down to threaten their unarmed victim.

I am not going to be their victim.

"Well, I have something to discuss with *you*," she said indignantly. Though she figured it would probably be smarter to keep quiet, her mouth willed her to speak—to be more than a trembling little girl. "How dare you follow me and my friend around and scare us half to death? Not to mention chase us with your motorboat and nearly get us killed."

Nolan stifled a curt laugh.

"My apologies," Owen said flatly, still tapping his watch.

"Like I said, desperate times call for desperate measures. But if you cooperate and listen to us, I can promise you the situation won't get any worse."

"Right," Jan snapped back. "Because chasing us with a motorboat and almost getting us skewered by rocks at the cove wasn't bad enough."

As soon as she said it, she regretted it. Why couldn't she just hold her tongue?

To her surprise, Owen only uttered a humorless laugh.

"Again, our sincerest apologies," he said, rubbing his chin. He stood up and walked over to Jan. With a surfeit of strained composure, he leaned down and said quietly, "I'd appreciate it if you gave that necklace back. The box you found it in too."

It was uncomfortable with Owen breathing down her neck, and to make matters worse, Nolan subtly tapped the barrel of the gun on the table, reminding her that it was still with him.

Jan observed the small room, taking in all she could.

"You never know what you may need to use," her dad would always tell her. Despite everything, Jan felt warmth when she thought about all of the little life lessons her dad taught her.

Jan's eyes rested on the framed picture atop the shelf. It was of a young woman, perhaps in her twenties or maybe younger, with short blond hair and dark eyes.

Jan tilted her head. The woman looked familiar.

Noticing where she was looking, Owen quickly stalked

over to the shelf and turned the picture on its face. He lingered by it for a moment as if it were a real person.

Jan groaned internally.

"Have you ever been in love?" Owen asked Jan, walking back to the table.

The question caught Jan off guard. "No, I haven't," she responded curtly.

"It changes you, I'll tell you that much," Owen said. "Something you won't know until it happens."

"That doesn't sound very pleasant." She didn't bother to mind her tone.

"It's not. Not always, at least," Owen said, somewhat absently. After a pause, he leaned against the table's edge with his hand and looked directly at Jan. "I need that necklace. And the box."

"I don't know what you're talking about."

"Don't act stupid," Owen said as he straightened up and walked to the other side of the small cabin. "You know very well. It was obvious you enjoyed wearing it around. After we ran into you and your friend in the cove and I saw it on you, I had Nolan dive for it just to make sure my suspicions were correct. And they were. The box and the necklace were gone."

"Maybe you lost it in the bathtub," Jan said innocently, reveling at the hint of rage that crossed both men's faces.

"Don't be a smart-ass," Owen snapped. "I didn't lose it

anywhere. It was stolen from me—intentionally or not, I don't care anymore. But I'd appreciate if you'd stop hiding it. It doesn't belong to you."

"Maybe Nolan just didn't see it." Jan stared at Owen, not daring to blink. "Maybe you should've looked yourself instead of having him do your dirty work for you."

Owen's lips disappeared into a thin line.

"I know where we hid it," Nolan hissed. His breath reeked of cigarettes and was even stronger than it had been in the car.

"Just give us the necklace and the box," Owen demanded. "It will save us all so much time and energy."

"I don't have it anymore," Jan said smugly, pointing to her neck. "See? After my friend and I almost got cut in half at the cove, we decided it wasn't smart to keep the necklace. So we gave it—*and* the box—to the police."

The fact that she was standing strong amidst the men's threatening glares satisfied her. Her pride slowly faded, however, when she saw both of their faces go white.

"You..." Owen paled. "You gave it to the police?"

"Yes," Jan said, narrowing her eyebrows. "We turned it in to them. So you can go ask for your treasure at the station. I don't have it anymore. I don't even *want* it."

She felt relief saying it out loud. Ever since Shelley had snatched it off her neck, the overwhelming attraction she once felt toward the necklace had completely disappeared.

"*Who* did you give it to?" Owen asked frantically.

Realizing the urgency in his voice, Jan's pride diminished further. "Your brother," she said meekly. "I figured you already knew that. Isn't he the Chief of Police?"

Owen dropped down onto his chair and closed his eyes, his face sallow and distraught. In a matter of seconds, he had become a very different man than the one who had greeted Jan.

Cursing loudly, Owen stood back up again and paced around the room. Nolan sat motionless, his gun lowered to the table as he rested his eyes on the cherry-wood floor.

Jan eyed the stairs leading up to the door. They were distracted: this could be the perfect opportunity for her to escape. Almost as soon as the thought crossed her mind, she sprang up from the chair and lunged toward the cabin door. Adrenaline pumped through her veins, motivating her every movement. It was a valiant try, but Jan was back in her seat before she could take another step. Two strong arms held her down.

"You obviously don't understand the severity of this situation," Owen breathed onto her head. "You got yourself into it when you found the box, and now you're going to deal with whatever consequences arise."

Jan stumbled over what to say. There was nothing she could say—nothing she could do. Still, Nolan hadn't used the gun. If he hadn't done so yet, maybe he wouldn't at all. That alone gave Jan a glimmer of hope.

"That necklace means more than just money," Owen said, his voice wrought with distress. His hands still held her down on the chair. "I did not hide it for my own benefit. I hid it for *everyone's* benefit. Do you hear me?"

Jan blinked back her shock. She parted her lips to answer, but her mouth and throat had gone dry.

"I'm not forcing you here because I want to have a nice conversation about a little box and a necklace. I'm doing this because I understand where this situation could lead if I don't try to fix what you screwed up. So knock it off with the smart replies and the escape attempts," he said, his words stiff and enunciated. He released his firm grip on her shoulders and stepped back. "There are some things that are not fit to fall into certain people's hands. My intention is to *prevent* those things from falling into the hands of the unfit. And you, Miss Jenkins, having pried your way into this situation, may have put us all in danger."

Chapter 20
AN UNSTABLE MAN

"I'M SORRY," JAN SAID, HER VOICE WAVERING. THE little that was left of her confidence had deserted her.

"If you promise to sit and listen quietly," Owen said, taking his seat again, "and if you promise not to make a bolt for that door, then *maybe* we can work this out. But I need your word."

Jan nodded numbly.

"Good. Glad we've come to an agreement." Owen leaned back in his chair, a supercilious look manifesting in his eyes— the type of look people in authority gave to their inferiors. It made Jan's blood boil, but she was careful not to let her irritation show.

"As appealing as that necklace might have seemed to you," Owen said, "and as fun and trivial as it might have been to wear it, it is anything *but* just a fancy trinket."

"I know that," Jan responded meekly, struggling to find her

voice. "Aiden told us that it's a family heirloom. He said it was worth a lot."

"It's a lot more than an heirloom. No amount of money can buy what's inside of it."

"But there *wasn't* anything inside of it. Shelley and I opened it when we found it and we didn't see anything."

"No, you idiot," Nolan snapped. "Not *literally* inside the locket."

"Okay, I'm sorry," Jan said. A lump in her throat began to form, but she did her best to appear emotionless. "I clearly don't understand."

"You wore the necklace for two days, am I correct?" Owen asked. Though he composed himself much more eloquently than his friend, Jan couldn't help but notice that he thought she was an idiot as well.

Fine, then. If they were to think of her as a child, then she had no reason to answer them.

A sour look crossed Owen's face when she didn't respond, but he tried again. "Did you ever feel anything slightly off when you wore it? Any strange feelings? A sudden illness?"

The episodes. The metallic smell. The unsettling desire to keep it close.

"No," Jan said, folding her arms. "I didn't feel anything."

"Liar," Nolan spat.

Jan opened her mouth to retort, but Owen spoke before

she could. "What do you think you'll gain by not telling us the truth?" he asked. "Do you think you'll maintain some sort of dignity? Do you just want to piss us off? You're doing a wonderful job, if that makes you feel any better. Now tell us the truth."

"I'm not lying," Jan snapped.

Owen opened his mouth but closed it just as quickly. He took one prolonged breath and folded his hands.

"How many days did you wear the necklace?" he asked. When Jan didn't respond, he flattened his hands on the table in an angry gesture. Jan nearly jumped out of her seat.

"Two," she said almost immediately.

"If you wore it for two days, I *know* you felt something," Owen said. "Stop lying." Leaning closer to her, he lowered his voice to a whisper. "Do us all a favor and just be honest so I can try to explain this mess to you. Stubbornness will get you nowhere."

Owen stared straight into her eyes, refusing to blink. Out of pure obstinacy, Jan returned the look.

"If you can't trust us," Owen added, "then you can't trust anyone at all."

Jan scoffed. "I'm never going to trust someone who held a gun to me."

"That was a precaution," Owen said, side-eyeing Nolan. "We wanted to make sure you didn't do anything impulsive. The gun was just a reminder to keep you in line until you got here. We were not—and are not—going to use it. Right, Nolan?"

Nolan responded with a curt nod, and Owen looked back at Jan. "You have my word," he said.

"Fine," Jan said after a moment's silence. "Let's say I did feel something when I wore it. Does that make me worthy of your explanations?"

Owen shrugged. "Depends. Did you *truly* feel something?"

Jan pursed her lips, her eyes darting from Owen to Nolan. Knowing it was brash, she spoke up before she had time to fully convince herself it was the right decision.

"Yes," she said, looking off to the side. "I felt something."

Admitting it out loud felt terribly disorienting.

Owen tapped his watch impatiently. "Care to elaborate?"

"God, I don't know," Jan groaned, still keeping her voice low. "I felt weird. Obsessive. Not like myself. I wanted to keep it on, like it was some sort of security blanket. I thought it was just me until my friend Shelley pulled the necklace off. Then I realized it wasn't me...my feelings were *because* of the necklace. I felt like a lunatic admitting it to myself." She clamped her lips shut, hating how much she had revealed.

When Owen realized she wasn't going to continue, he clenched his jaw and drew in a slow, steady breath. "Fine," he said. "You don't have to expand if you don't want to. Maybe after you hear what I have to say, you'll change your mind. My family has a long history with that necklace, and it's convinced me that absolutely nobody is fit to have it." Owen's eyes flit off to the side for a moment, as though he were mustering up the courage to speak. "There's a legend about a sea witch," he finally said. "The story claims that she hid dangerous and destructive power inside a treasure of her choice."

"And if you destroyed her treasure, you'd get the power of destruction," Jan said, uncrossing her arms. "I've heard the legend."

"Right. Well, I have reasons to believe that it isn't a legend at all."

"You mean you think it's real?" Jan asked, even though she knew exactly what he meant.

Owen nodded. "Moreover, I believe that the necklace you and your friend gave to the police—to my brother—*is* the treasure from the legend."

Jan opened her mouth to argue with Owen, but even she knew that she would be fooling herself if she tried to do so. In all other cases, his claim would seem outrageous. But whatever it was she had felt when she wore the necklace bid her to trust him—to let him continue.

"Power, magic, whatever you want to call it—something is contained within the necklace. Something that's near impossible for me to explain unless you've felt it yourself. Whatever it is, though, it doesn't reside in the locket, it resides *within* it. There's a difference."

"I know the difference."

Owen exhaled and began tapping his index finger against his watch again.

"My family is very secretive when it comes to the box and the necklace," he said, "but what I know is this: when my great-grandfather inherited the box and the necklace, his father told him to leave it alone—to lock it up somewhere, away from everyone else—and to not bother with it until he could pass it down to his own son or daughter. But my great-grandmother, who'd inherited it as well through marriage, was infatuated with the legend. She managed to find the box even after my great-grandfather hid it away, and after she found it, she figured out how to destroy the necklace so she could get..." Owen paused and took a measured breath before he finished. "So she could get what was within it."

"Figured out?" Jan asked, raising an eyebrow. "It's a locket. I don't imagine it's impossible to break."

"Not impossible. But you have to do it the right way."

Jan caught herself before she smirked. "The right way?"

"Not smashing it, not burning it, not running it over with a car," Owen said. He spoke in a slow, clipped voice that made Jan feel as though she was in grade school. "The hinge of the actual locket needs to break, and it needs to be done in a specific way. The *right* way."

Jan stayed quiet for a moment. Then, slowly—hesitantly—she asked, "What's the right way?"

"I don't know," Owen said. "My great-grandfather refused to tell anyone, and his wife never had the chance to. But the right way, according to what my great-grandfather *did* say, is the only way. The necklace is indestructible unless you break it the way it was intended to be broken. The box won't break either, which I believe is a hint that the two of them are connected. But that's the only information my grandmother managed to get out of him."

Jan sat painfully still, her lips parting and closing before she spoke.

"I'm confused," she finally admitted.

Owen scoffed offhandedly and rubbed his temples. "I believe that whatever created this locket—be it the sea witch from the legend or something else entirely—made it so that the only way the locket could be broken was by breaking the locket *itself* in half," he said. "But I'm certain there's no other way to do that than by following the message at the bottom of the box."

"The poem?"

"It's not really a poem."

"It's a couplet," Jan said. "Technically a poem. This one just doesn't rhyme."

Owen shot her an unamused glance. Though Jan saw the urge in his eyes to argue back, he controlled himself.

"Oval to oval, golden to green," he said. "I think once you figure out what that means, then you'll know how to break it."

"So you're saying there's literally no other way to break the locket?" Jan asked, raising an inquisitive eyebrow. "That sounds illogical."

"Well," Owen said, still tapping his watch, "I'd argue that the whole legend seems illogical, but here we are."

Jan sucked in a breath but ultimately decided to stay quiet.

"You can step on it, try to smash it with a hammer, try to pry it apart with your own two hands...it will not break," Owen continued. "Not until it's done the right way."

"And by 'break' you mean snap it in half?"

"Exactly," Owen said. "Right at the hinge. Whatever is within that necklace...I think it resides at the hinge. Breaking it there releases what the locket holds. The only question is how to do it correctly."

Jan went silent for a moment. "How do you know all of this? Have you tried?" she finally asked, not sure if she wanted to hear the answer.

"No, *I* have never tried," Owen said. A pinched expression manifested on his face. "If you stay quiet and listen, maybe I can get the whole story out."

Jan felt a scoff form in her throat. She took a deep breath to ease her nerves, then said, "Fine. Go ahead."

Owen shifted in his seat, adjusting his silver watch slightly to the side. "My great-grandmother somehow succeeded in breaking the locket, and in doing so, she gained the power within it. But it didn't turn out well for her." He rubbed his hand on the back of his neck and looked down at the table. "She went absolutely insane. And only a couple days after she broke the locket, she slit her wrists to end it all."

Jan tried not to look affected by the story, but she felt terribly nauseous, especially after hearing that bit.

Owen tapped his fingers nervously on the table. "That's all I know. It's all my grandmother told me. Mind you, she was nine when this all happened. If she were still around today, I'd try to get more information. But she isn't, so all I know is what I've told you: my great-grandmother figured out how to break the necklace—the way it was meant to be broken—gained the power, and then something went wrong. Something that pushed her to choose death over dealing with whatever it was the locket gave her." He paused for a moment, then said, "When my great-grandfather found his wife, he came across the necklace as well. But it was no longer broken as it had been only days earlier. It had pieced itself back together."

Jan narrowed her eyebrows. "What do you mean?"

"My great-grandfather claimed that the necklace restored itself somehow after her death," Owen said. "I don't know how and I don't entirely know why, but I believe the story. After living with that necklace...after seeing the things it can do...

stories like that become less and less hard to believe."

Haunting silence descended upon the little room. The discomfort was so tangible that Jan nearly said something—anything—to diffuse it, but Owen beat her to it.

"Having seen for himself what the locket was capable of, my great-grandfather hid it away again," he said. "But he didn't stop there. What happened to his wife sparked an obsession in him—not with the power, but with how it worked. My grandmother used to tell stories about how his life changed after his wife's death. Everything he did revolved around trying to figure out what the locket was capable of. At first, he tried to destroy the box and the locket, but not to gain the power. He wanted them out of his life so that they would be gone forever and never hurt anyone again. But no matter what he did, nothing worked, which led him to believe that neither could be destroyed entirely. The locket was different, though. He believed it could be broken if—and *only* if—it was done in the proper way."

Jan inhaled sharply, remembering how even after Shelley had thrown the mermaid box into a pile of rocks, nothing had happened to it. Though Jan originally had been overcome with relief, looking back at the situation, she realized how utterly unrealistic it was. Even if the impact didn't break the box, it should have dented it. There should have been a scratch. But it had emerged from the rocks completely unfazed.

"Since my great-grandfather was too scared to try to break

the locket correctly, he mostly just theorized about its abilities based off of what he'd seen with his wife," Owen continued. "He called it possessed. At least, that's what my grandmother said."

"But..." Jan said, pausing to find the right words, "do you think he knew the right way to break the locket? Do you think his wife told him how she did it?"

"Whatever he knew about the technicalities of the locket and how it was meant to break, he wouldn't tell anyone. All he said was that if it was broken correctly, it would come undone at the hinge and the nightmare within it would be released. He said nothing else. He even refused to tell my grandmother—his own daughter."

Owen shook his head. "Everything you just learned took years for my grandmother to get out of her father. I guess he was worried that if she knew exactly how to break the necklace, she would try to gain the power someday, and there was no way he was going to risk letting what happened to his wife happen to his daughter. If he did know how my great-grandmother broke the locket, the secret died with him."

Fiddling once again with his watch and tapping his foot nervously against the side of the table, Owen kept his eyes downcast before speaking again.

"My great-grandfather posited that the locket worked in stages," he said, finally daring to meet Jan's gaze. "First, it makes itself known to the person who is wearing it through episodes, strange sensations, and an overwhelming desire to keep it close. That's what you experienced, correct?"

Jan nodded, her words trapped in her throat.

"After a couple months, you begin to lash out. You become less obsessed with wearing the necklace and more obsessed with discovering how to break it. Then, if and when you finally figure it out, you gain the power."

"And then what?" Jan whispered.

"From what I've heard, my great-grandfather speculated that one of two things happen. Either the power suits you and you use it for destruction—for getting things you want in the worst way possible. If that doesn't happen..."

"Then you go insane with it," Nolan piped in.

Jan's stomach jolted. She had forgotten that Nolan was in the same room.

"If you aren't fit for the power, it revolts," Owen said. "That's what happened to my great-grandmother."

"Right," Jan said, remembering what Mr. Brown had told her and Shelley. "Doesn't the story claim that only truly evil people are capable of using the power?"

Owen nodded, tight-lipped.

Pinpricks ran down Jan's arms and legs. Even Mr. Brown regarded the legend as morbid, and he didn't strike her as someone easily spooked.

"But there's a catch," Owen said. "You can't claim the power, decide you don't want it, and give it back. Once you break the locket, it's yours until you die. According to my great-grandfather, that was why his wife committed suicide. She was unable to get rid of the power, but she was equally unable to go on living with it inside of her. Once she passed, my great-grandfather assumed that the power no longer had a physical place to exist. Since it was unable to exist on its own, it was drawn back to the locket, which repaired itself once the power had returned. After that, it waits."

"For what?"

"Another person," Owen said. "My great-grandfather supposed that this might have been going on for centuries in our family. I don't know who first found the box and the locket, but somehow it fell into my family's hands. I suppose eventually someone decided to put it away and instruct their descendants to ignore it until they passed it onto their children. And on and on the cycle went."

"Until your great-grandmother," Jan said.

"Until my great-grandmother."

Jan licked her lips, praying that the information would sink in. Everything Owen said made sense. She had experienced firsthand the episodes the locket provoked and the desires it conjured. But a nagging voice inside of her—one that clung to logic and science—yearned for an alternative.

"You've certainly done a lot of digging to know this much information," Jan said. "Still, you have to admit that all of this sounds like some kind of demented fairytale. I mean, come *on*. How does anyone actually believe this is true?"

Her words lingered in her mouth, leaving behind a rotten aftertaste.

"For God's sake, pick a damn side," Nolan snapped. "One moment you believe the story, the next you don't. Make up your mind, kid."

"I'm sorry," Jan said, tears forming in her eyes. "This is all a lot to comprehend."

"Make light of it if you will," Owen said, stiffening. "I didn't believe the stories at first either. I thought it was only a locket with a senseless story attached to it—one that was just used in my family for some kind of sick entertainment or some screwed up way of justifying my great-grandmother's suicide. But I was wrong."

Jan looked at the man in front of her. She took in his grim eyes and his pale face, realizing that anyone else would write him off as crazy. But she knew he wasn't. He was telling the truth.

"Fine," she whispered. "I believe it."

Oh, how those words were hard to say.

"I believe it," she said one more time, just so that the words would stick.

"My grandmother watched her mother go insane because

of that necklace," Owen said. "Even though she was only nine when it happened, she remembered all of it. She would always tell us that her mother was prone to fantasy, but she admitted that this was different. Whatever is within that necklace is real, and whether we believe it or not—whether the entire world knows or only we do—it doesn't matter. It's not going away."

He rubbed the sides of his face, gaunt in the dim light of the cabin cruiser. "It's hard to accept," he continued. "For years, even *I* didn't believe my grandmother." The sides of his lips pulled downward. "But Aiden did."

Jan tilted her head. "Is that why you freaked out when I told you I handed it over to him? Are you worried that Aiden is going to figure out how to break the locket and go insane?" Lowering her voice, she added, "Are you worried he's going to die just like your great-grandmother did?"

Owen shook his head. "No. I'm worried about the exact opposite. I'm worried he's going to figure out how to break it and live. I'm worried it'll fit him *perfectly*."

Jan pictured Aiden: his friendly, charismatic demeanor, his gentle way of speaking...

"But he doesn't seem..."

"Screwed up?" Owen said. "Of course he doesn't. He wouldn't be Chief of Police if he *seemed* screwed up. But that's his God-given talent. He's an amazing actor."

Jan sensed the bitterness—and fear—in his voice.

"The necklace was always a source of mystery to us when we were kids, mostly because of the legend," Owen said. "We never saw it much, though. My mother kept it hidden away. But about seven years ago, Aiden began to take an obsessive interest in it. He asked about it, talked about the legend, and finally, he managed to find the box and began wearing the necklace around."

"Why?" Jan asked.

Owen paused and raised an eyebrow. "Why what?"

"Why did he start wearing it all of the sudden?"

"I..." Owen paused, then let out a long sigh. "It's all a very long story. We knew someone who was close to our family, and she was interested in the legend. She knew we had the locket and the box, and I guess she got Aiden thinking about it. That's what led to his obsession."

"Who was it?"

"A friend," Owen said. Jan couldn't help but notice that he paled ever so slightly. When he spoke again, his voice was sharp. "That doesn't matter. May I continue?"

"Fine," Jan said, affronted by his unpredictable touchiness. "Go for it."

"I'd always tease Aiden because I thought the story was a load of rot," Owen said. "But no matter how much I got on him about how he looked—sporting a little golden locket and all that nonsense—he'd still wear it. He didn't care. It was like he *needed* it...like he had a craving that could only be satiated by the necklace. My mother told me to just leave him alone. According to her, he was going through a hard time in the years after my father passed away. She said that the necklace was a security blanket for him or some bullshit like that. But then, he started having episodes."

Jan's heart skipped a beat. Her mind raced as she thought about the erratic, painful episodes she had experienced the last two days.

"He started losing his breath, doubling over for no reason. It would happen once, maybe twice a day, and then he'd go back to normal. My mother forced him to go to the doctor multiple times, but they never found anything wrong with him." Owen looked past Jan as he spoke, as though he were gazing far into the past. "He would speak of smelling metal whenever he wore that locket...as if he *smelled* the magic inside of it. And then, after about a month, the episodes, the metallic smells...they all stopped. Aiden was still wearing that damn necklace. My mother dismissed it as a phase, but things just kept getting worse."

Jan instinctively reached for her neck. A chill snaked down her spine as she thought about those two days she'd worn the necklace. It took strength not to claw at her skin and will any remnants of it away.

"After the episodes stopped, violent outbursts took their place," Owen continued. "Aiden would act completely normal one moment, then go insane the next. He nearly strangled one of our maids without any provocation whatsoever. But because my mother was so terrified of our family's reputation being ruined, she kept the ordeal quiet. She paid the maid loads of money, all so she wouldn't talk to anyone about what had happened. She said it was *normal* for young men to act out. Anything to justify Aiden's actions and protect the Aimsworth family name, she did. She put up blinders and let everything fall apart, because as long as our reputation was safe, she didn't care."

"But didn't she believe the legend?" Jan asked when her voice finally obeyed her. "Didn't she realize something was up?"

"She never believed any of those stories. She claimed that my great-grandmother was a paranoid schizophrenic and that the story about the necklace was a manifestation of her psychiatric disorder. Then she'd argue that my grandmother was too young to fully understand what was happening at the time."

"But you said your great-grandmother had destroyed the necklace," Jan pressed. "How did your mother explain the fact that it pieced itself back together when she died?"

"My mother has an excellent way of ignoring facts that don't coincide with her version of the truth," Owen said bitterly. "She would argue that the story was made up to seem dramatic —that it was my great-grandfather's attempt to hide his wife's illness. Whatever it was she wanted to believe, she would claim was the truth." He paused for a moment and exhaled slowly, trying to curb his anger. "She spent more time trying to hide Aiden's outbursts than trying to uncover the reasons behind them. So, out of desperation, I stole the necklace from Aiden."

"How did you manage that?"

Owen tilted his head toward Nolan. "If it hadn't been for Nolan, I never would've been able to. Aiden didn't trust anyone except him. They'd been friends since grade school, and Nolan was the one person Aiden confided in."

Nolan licked his lips nervously, as though the sudden attention shift deeply discomforted him. When he spoke, his words were slow and enunciated, and his eyes darted between Jan and Owen.

"Aiden would talk about how one day he'd break the necklace and control everything—people, things...whatever he wanted," he said. "At first, I didn't know what to think because I didn't believe in the legend. But then, he began to describe to me in detail the lives he'd take, the power he'd gain...everything. I thought he was sick, so I confided in Owen. I hoped that maybe he'd take his brother to a hospital or wherever it is they take people like that."

Nolan coughed, his face tightening. "Aiden had always been my best friend," he continued in barely a whisper, "but he was troubled. Even when we were kids, he'd do things to other kids just to mess with them...just to hurt them. I wasn't the nicest kid either, but I never took it as far as Aiden did. And the necklace...the things he said...I can't believe I didn't draw the line sooner."

"It was a violent wake-up call when Nolan confided in me," Owen said. "I'd known it was serious, but it was only then that we decided to act."

"I betrayed my best friend," Nolan said. His glassy eyes held a kind of pain in them that made something in Jan sink. "I spiked his drink with sleeping pills one night when we were drinking together and stole the necklace from him. If he'd been awake, I wouldn't have had a chance. He was obsessed with it... never took it off."

"But here's the thing," Owen added, "almost immediately after Nolan took it from him, Aiden changed. He started acting normal—no more outbursts, no more episodes. Although he completely shut Nolan out of his life for betraying him, he faired pretty well otherwise. But I was terrified he'd find the necklace again, so I gave both it and the box to my mother so she could lock it away. I just wanted to forget the whole thing. And it worked, for a while at least." His expression hardened and resentment returned to his voice. "Aiden started working for the police department and moved up the ranks to reach where he is today. He quickly became the pride and joy of our family—the popular, successful, determined, charismatic man everyone praises. And I fell under the radar. I was the 'bum' of the family.

Rumors were even spread about me—blatant lies that only made Aiden seem more perfect."

Jan remembered the gossip that Gabriel had told her and Shelley about Owen and his roommate. For a fleeting moment, she felt guilty for believing him.

"All the while," Owen continued, "Aiden's past remained hidden. But last year, he started asking about the necklace again. I guess his rise to power in Aledale wasn't enough for him. He played it off as some joke—as if he were simply wondering what had happened to it—but we both knew it wasn't a joke at all. At first, I only kept an eye on him. He'd moved out, but every once in a while he'd come back home, asking about the necklace. A couple of days ago, I decided that the best thing to do would be to hide it from him. So I asked for Nolan's help again."

"Right," Jan said, a slight smile tugging at her lips despite the situation. "Your right-hand man."

"Hilarious," Nolan said. "This is serious."

"We used one of Mr. Brown's boats and dropped it in the cove so that only we could find it if need be. I'm assuming you know the rest," Owen said.

"Why didn't anybody try to get rid of the necklace before you?" Jan asked. "If it's really as dangerous as you say it is, why didn't someone just throw it into the ocean years ago and lose it forever?"

"I assume they were worried that someone else would find

it," Owen said, giving Jan a pointed frown.

Jan took a deep breath, daring to let the remainder of her guard down. "When I wore the necklace, I experienced those episodes you talked about—the same ones Aiden had. And I felt attracted to it too. It was like some kind of obsession that I'd never experienced before. I didn't want to admit it earlier because..." her voice trailed off. "Because I really didn't want it to be true. I didn't think it *could* be true. And the way I was when I wore that necklace...it wasn't me. I was so attached to it that I didn't even listen to my best friend when she told me to take it off."

After a moment's silence, Owen said, "Thank you for deciding to be honest with us."

Jan shrugged, trying to come across far less frightened than she actually felt.

"Whatever is within that necklace seems to hint about its power to the owner, as though it's trying to make its presence known," Owen said, still fiddling with his watch. "I hate that necklace. I absolutely despise it. But no matter how much hatred I have for it, it's not going to go away. And now, Aiden has it...all because of you."

"Hold up," Jan said, overcome with defensiveness. "I didn't know this was going on. Your brother just happens to work at the police department. Shelley's dad was the one who took us there to talk to him. And it's not *my* fault you two harassed us and scared us half to death."

"We didn't harass you," Owen said.

"You totally harassed us."

"I..." Owen stopped himself. "I'm not going to argue about technicalities with a teenager."

"You're what, like twenty-five?" Jan said, her face hot.

"Twenty-six."

"That's only like ten years..."

"I hate to interrupt your argument," Nolan said, "but maybe instead of fighting, we should discuss how to get a dangerous necklace away from an unstable man."

Owen's face hardened. "Right," he said, shaking his head. "When I said you needed to deal with the consequences, I meant it. My brother isn't going to give the necklace to anyone, let alone me of all people. I'm guessing that out of all the places he'd keep it hidden, it'd be where he always is—in his office at the police station. I need you to retrieve it. There's no way I'd be able to do it unnoticed, especially since my brother isn't too fond of me and probably more alert now than ever."

"Are you kidding?" Jan protested. "How the hell am I supposed to do that? Do I just waltz in there and say, 'Hi Aiden! Fancy seeing you in your own office! I just decided to pop in and take back that super powerful, potentially life-threatening necklace, if you don't mind.'"

Owen glared at her in response.

"Besides," Jan continued, "are we one hundred percent sure this is all correct? I don't mean to continue picking the story apart, but the legend, the magic...it's all a little much. Maybe it can be explained..." her voice trailed off when she met Owen's eyes.

"If you seriously think there is another explanation for what you've seen and felt," Owen said, "then you're fooling yourself."

Jan didn't respond. He was right. Ever since she had found the necklace, she wanted to know where it came from. She wanted to understand why she had felt so attracted to it—why she had fought so hard against the idea of taking it off. All she had wanted was answers, and now that she finally had them, she wished she'd never wanted them in the first place.

Although every fiber of her being fought against the possibility, Jan thought that perhaps not everything could be rationalized. Perhaps there were things the brain simply could not understand, and that was the way things had to be. Whatever the case, she didn't have time to let it all sink in—not now.

"Okay," she finally said, her voice quivering. "Shelley's dad is the Captain. He knows Aiden pretty well. Maybe we could use that to our advantage."

It was a suggestion that Owen approved of. "We could," he said. He stopped fiddling with his watch and sat motionless, consumed by his thoughts.

"My ring!" Jan exclaimed.

"What?"

"My ring," she repeated, showing Owen the yellow-orange gemstone on her finger. "I wear it all the time. If I pretend I lost it at the station when we spoke to Aiden yesterday, he may let me look around his office."

"Are you sure?" Nolan asked, lighting a cigarette.

"If I keep bugging Mr. Waldbauer to let me ask Aiden, he will," Jan said. Then, with a smug smile, she added, "I can be pretty persistent."

"Then what would you do?" The cigarette dangled on Nolan's lower lip.

"Then," Owen answered for her, "she'd have a chance to look around his office. I don't expect him to let her look alone, though. He may be unstable, but he's not an idiot."

"Maybe I can get Shelley to create some kind of distraction," Jan said. *If she isn't still too upset with me.*

"But what's a good enough distraction to get Aiden involved?" Nolan asked, his voice raspier than usual from the cigarette smoke.

"She can say she's being followed by us," Owen said, snapping his fingers. "That's it. If Aiden thinks I'm close by, he'll drop everything, especially if he thinks I'm after the necklace."

"And what if I can't find it?" Jan asked. "What if he's not keeping it in his office?"

"I know my brother well enough. He won't let something as powerful as that out of his sight. Wherever he is, the necklace and the box will be as well. He's at the station more often than anywhere else. I'm sure of it."

"If that's the case, then why hasn't he destroyed it already and taken control of whatever is within it?"

Owen shook his head. "Because he hasn't figured out how to yet. I remember he used to ask my grandmother over and over again if she knew anything else about how my great-grandmother destroyed the locket, but he never actually figured it out. The answer will come to him eventually, though. I know it. *Everything* comes to him eventually."

More bitterness. Jan tried to ignore it.

"What about you?" she asked. "Do you have any ideas about how your great-grandmother destroyed it? Any ideas about the right way to break it?"

Owen hesitated. "Only the *couplet*," he said, emphasizing the last word to satisfy Jan. "I assume that it has something to do with the shape of the locket."

Jan nodded absent-mindedly. "The skull of the sea witch on the box was oval as well," she said.

Owen paused for a moment. His fingers twitched ever so slightly. Slowly, he narrowed his eyebrows and said, "I guess I've never looked that closely at her skull before." He shrugged and resumed tapping on his watch. "To be quite honest, I don't care what it means. But I can't say the same for Aiden. Let's just hope we get it back before he figures it out."

All three of them—once adversaries, now co-conspirators—kept quiet, their eyes downcast, focusing their thoughts on the necklace and its power-hungry possessor.

Chapter 21
CRAZY BUT TRUE

IT FELT LIKE FOREVER BEFORE JAN COULD GET back to the Blue Bomb. Once inside, she took a moment for herself, inhaling the musty smell of leather seats and the lingering cigarette stench in the back where Nolan had been only a couple of hours ago.

It had taken them an entire hour to solidify their plan, and another for Owen and Nolan to trust Jan enough to let her leave. The paranoia that she would drive straight to the police and turn them in for kidnapping her made it hard for them to let her go.

"Regardless of what you find, we'll meet you and your friend at the Fun Zone parking lot this evening, seven o'clock. Correct?" Owen had confirmed with her for what seemed like the seventieth time.

"Yes, in the parking lot at seven on the dot. Preferably where there aren't many people. We'll be there, I swear it."

"Just remember that if my brother finds out, we're screwed. So *please* don't mess this up by turning us in instead. The gun was the only way we could ensure that you followed directions. We were never going to use it, I promise."

Though Jan vowed what seemed nearly a thousand times that she wouldn't turn them in and that she understood what she had to do, the uneasiness was evident on their faces as she left the cabin cruiser. She understood the reason behind it, of course. Even she would be nervous trusting a sixteen-year-old stranger.

But she was all they had—their best bet. Nobody else knew about this. Nobody else would believe it. They had no other choice, unless they wanted to get the box and necklace back themselves, which would be even harder.

Their explanations left Jan with no doubt that they were her allies. Everything Owen had said about the necklace, its effects, the episodes, and the cravings echoed Jan's experience. There was no way he could have made it all up.

If there was one person Jan wasn't so sure about, however, it was Shelley. Jan might have believed the story, but she wasn't so sure her friend would. As she turned into the Waldbauers' driveway, she racked her brains about the best possible way to tell Shelley what was going on.

Shelley hadn't experienced the necklace's power like Jan had. To simply ask her to create a random distraction at the police department for the sake of a very unassuming necklace would be ludicrous. Jan needed to go about it properly—she needed to explain the entire matter in a way that would not only be realistic, but also include all of the mind-boggling facts.

The Blue Bomb purred unevenly as Jan sat in the driver's seat, going over her plan of action. She would go upstairs, sit down next to Shelley, apologize for the boat incident, and brief her about what had happened. She would admit that the story seemed ridiculous, but explain that she'd felt the power herself. Eventually, Shelley would believe her. Composition was key.

Mr. Waldbauer was still at work when Jan got back. He usually came home late, even on Sundays, which meant that she and Shelley had the whole day to discuss and execute their plan. But first, Shelley needed to believe the story.

She was lying on her bed in the same position she'd been in when Jan had left that morning. A pile of magazines littered her carpet, and a few were scattered around her body as she read. Jan wondered if she had moved at all. Shelley did that when she was upset—she stayed hooked on the same mindless activity until she sorted out whatever was bugging her.

"Hey," Jan ventured softly.

"Hey," came the curt reply.

"Can we talk?"

Shelley put down the magazine she was holding and sat up on her bed.

"Yeah, sure," she said. Warmth returned to her eyes, and Jan rejoiced at the sight of it.

Still, her nerves had not subsided. She exhaled shakily and sat at the foot of Shelley's bed, smoothing the sheets with shaky hands.

She could do this. She had always been good at articulating her thoughts.

Come on, Jan. She opened her mouth, trying her best to seem confident.

And then she burst into tears.

Shelley shot a quizzical glance in her direction. "Jinx?" she said, scooting closer to her friend.

The tears wouldn't stop now that everything had caught up to her. For the past couple of hours, she had been running on pure stress. Now that she finally had the chance to react to all of it, everything flooded out.

Shelley shifted uncomfortably on her bed, at a loss for words. After a while, she finally said, "Jinx, if this is about the boat incident, I shouldn't have blamed it all on you. And I shouldn't have thrown the mermaid box. That was really immature of me."

"No. No, it's not about that." Jan wiped angrily at her eyes.

"Are you sure? Because you were right...I *was* interested in that whole necklace business too. And it was unfair of me to get so mad at you."

Jan shook her head. "It's not that, Shelley. It's the entire situation. I should never have grabbed that box in the first place, and you were right to be upset with me."

"Yeah, but you didn't know what was inside of it. How could you have known?"

"I know," Jan said. "But I still wish I'd just gone diving for the shells like we'd planned and not gone on that stupid goose chase. God, why can't I just leave things alone?" Saying it out loud made her cry even harder.

"But we got rid of it," Shelley said. "It's all done now."

Jan put her head in her hands. "No, it's not."

"I promise I'm not mad anymore."

"That's not what I'm talking about."

As painful as it was, Jan told Shelley what had happened. She barely paused for breath, and Shelley listened intently, her eyes fluttering as she struggled to process everything.

Though she worried that no words could do the story justice, Jan described how the necklace had drawn her in, and how she hadn't realized how serious it was until she heard Owen's story. She explained how Aiden's obsession with the necklace had evolved, just as hers had before Shelley pulled it off of her at the police station. She recounted every fact and detail Owen had told her to the best of her ability, all the while expecting Shelley to cut her off and call her crazy. But it never happened. The entire time Jan spoke, Shelley remained silent.

When the story finally came to its end, the two girls said nothing.

After about a minute, when the silence had become too much for her to handle, Jan said, "I know all of this is hard to believe. If you don't think I'm telling the truth, or if you think I'm insane or something, I understand. But..."

"I believe you."

Jan blinked back her disbelief.

"I think you're telling the truth," Shelley repeated. "I believe you."

Jan ran her hand across her cheek, still damp from the tears.

"I know you're not insane, Jinx," Shelley said. "Not in a bad way, at least."

Jan managed a weak grin. "You mean the story doesn't sound crazy to you?"

"It does, but that doesn't mean it isn't true. I know you wouldn't lie about something like this. And even I noticed your weird attachment to that stupid necklace. That's just not you. So yeah, I believe you."

Relief washed over Jan, lifting a weight off of her shoulders that eased her breath and slowed her heart.

"Thank God," she said. "I don't know what I would've done if you didn't."

"You'd probably try to fix it all by yourself." A sad smile appeared on Shelley's lips. "And then I'd be a real shit friend, wouldn't I?"

"You're right," Jan teased, nudging her softly. "You would be. So does this mean you agree to help me?"

Shelley looked down at the floor and sighed. "Are you sure we have to get involved? Why can't Owen and Nolan fix it?"

"Because Aiden knows they're after the necklace. It'd take them forever to find a way to steal it back from him, and I don't know how much time we have before Aiden figures out how to break it and steals its power. But he won't suspect me."

Shelley still looked apprehensive. "Isn't it dangerous?"

Jan shrugged, still sniffling. "I don't know. I've only met Aiden once, but based on how powerful this thing seems to be, it might be more dangerous *not* to do anything."

"You really felt something weird when you wore it, didn't you?"

"Yeah, I really did."

Shelley tugged nervously at her hair. "Well, what are friends for? Just don't get us killed, okay? I'd like to be around to enjoy the rest of this summer with no magic necklaces or any crap like that."

Jan grinned and gave a tearful laugh. "No promises," she said.

Chapter 22
A DISTRACTION

"MY DAD WORKS 'TIL EIGHT ON SUNDAYS, WHICH is earlier than usual," Shelley said as they drove to the station. "That means we have four hours to do this."

"Less than that," Jan corrected her. "Owen and Nolan want to meet us at seven o'clock by the Fun Zone. But that still gives us enough time. I'll go in and tell your dad that I'm looking for my ring. Then, maybe ten minutes later, once I'm in Aiden's office, you can come in and create a distraction. Ten minutes should be enough time for me to annoy your dad enough so he lets me speak with Aiden."

"Are you sure Aiden will let you look around his office?"

"Not by myself. If he thinks I'm only looking for my ring, he won't suspect me, but I bet he'll still be nervous about some kid snooping around his office. That's why I need you to distract him long enough for me to look around alone."

"And I just come in and say that I think Owen and his friend are following me, right?"

"Right. Owen and Nolan. Just act all freaked out, and say that while you were waiting for me, you saw them driving around the parking lot."

"Okay," Shelley said unsurely. "But I'm not an actress like you are. What if I'm not believable?"

"Just act scared. It's not that hard."

"Maybe for *you*, little Miss 'I'm the Lead Actress in Every Play Ever!' It's hard for me."

"Oh c'mon. Use something you're scared of to fuel your acting, then."

"Like what?"

"Like this: if I don't find that necklace and Aiden figures out how to break it, he'll have enough power to massacre and destroy anyone and anything he wants, probably including you and me. Scary enough for you?"

The color drained from Shelley's face and she nodded slowly. "Yeah. Scary enough."

"Great," Jan said, patting her on the back. "Think of that when you're spouting off about how Owen and Nolan are following you. Trust me, it'll be believable enough. Besides, you'll be talking to your dad. If he thinks anyone is after you, he'll freak out regardless of how believable you sound."

"You're right," Shelley said. Then, hesitating slightly, she added, "Why'd you have to include that part about massacring people?"

"Because it's true." Although Jan shrouded her voice in what she hoped would come across as determined confidence, what she had said scared her too. It *was* true, after all. From what she had heard about this man, it seemed like he would go to any lengths to acquire unfathomable power.

The rest of their ride to the station was steeped in silence. Jan kept her eyes ahead, focusing on the evening sun as it began its descent in the sky. She had never been very good at keeping her mind off her nerves; her stomach roiled mercilessly until they pulled into the station's parking lot.

"Okay, remember the plan," Jan said, trying to control her voice.

"Right. I remember it."

Jan could tell that Shelley was just as nervous, although perhaps "nervous" wasn't the right word. Nervous, Jan thought, was what she felt when she was about to take a test. It was the butterflies that swarmed in her stomach like angry hornets before she stepped onstage to sing or deliver a monologue. This wasn't nervousness. This was something else entirely.

Jan removed her ring and stuffed it into the shallow pocket of her jeans. She pulled her hoodie down to ensure the outline of her ring was hidden and gave Shelley what she hoped was a reassuring nod. Then, she stepped out of the Blue Bomb and walked cautiously toward the building.

It was larger and more ominous than she remembered it, but Jan supposed it was her nerves that made her feel that way. She lingered at the threshold, letting the salty air pass through her lungs and wishing the sea breeze would carry her away.

It's all just acting. You're good at this. He won't suspect a thing.

With a mighty reluctant push of the door, she entered the station. Warmth laced with coffee and cigarette smoke hit her face, enveloping her in a bubble so suffocating that she nearly turned around. When the eyes of a woman at the front desk locked on her, however, Jan pushed forward.

The woman's lips stretched into a wide, gummy smile. Though Jan supposed it was a polite gesture, the woman's face —plastered with so much makeup that she looked more puppet than human—made Jan's stomach churn even more.

Acting, she reminded herself. *You're acting.*

Jan grinned back at the woman and leaned onto the front of the desk.

"Hi there," she said, forcing herself to keep smiling despite the nausea that clawed at her stomach. "I'm looking for Earl Waldbauer. I'm a friend of his daughter's. I think I lost my ring here the other day, and I'm hoping he could help me look."

"Oh, of course, honey." The woman's voice was shrill, and Jan tried to conceal her wince. "I can go find him for you."

"Thank you, but I can find him myself," Jan said quickly.

Barely pausing to regard the woman's reaction, she slipped past the front desk, marching into the main room through its swinging door. Holding her breath and praying that the woman didn't come after her, she stepped into the lively scene that was the police station.

People bustled about, some carrying boxes and others stacks of paper. A couple of men in uniform leaned against a counter at the far side of the room, deeply engrossed in their conversation.

Jan scanned the room for Mr. Waldbauer, her eyes darting from corner to corner and desk to desk. When she realized that he wasn't in the main room, she approached a middle-aged woman who sat hunched over her typewriter. Her bloodshot eyes darted across the paper in front of her as she clanked away at the keys.

"Excuse me," Jan said. Though the woman's fingers didn't stop typing, her eyes shifted sideways. "Do you know where Earl Waldbauer is?"

The woman shook her head in response and adjusted her glasses with one hand.

Stifling a frustrated sigh, Jan stepped back. Everyone was so consumed with whatever it was they were doing that they probably wouldn't help her unless she was on fire.

Some police station, she thought.

Clearing her throat, Jan decided to adopt another approach.

"Excuse me!" she said loudly, remembering how she had been taught to always project and articulate when on stage.

Immediately, almost everyone quieted down. Thanking the heavens she had been blessed with a voice that carried strength, Jan smiled at those who were now paying attention to her and composed herself.

"Does anyone know where Earl Waldbauer is? I'm looking for my—"

"Jan, what in the world are you doing here?"

Never having felt so grateful to hear that stern Austrian accent, Jan whirled around to see Mr. Waldbauer standing at the entrance of a hallway. She could've *hugged* him.

"Mr. Waldbauer!" she said, swiftly moving toward him and maneuvering past the boxes and stacks of unfiled papers on the ground. "Thank goodness I found you. I realized this morning that I'd lost my ring. I'm one hundred percent sure I lost it yesterday when you brought us here to see Aiden about the Owen Aimsworth mess."

"Jan," he whispered, grimacing, "this isn't the time to be asking me this."

"I'm really sorry, Mr. Waldbauer, but my dad bought me that ring when he went to Switzerland three years ago and it's super expensive," Jan said. She emphasized the *expensive* part, knowing that the thought of wasting money sent chills down Mr. Waldbauer's spine. "It has my birthstone on it and everything.

It's my favorite ring." Her heart pounded against her chest as she spoke. She desperately hoped he didn't see through her lie.

The weight of the ring felt heavy in her pocket. Jan inhaled slowly to calm herself down.

"If I could just talk to Aiden and ask if he's seen my ring, I'd feel a lot better," she continued. "It won't take long, I promise."

"Jan," Mr. Waldbauer said in a low voice, "Mr. Aimsworth is extraordinarily busy. Can't this wait until the end of the workday?"

"I'll be quick, Mr. Waldbauer. I swear." Jan's stomach flipped as she side-eyed the entrance to the main room, praying her ten minutes weren't up.

Mr. Waldbauer let out a lengthy sigh, but something in his expression softened. It wasn't until she took a breath that Jan realized how visibly shaken she was.

"If it means that much to you, I'll ask him. Wait here."

"Could I come?" Jan asked eagerly. "Just to his office...that way I can ask him myself. I know what it looks like, so maybe I can describe it to him. Or...or maybe I'll even see it and then he won't have to worry about it at all."

Mr. Waldbauer gave her a curt nod and led her to the familiar foggy door. A rigid knock was all it took for Aiden to greet them.

Jan's breath caught in her throat when she saw him in the

doorway, his tall figure hovering above her. Everything Owen and Nolan had said rushed back to her, and it took all of Jan's strength to stop the fear she felt from showing on her face. She glanced down at his holster anxiously. The gun wasn't in it, but Jan imagined it wasn't far away.

A man like this should not have a gun, she thought. However, to everyone else unaware of his true nature, he was simply the young, charismatic Chief of Police.

Upon seeing Mr. Waldbauer and Jan, Aiden smiled. His perfect teeth and flawless face masked the vicious man beneath.

"Hi, Earl." He gave a friendly nod in Jan's direction. "And…Jinx, is it?" he asked, tilting his head.

"That's it," Jan said, forcing a laugh and trying her best to smile back at him.

"Glad I remembered. What can I do for you two?"

"I'm so sorry to interrupt," Mr. Waldbauer said. "Jan can't find her ring, and she seems quite certain she lost it here when we visited your office yesterday. She was wondering if you may have seen it."

"I was thinking maybe I could take a quick look around your office," Jan added. "It's an expensive ring that my dad bought from Switzerland. I'd be devastated if I couldn't find it."

Jan could have sworn she saw Aiden falter.

"I don't think I've seen a ring around here, but you're welcome to look," he said slowly. "What does it look like?"

Not waiting for an invitation into his office, Jan slipped inside.

"It's a silver ring with a citrine stone on it," she said. "It's really pretty. I wear it all the time. Citrine is the stone for November, which is my birth month." Noticing that she was rambling, she clamped her mouth shut.

Aiden smiled. "November is my birth month too."

Great. I share a birthday month with a psychopath.

"Ms. Johnson's birthday is also in November," Jan said, scrambling to find something normal to say. "She sells jewelry down by the Fun Zone. Shelley and I go there sometimes."

"I see. Well, let's take a look together then."

Jan nodded and forced another smile. If there was any time for Shelley to make her grand entrance, it was now.

"Mr. Waldbauer, I think I'll be fine now," Jan said. "I don't want to keep you from your work."

Mr. Waldbauer hesitated.

"You can go if you have work to finish," Aiden said. "I'll lead Jan back out to the main room when we finish looking."

Mr. Waldbauer responded with a curt nod. "Hurry up with your search, Jan," he said. "I don't want to waste more of Aiden's time than what's necessary."

"Nothing's being wasted," Aiden said gently.

After another terse nod, Mr. Waldbauer strode down the hall, leaving Jan with the man she knew more about than she cared to.

The office was small with not much more than a desk, three chairs, a mini-refrigerator, and a bookcase. A window behind the desk let in the dim evening glow, and unlike the rest of the building, Aiden's office smelled pristine—a welcome change from the smoke-filled, coffee-stained main room of the station.

"Do you think you know where you might have dropped it?" Aiden asked.

Jan felt her heart leap to her throat.

"I'm not sure," she said, trying to remain levelheaded. "I don't even remember losing it...I just know when we got back from the station yesterday, it was gone." She walked over to the bookcase, taking her time as she studied the three shelves. A potted plant sat on the bottom, scattered files and manuals on the second, and an array of plaques and medals at the top.

Well, it certainly isn't here, Jan thought. She had half-expected to see the mermaid box hidden somewhere amongst the files. Disappointed, she turned back to Aiden's desk where he stood watching her.

"Do you have janitors who clean the offices at night?" she asked innocently. "Maybe they put my ring in one of your desk drawers or something."

Though she knew it was rude, Jan strode over to Aiden's desk and stood, unyielding, in front of the drawers stationed on each side of the table.

"We do," Aiden said slowly, coming closer to Jan. "But I don't usually have them clean in here."

"Oh," Jan said, observing both drawers. "Can I open them?"

Aiden laughed uncomfortably. He positioned himself next to Jan and pulled open the drawer on the right, revealing sticky-notes, discarded pens, and a pack of paperclips.

"Well," he said, "I don't see your ring in this one."

"What about the left drawer?" It wasn't until she pointed toward it that Jan noticed a little lock at the top. Looking back at Aiden to gauge his reaction, she inched closer to it. To Jan's disappointment, his expression stayed the same. He was annoyingly good at maintaining composure.

"I can assure you that your ring isn't in there," he said, giving her a small, warm smile. "I use that drawer to keep all my personal belongings so I don't lose them during the day."

"Personal belongings like what?" Jan asked.

Aiden shrugged and chuckled softly. "Just my wallet and car keys. Boring things like that."

"Maybe you put my ring in there without realizing."

Aiden opened his mouth to say something but was cut short by a familiar voice that sounded from the main room. As soon as he heard it, he turned his head toward the door.

Thank you, thank you, thank you.

"That sounds like Shelley," Jan said. She did her best to

seem caught off guard. "She came with me today. I had her wait in my car."

Aiden shifted his glance between Jan and the door.

Shelley yelled something else, and Aiden motioned for Jan to follow him out of his office.

"I can stay here," she said, a little too quickly. "I'll just sit down and wait for you to get back."

"I'm really sorry, Jan, but I don't feel comfortable leaving you in my office," Aiden said. "Why don't you come out with me and wait in the main room until I see what this is all about?"

Shit.

"Yeah, of course," Jan said. As polite as Aiden tried to be, it was clear he wasn't going to argue with her. He sternly guided her out of his office, then shut the door behind them and led Jan down the hallway.

Shelley stood in the middle of the main room, her eyes wide. All heads had turned her way, and a few confused people whispered to each other. Even the woman on the typewriter had stopped what she was doing long enough to cast Aiden a perplexed look when he entered.

"Miss Waldbauer?" Aiden said.

Shelley turned her head swiftly, meeting Jan's eyes with a baffled look that Jan knew meant, *"Why aren't you in Aiden's office?"*

As subtly as she could, Jan nodded to Shelley—a signal for

her to keep going.

"Michelle?" Mr. Waldbauer emerged from a small hallway opposite the one where Jan and Aiden stood. On seeing his daughter, he tossed the files he was carrying onto an empty desk and rushed over to her. "What's wrong?"

Jan had never seen Mr. Waldbauer in such a frenzy. When she looked back at Shelley's face, she realized how *real* her friend's expressions were. If Jan hadn't known what was going on, she would have felt equally as terrified.

"I was waiting for Jinx outside in her car, and...and I saw Owen Aimsworth and Nolan circling the parking lot," Shelley said in a wobbly voice. She ran her shaking hands through her hair and leaned against her father, breathing heavily and, if Jan wasn't mistaken, on the verge of tears.

Jan held back a grin. Shelley was impressive.

"Try to stay calm," Aiden said. He left Jan, his hands clenched at his sides as he approached Shelley and Mr. Waldbauer. "Do you know what kind of car it was?"

Shelley paled. She instinctively glanced toward Jan before shifting her gaze back to Aiden and shrugging.

"I...I don't know," she said. "It was a nice one, but I don't know much about cars. I was so freaked out that I didn't waste time figuring out the brand."

Jan bit down on her lip to keep from laughing. Though Aiden and Mr. Waldbauer didn't recognize the condescending tone in Shelley's voice, Jan could pinpoint it anywhere.

"I'm *sure* it was them. I'd recognize those two anywhere," Shelley continued. "They kept driving around in circles. I think they recognized Jinx's car."

Mr. Waldbauer muttered something that Jan couldn't hear. Then, louder, he said, "Show us where you saw them, Michelle."

Aiden nodded in agreement. He had lost all color in his face. "We'll try to track them down. I'm assuming they're upset because you and Miss Jenkins did the right thing and turned in that necklace and the box."

Paying no mind to Jan, Aiden and Mr. Waldbauer rushed out of the main room. Shelley followed closely behind them, throwing Jan a quick glance over her shoulder before the three of them reached the station's entrance.

Realizing she had been forgotten, at least for the moment, Jan snuck down the hallway to Aiden's office. She needed to find the necklace and the box, and she needed to do it *now*.

Jan prayed that Shelley could stall as well as she could act.

Chapter 23
THE COLEUS PLANT

SHELLEY HAD COME IN AT THE PERFECT TIME. Aiden had been in such a hurry to see what the fuss was about that he'd neglected to lock his office door, making it easy for Jan to slip in unnoticed.

Quietly shutting the door behind her, Jan rushed toward the locked drawer. Though she knew full well that Aiden wasn't stupid enough to leave the key out in the open, she scanned his desk anyway. Cursing herself for not having asked Shelley to lend her a hairclip, Jan continued sifting through stray papers on Aiden's desk, desperate for even the smallest idea.

How long would it take until Shelley ran out of ways to stall? What if she already had? What if Aiden was on his way back? What would she say if he caught her in his office? The ring wouldn't be a good enough lie—he would see through it, if he hadn't already.

The thought evoked a paranoia so sudden and deep that Jan went cold.

"He believed you," she whispered to herself, if only to hear the words. "Your lie was believable. Focus on the box."

Heart beating in her ears, Jan reopened Aiden's unlocked drawer. There had to be *something* she could use.

"The box," she repeated under her breath. "Focus on..."

The paperclips!

Jan uttered a sharp sigh as relief washed over her in waves. With unsteady hands, she pulled two paperclips from the pack and began fashioning them into a pick. It had been years since she'd given complicated locks a try, but her dad's instructions remained at the back of her mind.

Kneeling before the drawer, Jan got to work, pushing the hooked end of the paperclip into the keyhole and moving it from side to side, trying to decipher which way the lock turned.

After a minute passed with no luck, Jan felt her heart rate increase even more. The beating in her ears grew to a pounding, so loud that it was impossible to listen for approaching footsteps. Rife with desperation, Jan jammed the clip as far back into the keyhole as she could. When nothing happened, she closed her eyes and willed her heart to slow.

Freaking out isn't going to do anything. Shelley will stall them as long as she can.

Jan's dad always told her that she was a quick learner with

a keen mind—it was her patience that needed work. But patience was the hard part, especially now that her time in Aiden's office was limited.

Jan pulled out the paperclip, steadied her hand, and tried again, straining to block the far off ringing in her ears.

Push one down...the other back...clockwise.

Between shallow breaths, Jan turned her hand as gently as she could until she heard a clicking noise. As quiet as it was, the sound brought tears to her eyes.

Hands still trembling, she tossed the paperclips aside and pulled open the drawer so violently that the wallet, keys, and dollar bills inside flew backward.

The blood drained from Jan's face.

No...shit. No, no, no. God, no, where is it?

The ringing in her ears grew louder. Jan ran her hands through her hair, her chin trembling as she angrily slammed the drawer shut.

A locked drawer made sense. It was logical...it was practical...it was *close* to him. Why didn't he choose it?

Unless it wasn't in his office at all. The thought made Jan's stomach sink. What if Owen had been wrong? What if Aiden had found a different hiding spot—one that not even his brother would think of?

No, it has to be here.

Why would Aiden hide it anywhere else? This was the best

place—a personal office where he stayed nearly all day and had complete and constant control of who came in and who went out. Hiding it anywhere else would be idiotic.

Maybe it's somewhere else in the room, Jan thought, opening the empty refrigerator and scouring through the neatly stacked folders at the side of his desk. Returning to the bookcase, she looked behind the plaques and the files, praying for a glint of the mermaid's green eyes.

Aiden wasn't going to make this easy for anyone, and he certainly wasn't going to risk having the necklace stolen from him before he could finally find a way to break it.

She *needed* to beat him to it.

The bottom shelf was empty minus the potted plant she'd noticed earlier. The serrated leaves, spotted with crimson and apricot, looked just like the plants in her mother's gardening catalogs.

A Coleus. Jan managed a weak grin. It seemed Shelley was right: her mom's love of botany did rub off on her.

If her mom were here now, she would probably complain that the shadowy corner of a shelf was not the proper place to house a plant. Intelligent as he may be—much to Jan's chagrin —Aiden certainly wasn't a botanist.

This plant, however, didn't seem to need much sunlight at all. It's leaves were so wildly colored—so bright and tropical— that they almost looked fake.

Knitting her eyebrows, Jan knelt down and inched closer to the plant. She reached her fingers out and ran them gently over the glossy leaves.

Plastic. Of course.

Jan wavered for a moment, her hand hovering in place. Once the realization dawned on her, she hastily removed the pot from the shelf and placed it before her.

Please, please, please.

She turned the pot upside down, silently praying as the Coleus fell to the carpet in a single bunch of hot-glued stems.

With a muffled clank, the mermaid box followed. The beady emerald eyes of the sea witch gleamed back at her, more sentient than ever.

Chapter 24
UNREADABLE

FOR A MOMENT, JAN ONLY STARED AT THE BOX. Then, slowly, she reached for it, opening the already unlocked lid. She wondered if there had ever been a key for the box, or if it had always required a pick. Breathing a sigh of relief that Aiden hadn't somehow locked it again, she peered inside at the necklace, which lay in a meek coil.

Seeing it now that she understood the magnitude of its abilities made Jan dizzy. *This* was the very necklace Owen's great-grandmother had broken and died as a result of. It was the necklace Aiden had become obsessed with—the one she'd felt drawn too as well.

With a shaky breath, Jan flipped the lid closed and placed the plant and pot back on the shelf. She slipped the mermaid box underneath her hoodie and rushed toward the door to Aiden's office, scrambling back out into the hallway toward the main room.

Shelley hadn't returned yet with Mr. Waldbauer and Aiden, which meant she was still stalling them.

As casually as she could, Jan walked through the main room and toward the entrance. The puppetlike lady at the front desk gave her a disapproving glare, her eyes flickering as Jan passed. It took strength not to return the look.

The cool evening air greeted Jan as she stepped outside. In the distance, seagulls cawed as they circled the sky. Jan tilted her head back in relief, feeling as though a weight had been lifted off her shoulders.

"I'm so sorry," she heard Shelley say. Jan turned her head to see the three of them standing next to the Blue Bomb. "I've been overly nervous since the whole boat incident."

"I'd rather you be safe," Mr. Waldbauer said. "I never want you to ignore your intuition because you're worried that you're wasting my time."

"Thanks for understanding. Both Jan and I have been kind of jumpy since yesterday."

Jan approached them, thankful her hoodie hid the box perfectly, which felt cold against her hip. She pressed on it with her arm to keep it in place.

"Sorry, I had to use the restroom," she said. "Is everything okay? Did you find them?"

"Luckily, I don't think it was Owen and Nolan," Mr.

Waldbauer said.

Aiden remained quiet. He glanced at Jan, giving her a subtle look that made her go tense. When he finally spoke up, she shook the feeling away. His demeanor was the same as always: professional, friendly, and otherwise unreadable. She must have just imagined it.

"Regardless," he said, "I'm going to keep some of my officers on the lookout as a safety measure. I don't want to risk anything."

"That makes me feel a lot better," Shelley said. She turned to Jan and smiled gently. "Maybe we should just go home and read magazines for the rest of the day. I don't feel like doing anything else."

"Agreed," Jan said, nodding. She tried to observe the emotion on Aiden's face, but he gave her no reaction.

"If you're at home and you get *any* weird feelings, I want you to call the office number right away," Mr. Waldbauer said. "I have it listed above the phone in the kitchen. I'll pick up and we'll sort everything out."

"Thanks, but I don't think we'll need to," Shelley said. "Jan and I are going to stay in for the rest of the night."

Mr. Waldbauer nodded and turned to Jan. "Did you find that ring you were looking for?"

Jan shook her head. "No, I didn't," she said, trying to sound disappointed. "I'm going to make Shelley help me look in her room when we get back." Turning to Aiden, she said, "If you come across it at the station, would you hold onto it for me, please?"

"Absolutely," Aiden said. He gave her a well-mannered, tight-lipped smile.

Though Mr. Waldbauer seemed reluctant to let them leave, it wasn't long before Jan and Shelley pulled out of the station's parking lot and were back on the main road.

"Did you find it?" Shelley asked, watching through the rearview mirror as Mr. Waldbauer and Aiden went back inside the building.

Jan pulled the box out from underneath her hoodie and held it up. "I got it."

"Holy shit!" Shelley shrieked, grabbing it from her. "Oh my gosh, Jinx, we pulled it off!"

"Now we just need to return it to Owen and Nolan, and then it'll be out of our lives forever."

Shelley leaned back into her seat. "So...where was it?"

"You'd never believe it. He hid it in a potted plant. He must've really been paranoid that someone would find it. I was beginning to think it wasn't in his office at all."

"Well, I'm sure glad you found it. I was running out of ways to stall."

"You did a real bang-up job of acting, though," Jan said. "I was impressed. How'd you manage to act so scared?"

"I *wasn't* acting," Shelley said. "I was terrified."

Jan tried to laugh, but it came out as more of a nervous exhale. "We shouldn't be now, though. We've got the box and the necklace, and soon we'll forget about all of this."

"What if Aiden realizes it's gone?"

Jan shrugged. "If he does, by then we'll have already given it back to Owen and Nolan. After that, it's their problem."

"Yeah, but..." Shelley's voice trailed off. "Doesn't it make you nervous that we can't get rid of the necklace or the box entirely? That's what you said Owen told you, right? It won't ever really go away. So how do we know someone else won't find it later and figure out how to break it?"

Jan bit her lip, staring ahead at the road. Her grip on the steering wheel tightened.

"For now, I guess we'll just hope that doesn't happen," she said. "Besides, Owen seemed determined to keep it away from people. I trust him. I'm sure he'll make sure it doesn't fall into the wrong hands."

"You're right," Shelley said. "We did our job. We shouldn't worry anymore."

Despite their mutual reassurances, the stubborn knot in Jan's stomach persisted.

Chapter 25
FOR A REASON

BY THE TIME SHELLEY AND JAN PULLED INTO THE Waldbauer's driveway, the evening sun had almost completed its descent behind the hills. Fragments of weak rays left the sky a dusky blue, and the faint outline of the moon began to grow clearer.

"We've got a little less than an hour before Owen wanted us to meet him and Nolan at the Fun Zone," Jan reminded Shelley.

"And around two before my dad comes home. If we go quick, he'll have no idea we were gone."

"Then the whole thing will be over and done with," Jan added, trying to sound hopeful. She took her ring out of her pocket and put it back on her finger.

For a moment, only the clunky hum of the Blue Bomb lingered in the air. Jan and Shelley sat motionless, listening to the sound of each other's breathing, their eyes flitting from the box to their own trembling hands.

"I don't know why we're so freaked," Shelley whispered. "We did it. We found the box."

"Just lingering nerves," Jan said absent-mindedly. "They'll pass."

The reassurance didn't do much. Once her limbs obeyed her, Jan turned the engine off, and the two girls scurried inside like frightened mice.

As soon as they reached Shelley's bedroom, Jan shut and locked the door. Shelley tenderly placed the mermaid box on the carpet, and in unison, they sat beside it, studying the hypnotic glow of the sea witch's eyes. With every glint of emerald, the room grew colder, though Jan supposed she was imagining it.

Nerves, she reminded herself. *That's all. Just nerves.*

"This thing sure did cause us a lot more trouble than we'd expected," Shelley said.

"So much for collecting shells, huh?"

"Maybe we can get back to it when this whole mess blows over. I'd like to have enough money to buy those friendship rings from Ms. Johnson."

"That would be nice."

The room fell silent again.

Finally, Jan leaned forward and opened the box. "I can't believe that one little thing could be capable of this much evil.

It's hard to understand."

She stared at the necklace in the box, which lay over the familiar words carved into the silver: *Oval to oval, golden to green.*

Shelley nodded. "Maybe it's not supposed to be easy to understand. What I don't get is why anyone would willingly take that kind of power."

"Because some people are just messed up." Jan sat back, folding her knees and wrapping her arms around her legs. "When I spoke with Owen, he said he thought the little poem might be a hint about how the locket was meant to break. But neither of us could determine what it meant."

Shelley shrugged. "We don't have to worry about that now. As long as Owen keeps it away from Aiden, it doesn't matter."

"Yeah..." Jan's voice trailed off as her eyes rested on the copper-golden necklace.

"Jinx?" Shelley whispered after quite some time.

"Yeah?"

"You said you trusted Owen. You're sure about that, right?"

Jan narrowed her eyebrows. "What do you mean?" she asked, her tone tinged with defensiveness.

"I mean...I mean are you sure that everything he said was true?"

Jan faltered for a moment, but finally nodded and said, "Yes. Everything he described about that locket and the things it does…I *felt* it. I felt those episodes and the metallic smells and that crazy need to keep it on. How could he be lying about all of that?"

"I know," Shelley said, nodding to herself. "If you say he's safe, then I believe you. You're a good judge of character."

Even though Shelley sounded sure, the certainty Jan had first felt wavered within her.

"Owen was willing to open up to me about the history of this locket," she said, this time trying to reassure herself. "It's much more than I can say for Aiden, who lied to us about it being an expensive family heirloom and then hid it at the bottom of a pot."

"You're right," Shelley said. "That's pretty sketchy."

"It totally is." Jan breathed a sigh of relief as her confidence returned.

For a long while, the girls were quiet. Jan kept her eyes on the locket and the box. She tried to fathom how something as unassuming as an eroded, tiny necklace could hold so much power.

"All my life, I never believed in magic or anything like that," she whispered, lifting her eyes to meet Shelley's. "Even as a kid, I never did. Then *this* happened, and I actually experienced the impossible. I feel like my whole world has been turned upside down."

"That's because it has. Mine has too. But I always like to

think that things happen for a reason."

Jan didn't respond.

Shelley clamped her lips together and sighed through her nostrils. "When my mom passed away, I was so angry," she said, picking at a stray strand of carpet. "I think I might've been more angry than sad. I didn't know why it had to happen to me when so many other peoples' mothers were still alive. I mean, God, she was only in her mid-forties then."

She looked down, blinking fervently. Jan remained quiet. Shelley *never* spoke about her mother. Any mention of Mrs. Waldbauer made her go quiet and cold, as though she had stopped feeling altogether.

"But," Shelley continued, "my dad told me that things always happen for a reason. He said that maybe we don't know what the reason is, and at times it may seem like there isn't one. But there's a greater plan for us all and we have to have faith in it, or else there's just no point in going on when bad or scary things happen."

Shelley looked up at Jan, their eyes meeting amidst the solemn silence of the house.

"I know you don't really believe in all that stuff, and it may sound like a cop-out, but what I mean to say is that right now, this whole thing seems rotten and crappy...and it is. But maybe you found the necklace and the box for a reason. Maybe if you hadn't, it would've fallen into the hands of someone even worse than Aiden. I don't know, the whole thing sounds stupid, but…"

"No, Shelley. It doesn't," Jan said. "Maybe you're right. Maybe this whole thing played out the way it was meant to. Maybe I truly did find it for a reason. We know who is trustworthy and who isn't, and we know who the necklace needs to be given back to." She paused and gave Shelley a tender smile. "Maybe we played a bigger part in all of this than we think."

Shelley smiled gently. "Maybe we did."

"And after all of this blows over," Jan teased, crinkling her nose, "you can go back to your obsession with Gabriel."

"Oh, dear lord," Shelley giggled. "It is *not* an obsession." Giving it a second thought, she shrugged. "It certainly would be nice to get back to thinking about him instead of this whole mess."

Jan playfully rolled her eyes and glanced at the clock on Shelley's desk. Upon seeing the time, her stomach flipped.

"It's a quarter to seven already?" she said.

Shelley followed her gaze and quickly stood up. "Let's get going then," she said with a confident nod. "I'll grab my jacket. I'd like to get this whole mermaid box crap out of my life. After all, I have an obsession to get back to."

Jan laughed, picking up the mermaid box and pulling herself to her feet. For a moment, despite her nerves and her spinning mind, she felt a bit of warmth. Watching Shelley as she trudged past the mess on her bedroom floor, Jan relaxed a little.

"You coming?" Shelley asked.

Jan nodded. "Just give me a second to get myself together."

"Okay," Shelley said, tilting her head quizzically. "Meet me by the front door?"

Jan nodded as Shelley slipped out her bedroom door.

She opened the box to look at the locket one more time and pressed her fingers down on the coiled chain. It was so fragile and withered that, if it were any other necklace, it could easily be broken with a single hand. But it wasn't.

Jan plucked the locket out of the box and held it out in front of her.

"I'm done with you," she said, as if to the sea witch herself.

Though she knew saying so meant nothing, it made her feel better anyway. After all the locket had put her through—after all the trouble it had caused—she felt justified scorning it.

A shiver coursed up her spine. It would be terrible to have to deal with this mess by herself. She wasn't even sure she would be able to.

At least I have Shelley, she thought.

At the moment, it was the only comfort Jan could find.

Chapter 26
THE LAMBORGHINI

THE FAMILIAR GLOW OF THE FUN ZONE'S LIGHTS was dim due to the remainder of the evening sun. Still, they promised vibrant colors with the coming night. Though the park was mostly deserted, staff members and early birds prepared for the nightly action that occurred like clockwork during the summer.

Jan pulled into the parking lot, scanning her surroundings for Owen and Nolan. The spot she chose was far enough away from the entrance to both the Fun Zone and the parking lot that it wasn't a popular first choice. Unless it was a particularly crowded night, this part of the lot remained empty. The thought comforted Jan. Considering how dangerous the locket and box were, she knew it would be best to exchange the items in an area void of potentially nosey people.

"A precaution," she imagined Owen saying.

Yes, a precaution.

"Do you think they're here yet?" Shelley asked as Jan turned off the engine.

Jan shrugged, looking over at the mermaid box, which sat in her open glove compartment. An apprehensive part of her wondered if it was cognizant of all that was happening. Every time she looked at the tiny emerald eyes, they seemed to grow even more sentient.

"Those eyes get more and more real every time I look at them," she said.

Shelley nodded in agreement. "Hopefully we don't have to look at them ever again. Although I guess it's *kind of* cool to have gone on a super screwed up adventure with the son of the Aimsworth family." When Jan didn't respond, Shelley poked her gently. "Come on, Jinx," she said. "Not many friends are going to have the type of adventure we've had these past few days."

Jan shrugged. "I guess. I know this is out of character, but part of me wishes that we had just stuck to collecting shells and wasting time at the Fun Zone."

"It *is* out of character," Shelley said. Softening, she added, "But it's understandable. Besides, I wasn't the one who had a gun held to me."

"Yeah, that was a first for me, surprisingly," Jan joked, trying desperately to stop the churning in her stomach. The knot hadn't budged.

Tapping her foot testily on the edge of the car's door, she scanned the parking lot again. "God, where are they?"

"It's probably not seven o'clock yet. We got here early."

"How are you so *calm?*"

"Jinx, chill," Shelley said. "I'm nervous too, but we're doing the right thing."

Jan pushed herself back into her seat and groaned loudly. "What if we don't see them and they don't see us? I don't even know how to get in contact with Owen, and I think I'd go insane if I couldn't get rid of the box and the necklace."

Shelley reached over and put a firm hand on her shoulder. "Jan Marian Jenkins. I'm ordering you to take a deep breath, calm down, and wait. Panicking won't accomplish anything."

A bit surprised by Shelley's resolve, Jan nodded and inhaled deeply, unable to stop herself from grinning. Though Shelley and her father were typically not that similar, Shelley's sudden firmness reminded Jan so much of Mr. Waldbauer that it was almost comical.

"What?" Shelley asked, noticing Jan's grin.

"You just reminded me of your dad, that's all."

Shelley rolled her eyes. "Great."

Jan opened her mouth to say something, but Shelley had already shifted her gaze to the rearview mirror. Tapping Jan repeatedly on the arm, she motioned for her to get out of the car.

"I see them," she said, pointing over Jan's shoulder.

Jan's stomach flipped and she whirled around, looking through the rear window. Sure enough, Owen and Nolan were approaching the Blue Bomb.

"Where's their car?" Shelley asked.

Jan shrugged. "Thank goodness I have a car that stands out, huh?" She grabbed the mermaid box and pulled the door open.

"Jan," Owen said when he finally approached them. He stood tall and confident as he gave the girls a warm smile. He hardly looked nervous at all. Nolan followed behind, staying solemnly quiet as usual.

"And you must be Shelley," Owen continued, extending a hand to her. "Pleasure to officially meet you."

"Same here," Shelley said, giggling nervously while shaking his hand.

"So what happened?" Nolan asked impatiently.

"I got it," Jan said, proudly producing the mermaid box.

Though Owen hadn't seemed anxious before, the relief and shock that manifested on his face was clear as day.

"I'm impressed," he said, grinning. "I wasn't sure you'd be able to find it so quickly. Thank God you did, though." He turned his head to Nolan, who looked even more surprised, and raised his eyebrows. "I guess our trust *wasn't* misplaced."

Nolan shrugged. "Forgive me for being skeptical about a

sixteen-year-old."

"Jinx can do anything," Shelley said, almost defensively. "She's crazy good at figuring things out."

Jan would have thanked Shelley for sticking up for her, but Owen spoke first.

"I don't doubt it," he said. "Nolan was just nervous about having things so out of control. If I'm being honest, I was too. It's very unsettling to know that someone as unstable as Aiden was in possession of something as dangerous as the locket, even if only for a short amount of time."

"We were nervous too," Jan said, feeling at ease now that Owen had admitted it. "But now you can hide it forever and we can just forget this whole thing and move on. Right?"

"Absolutely," Owen said. Pausing, he smiled. "Is that your nickname? Jinx?"

Jan nodded. "Shelley gave it to me."

"It's because she's always getting into trouble," Shelley added. "I guess it just stuck after a bit."

"So...what are you going to do with it now?" Jan asked after a moment, glancing at the box in her hands.

"Hide it in a better place than before," Owen said. "A place where two very adventurous girls won't come across it."

"We're done with adventures for the time being," Shelley said. Smiling, she looked over at Jan and added, "Hopefully."

"As long as the necklace stays away from people like Aiden,

everything should be fine," Owen said.

Nolan shifted impatiently.

"I can't thank you enough, Jan," Owen said. "And you too, Shelley. If anyone else had stumbled upon that box, I don't know what would've happened."

"Even if we did give it to Aiden?" Shelley joked.

"You got it back," Owen said. "And you did it quickly— before he figured out how to break the locket."

He slowly reached out with an open hand to take the box from Jan. For a moment, silence lingered between the four of them as faint music echoing from the Fun Zone began to flit across the parking lot.

Jan looked down at the box and thought of all the trouble it had caused.

So much for such a little treasure, she thought.

But it was over now. As she extended her arm and the box to Owen, Jan felt a welcome rush of relief course through her.

The relief, as comforting as it was, was also short-lived. Before Owen had taken the box from Jan's hands, a black Lamborghini hightailed into the parking lot, the tires screeching on the pavement and stopping right in front of them.

Jan jumped back. Both her arm and the mermaid box retracted toward her stomach.

Owen snapped his head toward the Lamborghini. The relief and self-assuredness once on his face had completely abandoned him.

With animal-like haste, the man in the car flung open the side door. It wasn't until he started to approach them that Jan realized it was Aiden.

Chapter 27
OWEN AND AIDEN

IN THE WEAK EVENING LIGHT, THE BROTHERS looked even more alike than Jan expected them to. Their dark eyes narrowed as their faces contorted into a mixture of rage and fear. Shelley moved closer to Jan as though she expected some kind of protection, but Jan was just as startled.

How could this possibly be happening? How could he have figured it out so quickly? The words failed to form on her tongue. Instead, Jan stood pressed next to Shelley, frozen like a deer in headlights, as Owen positioned himself between the girls and Aiden.

Aiden, however, wasn't interested in his brother. Looking over at Jan and the box, he put his hands up.

"Jan, stop," he said, heaving to regain his breath.

"Stop what?" Owen spoke before she could. "I think your issue lies with me, Aiden. Not her."

"She's the one with the box and the necklace," Aiden said, still panting. "Right now, it does."

Out of the context of the police station, Aiden looked unnervingly normal—not at all like the esteemed, wealthy, and well-known Chief of Police of Aledale. Minus the holster around his waist that carried his service pistol, he stood out no more than the average citizen. Still, Jan couldn't see past the person she knew he really was. Seeing him stand before them, his eyes wide and hungry, made everything about him the exact opposite of normal.

Jan gaped at him, remembering how he'd glanced at her outside the station. Had something in her demeanor given everything away?

"How did you...?"

"You forgot to throw away the paperclips you used to break into my desk drawer," Aiden said. He didn't take his eyes off his brother. "Not many people go through that much trouble to get a little ring. It didn't take me long to realize what you were actually after."

Jan's heart sank. Of all the things that could have given her away, it was two tiny paperclips.

"But how did you know we were *here*?" Shelley asked.

"I'm more familiar with this town than you may think, Miss Waldbauer," Aiden said, straining to steady his voice. "This isn't the only exchange that's happened in the Fun Zone parking lot."

"That box isn't yours," Owen said. He took a step closer to his brother. "I'm not going to let you take it back from her so you can hurt hundreds of people."

"I'm not arguing with you, Owen," Aiden said. Shifting his gaze back to Jan and Shelley, he reached out his hands. "Give me the box. Please."

"Oh, this is wonderful." Owen laughed dryly and shook his head. "Begging a sixteen-year-old? Really? It's too late. She knows who you are and what you've done."

Aiden glared at Owen with an expression Jan had never seen before. It was one so cold—so full of hate, rage, and indignation—that Jan could have sworn the temperature in the parking lot dropped. "What *I've* done? Are you serious? I haven't done anything, Owen. You and I both know that."

"You can't trick us," Jan said, her voice shaking. "Owen already told us what happened. There's no way I'm going to let you get ahold of something like this."

"Something like this?" Aiden choked on a laugh. "There's *nothing* like this, Miss Jenkins. I don't expect Owen told—"

"It's clear that someone with a power complex like your own is remarkably ill-suited for the necklace," Owen interrupted hastily.

"A power complex? Because I'm Chief of Police? Because you're angry that I *worked* for my position rather than lounge around with a silver spoon in my mouth?"

"Because you're insane," Shelley blurted out.

That time, Aiden did not respond. Instead, he stalked over to Shelley and pulled her away from Jan. His movements were so swift that neither girl could process what was going on until it happened. With trained dexterity, it took less than a second before the gun in his holster was pressed against Shelley's head.

Shelley didn't scream. Instead, she simply choked out a surprised sob. Her eyes landed on Jan, whose heart all but stopped.

In a cold rush of fear, the blood drained from Jan's face.

No. He couldn't.

"Give me the box, Jan," Aiden barked, violently extending his free hand. "Give it to me or I pull the trigger."

He could.

Shelley uttered another strained whimper.

"If you run, I shoot," Aiden growled through his teeth. Shelley nodded through tears.

Jan desperately wished that someone—*anyone*—would jump in unexpectedly and get her and Shelley out of the situation. But the parking lot was nearly empty, with only a few early-arrivals parked close to the flashing entrance of the Fun Zone. The five of them were yards away from anyone, isolated by the parking spot Jan chose.

"Okay!" Jan said loudly, her voice breaking. She held out the box to Aiden. "Get the gun away from her."

Nobody was going to help.

"Jan..." Owen said. His voice rang in Jan's ears, but she ignored him.

Aiden lowered his gun and snatched the box out of Jan's shaking hands. Shelley quickly scurried to Jan's side as he backed away from the girls and opened the mermaid box. In the evening glare, the sea witch's emerald eyes shined hungrily.

It took everything within Jan not to cry. Hot tears pricked the corners of her eyes and her head spun, but she directed all her energy toward staying composed. She focused on Aiden, observing his face as he peered inside the box. Though he hardly showed any emotion at first, it didn't take long for the panic to set in. The color leached from his skin as he gaped at the opened box—his lips parted as though he were going to say something but found he could no longer use his voice. It wasn't until Owen began to laugh—cackle, even—that he looked up, casting a flinty stare both at and beyond his brother.

Jan stuffed her hand into the pocket of her hoodie and produced the little locket, which reflected the weak light of the parking lot off its tarnished face.

Shelley gaped at her. "How did you...?"

Jan shook her head to quiet her friend and mouthed, *"Later,"* all the while fighting back persistent tears.

It had been pure impulse to separate the locket and the box, but after Shelley had questioned the validity of Owen's story back at the Waldbauers' house, Jan had decided to wait until she knew his intentions for sure before giving him the locket. Now she did, and it was clear that he had been telling the truth about Aiden.

She turned her attention to Owen, who hadn't stopped laughing, and at Nolan, who wavered hesitantly beside him.

"Owen," she said softly. When he looked over at her, she tossed the necklace to him. With a quick reflex, he caught it in his hand.

Still laughing with both relief and amusement, Owen grinned at Jan and said, "I'm impressed. You really gave this exchange a lot of thought."

Jan ignored his praise. She turned back to Aiden, who stood motionless. He looked down at the box, then up at Owen, and then down at the box again.

"You idiot," Aiden said, finally focusing on Jan. "You—"

A deafening clap rang throughout the parking lot. Jan shrieked and jumped back, colliding into Shelley. Completely dumbfounded, the girls gaped at Nolan, who held his pistol out in front of him. His hands shook just like they had when he'd held the gun to Jan earlier that morning, but he managed a precise enough shot.

Though the bullet only grazed Aiden's arm, it shocked him enough to make him drop what he was holding. A clank sounded as the mermaid box hit the pavement, and another followed with his gun.

Acting without thought, Jan rushed over to the box and kicked it to Owen. It slid unevenly across the bumpy asphalt, landing just by his feet. Owen bent down and swooped the box up, still grinning.

Once Aiden realized the shot hadn't been fatal and managed to regain his wits, he started back for his gun.

"Stay away from it," Nolan hissed, still keeping his pistol out in front of him.

Aiden held up his hands in surrender, but he had already succeeded in getting his gun, which dangled above his head.

"Okay," he said. "I won't shoot."

Nolan eyed him suspiciously.

"I won't shoot," Aiden repeated.

The night had already begun to take its turn. More cars pulled into the parking lot while screaming children at the far end of the lot pulled their parents into the Fun Zone, mesmerized by the flashing lights and the multi-colored Ferris wheel that towered above the boardwalk. The sound of the gun had caught the attention of a few people, who craned their heads to make sense of the commotion.

Aiden lingered in his place, watching his brother with wide and unyielding eyes.

"Owen," Nolan said. "Do it."

Jan and Shelley looked back over at Owen, who stood just

as still as his brother. He was still grinning down at the locket and the box, now both in his possession.

"Owen!" Nolan said, louder. "Do it. Break it!"

The sliver of hope Jan felt evaporated, replaced with thronging panic that shrouded her senses. Shelley shot her a look rife with desperation, but Jan was too shocked to return it.

"What do you mean *break it?*" she finally said, swallowing a gasp as the parking lot began to spin. "I thought..."

No, it wasn't supposed to happen like this...

"Owen," Aiden said, his eyes wide. "Put it down. Please. Walk away. It's not worth it."

Owen took a deep breath and looked up. "But that would be such a waste. I've been looking forward to breaking this thing for such a long time."

Jan tried to cry out, but all that emerged from her constricted throat was a broken wheeze. For what seemed both hours and seconds, she felt nothing but the primal fear that surged throughout her body in currents. The sounds of faraway car horns and voices from the Fun Zone grew to a deafening pitch, then died down again, leaving Jan's head foggy as she struggled to ground herself.

When she finally managed to surface from her dumbstruck state, she shifted her gaze to Shelley, who stood motionless. Her eyes fixed on Aiden, as though she were waiting for him to act. When he didn't move, her face grew pallid as the despair set in.

"Don't look so upset, Aiden," Owen said, fiddling with the necklace in his hand. Nolan watched intently from behind him. "I put on a pretty convincing performance."

He turned to Jan, looking her over with a derisory gaze. *"Jinx,"* he said through a grin. The satisfaction in his voice made Jan go cold. "That's fitting. The name suits you." He paused and took a step toward the girls. "You two need to learn to be less gullible."

"Move away from them," Aiden commanded, his grip on his gun tightening.

"I'm just giving advice," Owen said softly. "Honestly, I appreciate their efforts. If it weren't for them, I'm not sure I would've gotten the necklace back from you at all. Of course, I probably wouldn't have lost it in the first place."

"You don't even know how to break it," Jan said, her voice so weak and unsteady that she could hardly hear herself.

Owen cocked his head and grinned. "For what seems like the thousandth time today, you're wrong, *Jinx,*" he said.

The sound of her nickname coming from his mouth evoked a churning so sickening that Jan reached for Shelley, desperate for what little solace she could find. When their hands met, they locked fingers so tightly that Jan could feel every movement Shelley made—every infinitesimal, terror-stricken twitch.

"I spent so much time trying to figure it out," Owen said.

"That's why I dropped the box and the necklace into the ocean in the first place. I needed time to think...to figure out the correct way to break the locket without anyone interfering. These past few years have been a vicious cycle of hiding and re-hiding the box from Aiden. He even found it once, and taking it back was almost impossible. I never had the time to think about the technicalities—about how to actually *get* the power—because I was so busy dealing with my intrusive, self-righteous brother."

He laughed and rubbed the side of his chin. "The plan was to dive for the box and necklace again when I figured everything out, but that got a little messed up. But that's okay. In fact, Jan, you actually *helped* me when you made that comment about the shape of the sea witch's skull. It's funny how little details seem so obvious after they're pointed out."

"That...that doesn't mean you know," Jan choked, feeling bile rise in her throat. "That doesn't mean it'll work."

Owen only grinned in response. Though his eyes shined hungrily, he was unable to hide the apprehension on his face.

"Owen," came Aiden's strangled plea. "This isn't worth it. What you're feeling...it's the necklace. You know that. You've seen it happen. You know what it does—"

"Five years...almost six, now, since she died," Owen said, his chest rising and falling rapidly with every breath. "You remember that, Aiden. Of course you do. You don't know how long I've been waiting for this moment. God, if only she were here to see it."

The situation began to attract the curious eyes of even more people, who looked on from a distance with befuddled concern. Some whispered amongst themselves, lingering by their cars as they tried to decipher the situation. A few stopped what they were doing entirely, no doubt wondering why a gun had been fired.

"Isn't that the Chief of Police?" Jan heard someone say.

The ringing in Jan's ears increased tenfold.

Aiden stepped toward his brother, but Owen did not heed him. Instead, he snapped open the locket and positioned it over the sea witch's skull on the box.

The two shapes were exactly the same—both tiny ovals the size of a thimble—and looked as though they fit together like pieces of a puzzle. But it wasn't only that. The shining emerald eyes of the sea witch reflected onto the locket, which shined more golden than copper in the evening light.

Oval to oval, golden to green. How had she not noticed?

Jan looked over at Aiden, who had lowered his hands and was now holding his gun tentatively to his side. She desperately willed him to shoot and stop this all from happening, but Aiden stood paralyzed.

He won't do it, Jan thought. She imagined having to kill someone she loved. Even if they were a dangerous, wicked person, she wasn't sure she would be able to do it either. Still, an adrenaline-filled part of her wanted Aiden to pull the trigger—to stop his brother and whatever he intended to do.

"Put your gun down, Aiden," Owen said through the side of his mouth. His voice trembled, but he suppressed it. "We both know you aren't going to shoot. I want you to watch this. I really, truly do."

Stop him, Aiden.

Although Aiden remained otherwise frozen, he managed to move his gun out in front of him. The horror in his eyes swelled outward as he placed his finger on the trigger.

Owen took a shaky breath. For a fleeting moment, Jan wondered if he was scared or excited. Perhaps both. It was clear he needed to gather courage to do what he planned, and Jan prayed his fear would stop him.

"Owen," Aiden begged again.

Clenching his jaw and drawing in another breath, Owen pressed the opened locket down onto the skull of the sea witch. A sickening click reverberated through the air as the two attached to each other. With a violent tug, he pulled the necklace toward himself.

Jan braced herself. For a moment, nothing happened. Aiden stood with his gun pointed at his brother, Nolan watched like a vulture from the side, and Jan and Shelley gaped at Owen as if in a catatonic stupor, riddled with paralyzing fear.

And then, as if the sea witch herself had been there to do

it, the necklace broke in half at the hinge.

The last thing Jan heard was Aiden's gun, followed by a blinding flash of green.

Chapter 28
NATURALLY

A SPLITTING BRIGHTNESS, WHICH JAN HAD NEVER thought possible, lit up the parking lot. Though she steeled herself for some kind of excruciating impact, she didn't feel it. A few people from an unknown distance shrieked loudly, and a nearby car alarm began to ring.

When Jan opened her eyes, she remained standing just as she had been before. Shelley stood beside her, blinking rapidly, having impulsively flung her arms upward to shield her face.

Slowly, the light began to fade, and Jan prepared for the worst. Despite the thousands of possibilities that flooded her mind, however, once the green glow dimmed down and the late evening shadows swarmed back in to fill the void, she was met with nothing.

Her eyes darted across the parking lot, half-expecting some sort of mass devastation to have started its descent upon the world. But everything was as it always had been. The Fun Zone's lights twinkled and faint carousel music flit out and above the little amusement park. Crashing waves echoed in the distance, and cars on nearby roads gave off their low hums as they passed.

Finding herself both present and removed, Jan directed her attention back to the people around her.

A swarm of perplexed witnesses had stopped in the parking lot, shooting frightened glances at the scene. They lingered uncertainly in their tracks like lost children, as though they were waiting for someone to come out and direct them in a round of applause—someone who would assure them that everything happening was all part of some dramatic show.

Drowning out their murmurs, which had now crescendoed to a mass of confused prattle, Jan looked back at Owen, who stood unnervingly still. For a moment, he kept his gaze locked on his feet. Next to them rested the mermaid box and the broken halves of the locket.

Jan hardly needed to observe Aiden's distraught face to understand the severity of the situation. Whatever emerged from the locket had, in the matter of a split second, been so strong and bright that Aiden missed his shot.

Jan looked around to spot the blaring car parked a few yards away. What had once been a quaint vinyl-roofed buggy now looked like something out of a junkyard, complete with shattered glass and dented metal from Aiden's bullet. Its alarm, however, rang shrill, refusing to be silenced despite its condition.

Owen stood smiling, looking down at the ground. He was untouched, unharmed, and on the verge of laughter. Finally, pulling his lips back into a straight line, he leveled and composed himself.

"Do you feel anything?" Nolan asked eagerly.

"Give me a minute," Owen hissed. He shifted his gaze to his hands, which although were quivering, did not look any different than before. When he looked back up, however, Jan noticed his eyes.

Though Owen looked disconcertingly normal, his once fully amber eyes held a very familiar green hue. It was as though the eyes of the sea witch on the box had merged with his, leaving him somewhere between human and beast.

He held out his hands and flexed his fingers slowly before directing his attention to his brother.

"If there's *anyone* I've been waiting to use this on, it's you, Aiden," he said, struggling to overpower the sound of the car's blaring alarm with his voice.

"You don't even know if you can control it," Aiden said. It was clear he was feigning confidence. For once, Aiden was unable to maintain his collected, self-assured composure.

"You're right," Owen said. The look on his brother's face made him grin even wider. "I guess we'll just have to see if it comes naturally."

Jan watched in horror as Owen inhaled and stilled his shaking hands. Then, slowly, as though he were trying to crush steel, he curled his fist into a tight ball.

Aiden uttered a piercing shriek as he dropped his gun and fell to the ground. Jan and Shelley instinctively embraced, paralyzed with immobilizing fear that left them clutching at each other's bodies and praying for safety that neither one could provide. Jan's stomach coiled and soured as she watched Aiden's hand distort under an invisible force—a force that Owen had complete control over.

Another muffled howl of pain escaped Aiden's mouth as he pulled his hand toward his body, his fingers bent backward over one another. The tip of a bone had broken through his skin, leaving his hand little more than a mangled jumble of bloody flesh.

"Well! It looks like this *is* all coming quite naturally," Owen remarked, if only to taunt his brother further.

"Owen," Nolan whispered, crossing his arms. From what Jan could see of his face, his gesture was anything but casual. Though he masked his emotions with a smirk, it was obvious that even he was shocked.

Owen didn't acknowledge him. Instead, he lifted his arm up and brought it back down sharply, slamming Aiden's head onto the ground from a distance. The laugh he gave when his brother cried out bordered on euphoric.

Jan could not think. She could not move. There was nothing that could describe what Owen was doing—nothing but the broken locket at his feet and the growing emerald in his eyes.

Shelley whimpered. She gently reached her hand out and brushed it against Jan's arm, as if to say, *"We need to run."*

Jan grasped Shelley's hand in her own, keeping her in place. She didn't know the extent of Owen's abilities yet, but she knew he could harm them from a distance, just as he was doing to his brother. Running would be more dangerous than staying put.

Owen laughed, finding twisted joy in the ordeal. It reminded Jan of a child finding pleasure in breaking his toys.

"I think I'm warming up to this," he said, more to himself than anyone else. Eyes wide and hands shaking in manic excitement, he cocked his head to the side, evoking another terrible shriek from Aiden, who lay on the pavement in a ball. Jan wasn't even sure what Owen was doing to him. Still, it was a terribly unfathomable sight to see someone reduced to this.

"Owen," Nolan said, louder this time.

Owen snapped his head toward him. "What do you want?" he said, shooting an annoyed look at the buggy.

"People are looking," Nolan hissed.

Owen looked up. Now, the bystanders were more than just confused; they were noticeably panicked. Families gathered around their cars and shielded their kids as distressed onlookers backed away.

"Someone needs to find a phone!" Jan heard someone yell.

"We need to call the police!" came another voice.

Owen heard them too. "No, no, no," he said, loudly enough so that the people close to him could hear. "Nobody is getting the police." He raised his voice, projecting across the parking lot so that even those closest to the Fun Zone could hear him. "The police aren't going to help you. Don't you see?" He pointed at his brother, who lay on the pavement moaning deliriously.

Blood pooled around Aiden's body, though Jan wasn't sure where it was coming from. It was only when he lifted his head off the ground that she noticed the blood matting his hair, seeping out of an open wound by his ear.

"Your Chief of Police, everyone!" Owen shouted over the persistent car alarm. "Not so heroic now, is he?"

The green glimmer in his eyes lit up as he spoke, growing with the same amount of energy as his rising voice.

The car alarm blared again, and Jan could see something crack in Owen's eyes. He turned toward the buggy and violently extended his hand. The little car erupted with a deafening bang. A fist of orange flames catapulted upward, replaced with gusts of dense smoke. The vinyl roof flew back as bits and pieces of the car propelled toward Jan and Shelley, who ducked and covered their ears.

Owen didn't wait for the crowd's reaction. He made

another movement with his arms—this time, a wide-sweeping motion rather than a flick. Jan gasped as several parked cars flew sideways and slammed into each other, knocking over one after another like dominos. They moved with so much force that one skidded diagonally into a group of teenagers who had been standing in a huddled group, watching in disbelief.

It was at that moment that screams erupted in the parking lot. Someone had been hit. With all the movement and chaos, Jan could hardly focus on what was happening. The ringing in her ears was so loud that even the screams seemed silent.

Chapter 29
LIES AND OBSESSIONS

RAPT IN HIS NEWFOUND ABILITIES, OWEN MADE another gesture that caused four more cars to topple over, which skidded across the ground at the will of an entirely invisible force. He was so immersed in the mayhem he was creating that he failed to notice Aiden, who had found a way, despite his shaking limbs, to pick himself up.

"Owen!" Nolan yelled.

Owen spun around, but he wasn't quick enough. Aiden flung himself toward his brother and tackled him to the ground.

Caught completely off guard, Owen struggled to wriggle out of Aiden's firm grasp. Upon realizing his brother's strength surpassed his own, he pressed his hand down onto Aiden's arm.

Immediately, Aiden let go and cursed so loudly that Jan was sure even those atop the Ferris wheel could hear him. He jerked his arm back, revealing the ripped sleeve of his coat and the searing red, blistering flesh beneath it. The pain, as agonizing as it seemed, did not deter Aiden. Through gritted teeth, he flung himself at his brother again. Another flash of green light catapulted from Owen's hands, hurling Aiden backward with so much force that when he hit the ground, Jan nearly expected the pavement to break.

Owen pulled himself to a standing position. "You're not winning this time," he said between breaths. He approached Aiden's body like a starving snake nearing its prey, then gave his brother a hard kick to the ribs. "I'm not letting you win. I'm tired of it. Game's over."

He raised his leg to kick Aiden once more, but before he managed to deliver it, Aiden grabbed his ankle, sending Owen to the ground. He piled on top of him, boxing his face with his unscathed hand.

Jan braced herself, waiting for Owen's counterattack. When it didn't come, she blinked back her confusion, watching as he lay with his arms in front of his face, shielding himself from Aiden's persistent punches.

For a fleeting moment, Jan wondered if perhaps he had pushed himself too far. When he finally managed to launch another burst of green light, it was duller and weaker than before. Aiden only fell slightly to the side, giving Owen enough time to roll out of the way and jump back up.

He was pale and breathless, as though he had exerted

himself to the point of collapse. He wiped blood off of his lips and from underneath his nose, giving Aiden just enough time to attack again. Seizing the opportunity, Aiden collided into his brother, this time shouting at Jan and Shelley.

"Go! Leave!" he yelled, making a frantic gesture with his arm.

The command was enough to snap the girls out of their paralyzed state. With only a wide-eyed glance to each other, they whirled around and sprinted to the Blue Bomb.

As powerful as the magic from the locket was, the man who wielded it was only human. That in and of itself offered Jan some hope. Perhaps there was a small chance they could escape—that they could live through this.

When Owen spoke, desperation plagued his voice. "If you leave, I'll kill him!" he shouted.

Jan and Shelley stopped in their tracks. Though she couldn't see his face, Jan could feel Owen grinning from behind her. Slowly, she turned back around to face him.

"Good choice," he said through an exhale. He managed to push Aiden away with the help of Nolan, then stood up unsteadily. "Stay put or his death will be your fault."

Shelley uttered a distressed cry.

"I said *go!*" Aiden yelled again.

"God, you're perfect, aren't you?" Owen spat. "Such a martyr. It's disgusting."

"Is that why you want to kill me, Owen?" Aiden snapped, wriggling free from Nolan. "Because you think I'm a martyr?"

Owen responded to his brother by uttering a low laugh. He was noticeably winded, but his laugh still held enough venom to make Jan's body go cold.

It was that very laugh—weak, yet simultaneously filled with burgeoning power—that made Jan realize how useless she was. Part of her wanted to tackle Owen just as Aiden had, but she knew that wouldn't end well for her or Shelley. Another part of her wanted to pull Shelley into the Blue Bomb and speed away as fast as possible. But after the mistake she had already made, she wasn't sure she could live with herself for having abandoned Aiden. All she could do was stand frozen next to Shelley, wavering between two equally dreadful options, feeling no more useful than a doll as she observed the nightmare through wide and stock-still eyes.

If they didn't act now, then what? Within an instant, everything Jan had been told about the legend became real. It was no longer a story or some otherworldly possibility she hoped she would never truly witness. Now, Jan saw the locket's power at work as Owen blinked through the inhuman emerald glow in his eyes. Though he struggled to regain energy, Jan knew it wouldn't take long before he could exercise the curse within him again. It was a gut-wrenching feeling—knowing that time was ticking, yet blind as to when it would be up.

"If you want to kill me, then do it now, Owen," Aiden hissed. "I'm not going to beg for my life."

"No...no. Not now. You don't get off that easily. I want you to *know* what you're dying for," Owen said through his teeth. "I've lived my entire life in your shadow, and you've taken away the only person I've ever cared about."

"I've apologized about Tanya. But what I did needed to be done."

Tanya.

"You truly believe she needed to die?"

"That was never my intention. You know that. She brought that on herself."

Owen choked out a nasty laugh. "There you go again, Aiden—blaming the victim. You never gave a shit about her, but you pretend to be sorry anyway because it makes you look better. You stand there on your moral high-ground refusing to admit that *you* caused her death."

"She was unhealthy. She was the reason your obsession with the locket began in the first place. Don't you see that I was only trying to help?"

Finally, the truth clicked. It was Tanya Day whom Jan and Shelley had read about in the newspaper archives. She was the woman whose face was framed in the cabin cruiser—the picture Owen had turned over so hurriedly.

"Help by throwing her into a psychiatric ward? By forcing

her to resort to hanging herself?" Owen spat. "She was *twenty*, Aiden! She was alone in that hospital because *you* used your power to put her there. And now she's dead."

"I did that to help her...to separate her from her obsession with the necklace. You know that. She changed the day you told her about the legend, but you refused to see it." Aiden clenched his jaw and pushed on, trembling as he spoke. "You were so infatuated with her that you let her wear the locket for over a *year*. You knew what it was capable of...you knew what it could do to the person who wore it, but you *still* encouraged her insanity. You knew the locket wasn't safe, but you gave it to her anyway because you thought it would make her love you more. It's your fault that she couldn't shake those feelings, even after the necklace was taken from her. She had worn it too long...all because of *you*. You were the one who disregarded her safety because of some juvenile romance, not me. I only tried to help when she began suffering because of your choices."

"She wasn't suffering until you had her hospitalized against her will," Owen bit back. "Tanya opened my eyes to the possibilities of the locket."

"She led you into your obsession, Owen. You both made a lot of bad choices, but none worse than this. If it weren't for Tanya, you would have never started wearing that necklace after she died. It wouldn't have corrupted you the way it has. You were both so young, I don't blame you for—"

"Don't patronize me, Aiden," Owen snapped. "And don't pin this whole thing on me and Tanya. You never intervened because you cared for her. You did it for you—so that you could be the hero. Bravo, Aiden! Because of your insatiable need to feel better than everyone else, Tanya lost her life."

The story came together like pieces of a sick and morbid puzzle. The story Owen had told about Aiden hadn't been about Aiden at all, but instead about himself—that much Jan knew. But the young woman in the paper played a bigger role in the story than she had previously thought.

Idiot, idiot, idiot, Jan chided herself. How could she have missed it?

"The only person who thinks you're a martyr is yourself," Owen continued. "But you're not. You weren't back then and you aren't now."

"Do you feel no remorse at all?" Aiden said, ignoring his brother's remark. "Do you feel any sympathy for the people you want to hurt?"

"The people I want to hurt are the people who hurt Tanya," Owen said. "Aledale failed her. *You* failed her. And now, I can finally take back what they took from us. I can finally avenge her. I have more power than anyone here ever will, and I know how to wield it. It comes naturally. Without Tanya, I would have never seen that."

"Owen, listen to yourself. *Please.*" Aiden's voice cracked, and his eyes shined with brimming tears. "You aren't like this. Not...not really. All those months you wore the locket after Tanya's death...they changed you, just like they changed her. The necklace brought out the worst in you. Don't you see that?"

Jan's eyes darted between the two brothers, but the rest of her body remained frozen. The panic, confusion, and shock was too much. She felt her senses slowly drift away from her one moment, then come back with overwhelming force the next. The figures of Aiden and Owen blurred, then cleared, then blurred again, and Jan blinked hard to stabilize her vision. When her surroundings finally unclouded, she noticed that Owen's eyes had grown just as shiny as his brother's.

"I know you loved her," Aiden continued. "I know you're angry that she's gone. But please—"

"For once, Aiden, stop trying to manipulate the situation," Owen said, his voice low. His hands, which he held close to his sides, trembled. "And stop trying to change things. You've done enough."

"I know you're angry—"

"You don't get to talk anymore," Owen barked. The sudden change in his voice made Jan jump. "This time, I make the rules. This time, *I'm* the one who comes out on top."

Aiden looked over at Jan and Shelley. He opened his mouth to say something, but the blare of police sirens in the distance interrupted him.

Blind relief washed over Jan.

Someone must've called the police. Someone must've gotten help.

Owen heard the sirens too. He looked around at the parking lot, observing the panicked people, the overturned cars, and his brother. As the red and blue flashing lights came into view, speeding toward the Fun Zone parking lot, Owen sighed. Exhaustion consumed his face, blocking out the potential for any kind of emotion.

The luster of the siren lights came to a surge as police cars shot into the parking lot like bullets. As soon as they entered, they pulled toward the center of the mayhem where Owen and Aiden stood.

They've noticed Aiden, Jan thought. *They're going to help. It's all going to be okay.*

Nolan shot Owen a look rife with panic.

"I've got it," Owen snapped.

Before the officers could get out of their cars, Owen turned to Aiden.

"One more thing," he said.

"What?" Aiden asked, eyeing the police cars nervously.

"See you in Hell."

Following a quick movement of Owen's hand, Aiden's body convulsed. There was no flash of blinding green light and no loud sound—only the thump of Aiden's limp body on the pavement.

Though Shelley uttered an anguished, inhuman howl, Jan could not find her voice. She didn't flinch or turn to run, but instead numbly watched as police swarmed out of their cars. The ringing in her ears had gone away. Now, all she heard was a heartbeat—*her* heartbeat—as she observed Aiden's body.

When she saw him, lying on the ground amidst flashing lights and Owen's shadow, she knew he was dead. The life in him slowly faded as his chest rose and fell. A low gurgle emitted from his mouth for a few moments and then stopped. After that, he did not move again.

Chapter 30
A BONE TO PICK

DEATH PRESENTED A SIGHT UNLIKE ANY OTHER. Aiden's skin morphed from pink to pale purple, and his lips turned a dappled gray, every second draining him of color and life. He was no more the Chief of Police than he was a pile of flesh and bones, made that way by his brother, who stood—breathless and grinning—in the flashing lights of the sirens.

Jan did not remember moving, but when her senses returned to her, she found herself once again embracing Shelley. The two clung to each other like children refusing to leave their mothers, pressed so close that Jan could not tell whose heartbeat was whose.

There must have been about ten cops surrounding them, all with their guns out and their fingers on the triggers. Nolan inched closer to Owen for protection.

Though Owen was winded, the green glint in his eyes

remained—brighter, as though taking Aiden's life had given him more power.

"Put your hands up!" a cop yelled. He stood in a defensive position behind his car's door.

In fact, all of the police had positioned themselves behind their car doors, unsure of what Owen was going to do. They knew what they had seen, but they could not fathom it. Jan desperately wanted to explain everything to them—to tell them that no amount of guns or ammunition could stop Owen.

But she didn't have to.

Owen shot his hand out, igniting a lance-like yellow and red flame that swelled outward and slammed into the cars. It was so quick and unexpected that the officers hardly had time to move. Within seconds, the place they had been standing was engulfed in flames, cars and all, leaving only a thick pillar of gray smoke in its place.

This time, Jan did not cry out. She did not take time to observe those who had witnessed the explosion, and she certainly did not take time to listen to their screams. Instead, she grabbed Shelley and sprinted toward the Blue Bomb. Though she knew their escape was fruitless, she had to try.

Heart pounding in her ears and adrenaline fueling her every move, Jan prayed for a miracle that would get them out alive. She felt like one of the gazelles she'd seen in nature films or textbooks—running away from her predator but knowing deep down that she was too slow.

If only they could escape, then they could get help. They could end this. They could explain everything. They could...

Before Jan could reach the door of the Blue Bomb, she felt her body jolt backward. Her breath left her as she hit the pavement on her back.

"Jinx!" Shelley screamed.

Pulling her by her hair, Owen wrenched her off the ground and up toward him. Blotches of color obscured her vision. Jan tried to blink them away.

"You're not going anywhere," Owen said. "I'm not done yet. I want you to watch all of this. I want you to remember that *you* were the one whose stupidity caused hundreds of people to die. I want you to watch as your friend dies as well, and then, when I've finished with everyone else, I'll kill you."

As Owen breathed onto Jan, the scent of something not quite human escaped his mouth. It was the smell of a metal teapot set that spent years collecting dust in an attic—the smell of blood and iron. Jan recognized it immediately. Owen reeked of the same metallic smell that she had sensed when she wore the necklace. Whatever power was inside of him swelled outward, consuming him in a suffocating, ferric aroma.

Shaking violently, Jan grabbed Owen's arm, trying to claw her way out of his grip.

"Nolan," Owen ordered, cocking his head toward Shelley.

Nolan started toward Shelley, but stopped in his tracks abruptly.

"*Nolan,*" Owen said, this time louder.

"I know. I will. But..."

"But what?" Owen clenched his jaw impatiently.

Jan struggled, but to no avail. With or without the power, Owen was too strong for her.

"But," Nolan said, coughing to clear up the hoarseness in his voice, "I just want to make sure I'm benefitting from this too."

Owen paused. His grip on Jan loosened. "Is this really the time to bring that up?"

When Nolan didn't respond, Owen exhaled sharply. "You will," he hissed, "if you do what I tell you."

"Yeah, I understand, and I said I will," Nolan said. "But I just want to make sure I'm getting what you promised me."

Owen released Jan, who fell to the pavement on her knees. The impact sent a sharp current of pain up her legs.

"Of course," Owen responded. He didn't move away from Jan, ensuring that she stayed put. Shelley lingered by the Blue Bomb, clutching the opened passenger door. "And what exactly did I promise you?" Owen mused after a few moments of silence. Though he tried to sound genuine, venom resided deep within his voice.

Nolan paused, as though he hadn't expected the question.

"Well," he started slowly, "there's a couple of people I want to get rid of, which you said you'd help me do. And..." Nolan stumbled over his words. "And I'd like to get money from a couple of fellas."

"I *do* remember you mentioning that." The forced softness in Owen's voice had quickly become cloying. "Anything else?"

Nolan shrugged. "I figured I'd know when the time came, you know?"

"Let me make sure I understand this correctly. You want to use the power that now belongs to *me* for whatever trivial bullshit your heart desires?"

Nolan wavered.

Jan inhaled the smoke from the destroyed cars. She willed herself not to look, knowing that all she would see was burnt bodies and pulverized steel.

"The thing is, though, *I* have a couple of people I'd like to get rid of as well—preferably everyone in this pathetic town," Owen continued. "And, honestly, Nolan, I don't *need* any more money. So, if you think about it, everything you want is just unnecessary work for me."

Nolan glowered at him. "You promised me."

"That was before I knew this would all work out. Things have changed."

"After all I helped you with?" Nolan said in a choked voice. "Without me, you wouldn't have gotten the necklace back from

Aiden after he hid it from you. You're too lazy to lift a finger, so you make everyone else do your dirty work."

"Maybe. Or I would've gotten someone else to do it."

Nolan ran his hands through his hair, his eyes rigid and cold. "I deserve this power too," he said, his lips shaking. "I deserve *something*. After Tanya died and Aiden managed to steal the necklace from you, I drugged him to get it back. I was his friend. He trusted me, and I betrayed him. He was hiding that necklace from you because he knew what you wanted to do with it. But...but I stole it anyway because you promised to reward me when you figured out how to break the locket and get the power."

Owen kept quiet, clenching his fist. Still by his feet, Jan looked over to Shelley, shooting her desperate glances.

"Go," she tried to say with her eyes.

Either Shelley didn't understand what Jan was trying to say or she didn't want to leave her friend, because she stayed put, grasping the side of the Blue Bomb with white knuckles.

"Now you've figured it out. Now you have the power," Nolan continued, "and I want what I was promised."

When Owen refused to respond a second time, Jan swore she saw something in Nolan crack.

"I helped you hide that necklace in the cove," he snarled. "*I* dropped it, *I* dove for it, and when it went missing, *I* followed *them* around!" He pointed to Shelley and then to Jan. "*I* put a gun up to a sixteen-year-old, *I* risked getting arrested, and all you did was sit in your yacht, telling me what to do. But I did everything you asked anyway because you promised me it would be worth my while. So make it worth my goddamn while."

Owen's hand unclenched above Jan's head. "You're right," he said finally.

The anger quickly left Nolan's eyes, replaced by a quizzical stare. "I'm only asking for a little bit," he added softly.

"I know. You're right. You do deserve something. And I did promise you." Owen smiled as the subtle green glint flashed in his eyes. "But since when have you ever known me to keep promises?"

Realization registered on Nolan's face, but almost as quickly as his expression changed, his body catapulted backward and landed yards away. His head hit the pavement, just as Aiden's had only minutes earlier. The sound of a stick breaking pierced Jan's ears, but it wasn't a stick at all. It was Nolan's neck.

Nolan's eyes remained open upon impact. Jan watched as their once gray-green color grew duller by the second until she could have sworn they'd become entirely gray.

Someone in the distance screamed, but Jan couldn't tell who it was or where the scream had come from. Though several people had abandoned the parking lot, those who remained hid behind their cars for safety, paralyzed with fear and shock.

"Two down," Owen said gleefully. Turning to the column

of smoke that lingered above the police cars and bodies of the officers—partly burnt flesh and fabric, partly ash—he shrugged. "And them, of course."

The pride in his voice was unmistakable. He was *bragging*. It was with horror that Jan realized the dead were not human to him; they were just pawns in his twisted game.

A lurid jolt coursed through her body. Fear replaced with burning anger, she jumped at Owen, clawing and slashing at his neck with her fingers. He smacked her across her face, causing the tiny multicolored blots to reappear in her vision. The world spun around her, but Jan didn't stop fighting. She lunged toward Owen again, but toppled forward as he stepped out of her reach.

His attention was no longer on her. Instead, he began to move toward Shelley, who had raced over to where the mermaid box and broken locket lay on the asphalt.

"What do you think you're going to do with that? I already broke the locket, you idiot. Do you really think that means anything to me now?"

Shelley didn't respond. Instead, she scooped up the box along with the two halves of the locket, holding the items close to her chest.

Owen chuckled and half-shrugged. The green glow in his eyes grew brighter as he raised his hand. Though Shelley stood her ground, the tortured dismay on her face made Jan snap.

Jan lunged toward Owen once again, this time faster and

harder. To her short-lived satisfaction, she managed to get him to the ground. Pins and needles pricked her arms as she hit the pavement and braced herself for Owen's response.

Before Owen could react, however, blaring sirens in the distance caught his attention. This time, the sound had increased tenfold. When Jan looked up, she saw at least twenty cars tearing toward the parking lot entrance. She didn't even think Aledale had that many policemen, let alone cars, but there they were—an army of flashing lights and screeching tires, hurtling head-on into the Fun Zone parking lot.

"Let them try," Owen muttered as he got up. He exhaled, then flashed Jan a sickly-sweet smile. "I'll come back for them at some point tonight, as well as you and your friend. As for now, I have more important things to do. People are visiting the Fun Zone tonight and I still have a considerable bone to pick with the residents of Aledale—one that I'd prefer the police not get in the way of."

The breath in Jan's throat constricted as the glow in Owen's eyes grew even more. The presence of the curse utterly consumed him, producing an intoxicating high that left him reeling in his power. Though Jan supposed he had never been able to think clearly, it was obvious that he was further gone now than ever—that he believed he was invincible and could do what he wanted whenever it suited him. The worst part, Jan realized, was that he seemed to be right.

He gave Jan another nauseatingly sadistic grin. "I suggest sticking around so you can watch."

Starting off with a slow walk, he pushed his pace to that of a sprint as he ran toward the flashing lights of the Fun Zone. Within seconds, the black of his hair and his coat were veiled in the night. It was only when he disappeared from view that the police loaded out of their cars.

Chapter 31
LITTLE LESSONS

THE SHOUTING OF THE POLICE ONLY ADDED TO the confusion.

Jan stayed put on the pavement, her head in her hands as she desperately tried to piece her thoughts together. Firm hands gripped her shoulders and brought her up, steadying her as she tried to balance on trembling feet.

"Are you okay, miss?" a stocky middle-aged man asked. The flashing lights of the sirens reflected off his badge.

Jan shook her head. She looked over at Shelley, who was being calmed by a short policewoman with dark hair tied back into a slick bun.

"Did you see what happened, miss?" the man asked.

Owen had gotten away. He was in the Fun Zone.

Jan nodded, her words pouring out in stutters. "Fun Zone," she managed. "He's...he's in the Fun Zone."

The man shouted something to about a dozen officers, who started toward the other end of the parking lot.

"No..." Jan sputtered as they ran off. "They can't go in there!"

"I assure you, our men and women are highly trained. They'll be able to handle—"

"No!" Jan shouted, grabbing the policeman by his arms. "You don't understand! He can kill people without touching them! He's cursed...he has some kind of deadly magic and he's going to try to hurt people!"

The policeman gestured to another officer who came over and pulled Jan aside to where Shelley was standing.

Someone shouted something about setting up a blockade and others hollered indistinct commands as officers rushed toward the civilians who remained in the parking lot. A couple of policemen approached and identified Aiden's body, then covered it with a plastic sheet.

"EMTs and the coroner are on their way," a woman said.

Jan's head spun. The dreadfully unnatural metallic smell lingered in her nostrils.

They were all going to die.

"Michelle! Jan!" Mr. Waldbauer's familiar Austrian accent boomed from behind several policemen. He pushed his way between them forcefully, shoving some off to the side as he ran toward Jan and Shelley.

He embraced Shelley instantly, holding her so close that Jan thought he might crush her. When he backed up, she realized how shaken he looked. His dark, widened pupils starkly contrasted his sallow face, and his hands shook as he smoothed his daughter's hair.

"Are you okay? Both of you?" he asked, turning to Jan and putting a hand on her shoulder.

"No," Shelley said, and she began to sob. The tears poured out and down her face in reams.

Though Jan desperately wanted to cry as well and let out the sickening feeling inside of her, she could not find any tears. It was as though they had been stolen from her, forcing the terrible lump in her throat to persist.

"What happened? What's going on?" Mr. Waldbauer asked frenziedly. The terror in his eyes was heartbreaking.

"We made a mistake," Shelley said between sobs.

"What mistake?"

"The necklace and the box. We gave it to Owen, and now Aiden is dead. Owen killed him." She began to sob even harder.

"Why did you...?"

"We don't have time to explain!" Jan snapped. "Owen has a terrible power and he's going to use it to murder as many people as he can. He's stronger than everyone here...he can kill anyone he wants without weapons...without even touching them—"

"What in the world are you talking about?" Mr. Waldbauer interjected.

"She's telling the truth," Shelley said frantically, furiously wiping the tears from her face. "Please...you have to believe us...I know it sounds crazy, but it's true. Owen broke the locket and it gave him some kind of horrible magic that he's going to use to kill even more people!"

"Magic?" Mr. Waldbauer blinked back his confusion. "Michelle, do you hear yourself?"

"Just *listen*," Shelley pleaded. "You can't understand it until you see it...I promise we're not crazy. We're telling the—"

Shelley was cut off by the sound of distant screaming that flit out of the Fun Zone alongside the carnival music.

A nightmarish tremor shot up Jan's spine and ended at her fingertips. "He's going to kill everyone!" she yelled.

Shelley's eyes widened. "Gabriel is in there! Dad, we need to get more officers in there to help!"

"What we need to do is calm down," Mr. Waldbauer said. "Nothing's going to be solved if we panic. We need to—"

"No!" Jan shouted, her voice breaking. "Nothing's going to be solved if we stand here and do nothing!"

"We have officers on the scene and more coming," Mr. Waldbauer said. "I want you two to come with me."

Jan shook her head forcefully. "I can't," she said. She looked at Shelley, who still held the mermaid box and the broken locket in her hands. "I screwed this all up," she said.

"This isn't your fault," Shelley said, her voice still quaking.

Jan didn't respond. Instead, in a flash of impulse, she turned around and sprinted toward the flashing Fun Zone lights with all the strength she could muster. Though she heard Shelley and Mr. Waldbauer yell, followed by the shouts and footsteps of officers behind her, she pushed on, refusing to look back.

Owen had told her that he would kill her last. He wanted her to watch everything he planned to do because of some deep resentment that she had stolen his precious locket and put him through all that trouble to retrieve it.

She had worn the necklace herself. She had felt the hints of its magic: the metallic smell, the episodes, and the mind-numbing need to keep it on. No other living person, minus Owen and perhaps Shelley, understood what the locket was capable of. The police, as large as they were in number and as powerful in practice, were certainly not prepared for this.

As Jan came closer to the Fun Zone's entrance and the bloodcurdling screams of the people inside, she thought about her father. Even though he was thousands of miles away, his little lessons stayed with her.

"It's only a mistake if you don't try to fix it," he would always tell her.

She pushed on, ignoring the sting of the briny air on her face and remembering that early morning at Azuline cove—the morning she'd made her first mistake. Perhaps Shelley had been right when she said Jan's curiosity would kill them.

Though she knew dwelling on her mistakes would do nothing, it became impossible to ignore the regret that grew with each passing moment. She thought of Aiden, who although perhaps had made mistakes of his own, only wanted to keep the necklace away from his vengeful and power-hungry brother. She thought of Tanya, whose death had been the catapult for Owen's rage, and then Nolan, who—despite the terrible person he was—had been betrayed by Owen just the same. But it was when she thought of Shelley that the regret hurt most. Out of everyone involved, it was Shelley who had played into Jan's curiosities because she was a good friend, who had put her own safety on the line to help Jan, and who did not deserve this at all.

I'll fix this, Jan thought, wishing Shelley could hear. *I'll fix what I started.*

Chapter 32
GET THEM OUT

JAN GOT TO THE FUN ZONE BEFORE THE OFFICERS managed to reach her. Though the music went on playing and the decorative lights continued to flash myriads of color, the Fun Zone had turned into more of a madhouse than an amusement park.

A stampede of people shoved past her, sprinting toward the parking lot. Realizing that the mass of bodies formed a barrier between her and the officers, Jan slipped farther away, praying that she wouldn't get caught. She scanned the boardwalk for Owen, but she didn't see him. Her windpipe burned and her lungs ached, but she refused to rest.

Jan pushed past people running in the opposite direction, feeling like a fish swimming against a current ten times stronger than she was. She violently slammed into the arm of a girl in her teens with dark, curly hair, who stopped just long enough to gape at Jan with wide eyes.

"Did you see what's happening?" Jan asked frantically.

The girl shook her head. "You need to get out of here," she said, trembling like a leaf. "There's been a bad accident...I think I just saw people die."

Jan opened her mouth to ask the girl where she saw the accident, but she had already left. She ran toward the parking lot with the rest of the panic-stricken crowd, which had all but become one being, writhing in fear and abandoning any sense.

Despite the fact that almost everything within her told her to turn back toward the parking lot, Jan pushed on, her eyes darting every which way, praying against her better judgment that she would see Owen.

She passed the recently deserted carousel, filled only with riderless plastic horses that moved up and down to the tune of a shrill song, and continued ahead toward the House of Mirrors, which had also been abandoned.

Once she moved out closer to the Alpine Slide and the Bamboo Shoot, Jan was finally able to see the rest of the Fun Zone. Only a few disoriented people remained, scurrying around like ants under a magnifying glass. It made her sick to imagine how satisfied Owen probably felt watching them topple over one another.

Looking over her shoulder to ensure that no officers had followed her, Jan maneuvered past a group of several people who were closer to the end of the boardwalk, gathered below the Ferris wheel. It towered above the pier, its lights reflecting blurry hues onto the water below.

A few officers attempted to guide the remaining crowd out of the Fun Zone, while a group of policemen stood around two bodies—one of a grown man and the other of a young girl. A father and daughter, Jan suspected.

She lingered by a clothing shop as she strained to get a closer look. When a few of the officers stepped to the side, Jan studied the girl, who lay motionless on the wooden pier. Even from where she was standing, Jan was able to make out the girl's face, which, just like Aiden's, was pale and lifeless.

Jan gasped as a wave of nausea overcame her. She stumbled over to the door of the empty clothing shop, leaned inside, and vomited onto the floor.

The shock was unbearable. It twisted itself around every organ in her body, constricting with so much force that Jan lost all feeling in her limbs. She leaned against the door, resting her head against the cool glass and squeezing her eyes shut as she tried to stop the terrible sensation surging in her stomach.

"Jan?" The familiarity of the voice struck her. She opened her eyes to Gabriel, who rushed toward her and grabbed her by the shoulders. "Have you seen my dad?"

Jan shook her head.

"God, I can't find him!" Gabriel clasped his hands over his

head in distress, shaking so violently that he could hardly stand still.

"He...he may be in the parking lot," Jan said. It wasn't until she spoke that she realized how broken her voice was.

"We need to leave," Gabriel choked out, grasping Jan's arm and pulling her in the direction of the parking lot. "Right now...we need to leave *now*."

Jan wriggled out of his grip. "I can't."

Gabriel narrowed his eyes and nodded his head to the nearby officers. "Don't you see what's happening?"

"That's exactly why I'm *here*. Get yourself out of here now before anything else happens."

"Jan...what's going on?"

"If you stand here asking me questions, you're going to end up like them!" Jan shouted, pointing at the bodies of the man and the young girl. "Get out of here now. Find your dad...find Shelley and Mr. Waldbauer...and get as far away from here as possible. And *don't* come back. I swear to God, Gabriel. Don't you dare come back."

As soon as she said it, a loud creaking sound from above jolted both Gabriel and Jan backward.

The Ferris wheel uttered another low, thundering groan as a spoke came unhinged, throwing the carriages into bedlam. They rocked back and forth wildly, and Jan thanked the heavens that it had been fully evacuated. The lights flickered on and off

sporadically and two other spokes broke free. As a rim came undone and several carriages tilted sideways, the officers standing by the bodies stepped backward, shouting indistinctly. As loud as they were, it took only seconds before another deafening noise quelled them.

Jan gasped, horror seizing her limbs as she watched the Ferris wheel. With the ease of a twig breaking, the lateral support arm snapped in half and the wheel came down on its platform, moaning like an angry giant as it toppled sideways. The officers beneath it scattered as it broke through the wood of the pier and hit the water below, suspended only by the backstay cables.

Gabriel seized Jan by her arm, pulling her away from the clothing shop and back toward the parking lot. Another snap sounded as the Ferris wheel collapsed backward, stunning Gabriel long enough for Jan to twist out of his grip.

"What the hell are you doing?"

"I need you to listen to me!" Jan shouted over the groan of the Ferris Wheel. "I need you to go to the parking lot and find Shelley and Mr. Waldbauer and your dad. And when you do, I need you to tell them something—*anything*—that will get them out of here. Do you understand?"

"What are you...?"

"Gabriel, *please*," Jan begged, taking Gabriel's wrists in her hands. "I need to know I can count on you. I know what's causing all of this to happen, but you have to take them and get out of the parking lot *now*."

Gabriel blinked rapidly, his eyes darting from point to point on Jan's face.

"He's going to target the parking lot next," Jan said between breaths. "I know it. He's doing all of this to herd them into the same spot."

"Who's going to target the parking lot?"

"Owen. It's all Owen."

"Owen Aimsworth?"

"He's causing all of this. He's going to kill as many people as he can." Jan held Gabriel's wrists so tightly that her knuckles ached. "Get them out *now*. I'm begging you."

Gabriel's mouth contorted and his eyes narrowed, but he nodded furiously nonetheless.

"I'll get them out," he said in a low voice. "But you better know what you're doing."

Jan didn't respond. Instead, she gave Gabriel a hard push forward and watched him sprint down the pier. He fought his way past the few people that remained inside the Fun Zone, only looking back once before continuing ahead.

Chapter 33
FOR TANYA

AS SOON AS GABRIEL DISAPPEARED, JAN TURNED back to observe the Ferris wheel. It leaned against the edge of the pier, crammed into a niche of broken wood that had been created upon its collapse.

Jan didn't bother to see what the police officers did next. She knew Owen had to be close, and more importantly, she knew where he was headed.

Shattered bits of glass from shop windows crunched under Jan's shoes as she edged along the walkways near the House of Mirrors. Although she knew exactly who she was looking for, she had no idea what she would do when she found him. Perhaps she would stall him long enough for Gabriel to get Shelley, Mr. Waldbauer, and his father out of the parking lot and take them as far away as possible.

Yes, that sounded like a half-decent plan.

Jan stopped between the House of Mirrors and the Sea Witch's Castle where Ms. Johnson's shop was. The door to the little store was opened, but it was completely dark inside.

Leaning against the shop's outside wall to catch her breath, Jan tried to calm herself by thinking about the friendship rings she and Shelley planned to buy. Perhaps when all of this was over, they would finally get them. The thought evoked the tiniest flicker of warmth within her. As welcome as the warmth was, however, it didn't last. As soon as Jan stepped forward, a cold hand smacked over her mouth and brought her sharply back.

Jan tried to spin around, but her effort was fruitless. Though she thrashed about, struggling to turn her head, she knew to whom the cold, shaking hand belonged; the metallic smell was evidence enough.

"You can try to scream," Owen said as he pulled her into Ms. Johnson's shop. "Those valiant officers won't resist the cries of a helpless civilian. My brother certainly wouldn't have, and he was the epitome of a hero, don't you think?"

Jan ushered a swift kick to Owen's legs, but it didn't faze him. Whatever he was running on—adrenaline, delirium, or the power within—left him unfettered by her attempt. It wasn't until Jan bit down on his hand that he let go, cursing.

For a moment, he only stared at his hand. Then, he uttered a low laugh and wiped it on his coat. Crimson blood dripped onto the ground, spotting the floor. Jan could see the bite marks she had made and, if only for a second, felt rather pleased with herself.

"Do you know what 'jinx' means?" Owen mused as he studied his hand. Without waiting for an answer, he said, "It means 'bad luck,' which you seem to be dealing with quite a lot lately." He twisted his lips into a half-smile. The emerald glare in his eyes flashed in the darkness of the shop. "Like I said earlier, it's quite the fit for you."

"Screw you," Jan spat.

Owen clicked his tongue. "If I were you, I wouldn't be such a bitch to a person who clearly has more power."

"That must be a first for you," Jan said. "That's why you wanted the power so badly, so you could finally understand what it was like to be noticed." She was taunting him, but she hardly knew why—to stall, to keep him away from everyone in the parking lot, or perhaps it was all just to make him angry.

Owen gave her a tight-lipped smile. The side of his face, illuminated by the lights outside, was riddled with cuts and bruises from Aiden's attack.

"Every time you piss me off, I think about how much longer I'm going to keep you alive," he said. "I think about how slow I'm going to make this for you—how I'm going to make you watch everyone die before you meet your end, all the while reminding you that if you hadn't been so gullible and naive, none of this would have happened." He paused for a moment as the emerald glow in his eyes grew brighter. "You really slowed things down for me by stealing my locket, *Jinx*, and you put me through a lot of trouble to get it back."

"I didn't steal it," Jan said. She knew it wasn't the right time to argue, but she said it anyway. "I didn't know it belonged to you. You were the one who dropped it in the ocean. That kind of relinquishes your ownership."

Owen did not respond. Instead, he flicked his eyes to the side. A large glass case, stuffed to the brim with necklaces, bracelets, rings, and souvenir snow globes, shuddered in its position. Though Jan thought it was bolted to the wall, it only took a second before it came crashing down toward her.

Jan shrieked and jumped out of its way, watching with horror as it landed front-first on the ground. Glass shards shot outward, scattering so quickly across the floor that a few hit Jan's shoes.

"I thought you said you weren't going to kill me yet." She put her hand to her heart, wishing it would stop beating so quickly.

Once again, Owen didn't respond. Following another movement of his eyes, Jan slammed against a little wooden table that displayed handmade ceramic souvenirs. She let out a yelp as the corner of the wood rammed into her back. The table fell backward with the weight of her body, and the ceramic goods shattered as they crashed to the ground. Jan landed on the floor amidst the fragmented bits of glass, her fingers brushing over the cool surface of a shard.

Her head throbbed as she tried to push herself up, but she quickly realized, much to her dismay, that some occult force held her down. She could not feel it until she tried to move, but when she did, it was so strong and unrelenting that Jan wondered if she would ever be able to stand again.

With what little movement she could manage, Jan pressed her palm down on the fragment of glass. Though she couldn't lift her arms, she was still able to move her hands. Slowly, she ran her fingers over the shard's jagged edges and began inching it up toward her hips. Perhaps she could use it as some kind of weapon. At the moment, she was desperate for anything.

Owen knelt down next to her. "The power isn't very complicated," he said. "I thought maybe you'd want to know how it worked, seeing as though you spent so much time with *my* locket these past few days."

Jan lifted her chin and glared at him. "Burn in hell," she said, though her voice sounded far weaker than she'd hoped.

A wry smile tugged at Owen's lips. "I probably will, someday," he said. "Right next to my brother."

Jan continued inching the piece of glass upward with her fingers in small, measured movements, praying that Owen wouldn't see what she was doing. Slowly—and then even slower—she pushed it into the pocket of her jeans. A wave of relief washed over her when she realized Owen hadn't noticed.

"Unfortunately for you," he continued, "today is not that day. I haven't had enough time to use this yet, and Tanya would be disappointed if I let it all go to waste."

When Owen lifted his hand, Jan noticed the little gashes she'd made with her teeth. She didn't have much time to feel proud, though; as soon as he lifted it, he brought it back down, smashing Jan's head back onto the tile. A thousand lights flashed before her eyes.

"It's all very natural," Owen said. "I feel like I've been doing this forever. I just look at the person or thing I want to hurt or destroy, and it happens, like *that*." He smiled and shrugged. "There aren't a whole lot of options, but what I'm able to do, I absolutely love."

"Destroying things? Hurting people?" Jan said, trying to shake the shooting pains at the back of her skull. "That's what you love?"

A snapping sound echoed throughout the shop, followed by blinding pain. At first, Jan could hardly tell where the pain was coming from, but after a few moments, she realized it was located in her left arm. A chilling, current-like sensation surged through her body, coupled with churning nausea that left her disoriented and out of touch. She had never broken a bone before, but she knew what it was as soon as she felt it. She grasped her arm tightly and uttered a strangled cry. Her eyes burned as if she was about to cry, but there were still no tears.

Owen leaned down even farther, his breath on her face. "Absolutely," he said.

The invisible weight on Jan lifted as Owen grabbed her right arm and pulled her up. Jan yelped, pressing her broken forearm against her body, wishing desperately that the deep ache would go away. She was grateful, if even for a moment, that her sweatshirt hid her arm. Seeing the damage would only make it worse.

Owen dragged her out of Ms. Johnson's shop and in the direction of the parking lot. She squinted in the blinking lights, wincing as the glass shard in her pocket dug into her thigh.

In the distance, she could see the lights of the police cars and yellow tape that glared against the dark backdrop of the parking lot. Panicked voices drifted over the blockade.

"Owen, none of this is necessary...please don't kill them," Jan begged, gritting her teeth in response to the pain. She wasn't even sure she would be able to use the shard of glass if she needed to, especially now that her good arm was broken. She tried to shift her weight backward so Owen would slow down. "They've never done anything to you," she added when she realized she was being ignored. "They're innocent."

Owen didn't respond.

"What do you gain from this?" Jan stammered, desperately trying to buy more time. "You're just going to kill innocent people...people who've never done anything wrong."

When Owen still didn't respond, Jan braced herself and whispered, "People like Aiden."

This time, Owen's response was immediate. He shoved Jan into a nearby wall so violently that she lost any potential to cry out. She readied herself for another attack, but Owen only stepped back and grinned. It took everything within Jan not to let her confusion show.

"You've tried me these past few days, Jan," he said through a laugh. "More than he ever has. You stole my necklace, wore it around, and now you have the gall to pretend like Aiden was innocent?" Though anger flickered in his emerald-brown eyes, his laugh grew increasingly hysterical. "*Aiden*, who used his power to stick his hands where they didn't belong...who was an arrogant, selfish son of a bitch...who didn't care if lives were lost as long as he looked like a hero. And somehow, a sixteen-year-old girl has tested me more than my brother. I'll give you that."

Owen licked his lips, blinking rapidly against the glow in his eyes. "But even you see it, don't you?" he said, his voice shaking. "This town *worships* people like Aiden...not because of the person he was, but because of the position he held. People will mourn his death...those of them that are left to mourn, anyway. But Tanya? Nobody mourns her. Nobody but me." In a violent motion, he shot his hands up to the sky, as if he were gesturing to Tanya herself. "*This,*" he said, "is her redemption."

"That's why you're doing all of this?" Jan choked out. "As some kind of revenge for Tanya?"

Owen leaned in closer to Jan. The chilling metallic smell lingered at his lips. "For Tanya."

But it wasn't only that. The look in Owen's eyes was so sadistic—so full of demented thrill—that Jan knew he enjoyed what he was doing. That, above all reasons, she knew was the truth. As much as Owen hated Aiden and Aledale and everyone who lived there, and as much as he scorned the world for Tanya's death, Jan knew that at his core, he reveled in the idea of watching people suffer. And now that he believed he was too powerful for consequences, he could do anything he wanted.

It was people like Owen that the sea witch's power was intended for—people who wanted to watch others hurt.

"The very spiteful and wicked few with bad intentions would be well-suited for it," Mr. Brown had said.

Owen was certainly well-suited for it. Even the way the emerald glare flashed in his eyes as he spoke hinted at his uncanny compatibility with the power.

There was no time left for Jan to stall him. The rage in Owen's eyes had turned into hungry resolve, and the befuddled officers and civilians were his target.

This time, he grabbed Jan by the back of her neck, pulling her forward at such a brisk pace that she could hardly keep her balance. The pain in her arm had not gone away, so Jan pressed it to her stomach and tried to block it out of her mind. As much as she tried to keep it elevated, the numbness she hoped would set in didn't come.

Despite the pain, Jan fought with as much zeal as she could to pull back, all the while knowing that struggling was useless.

The worst feeling, she decided at that very moment, was fighting a pointless battle. Jan felt her inevitable defeat draw nearer with every agonizing second. Owen dragged her closer to the officers, who although had formerly given her hope, were no longer the invincible force she used to think they were. There was no way they could go up against something like this, especially when they didn't understand what was going on.

The moment they reached the entrance to the parking lot, the officers began to shout. Owen didn't seem to mind; he continued walking until he was only a few feet away from them.

Guns drawn and voices loud, the officers faced their suspect with confidence that Jan knew would be short-lived. Witnesses who remained in the parking lot stepped back, away from the unit of officers and the strings of yellow tape.

Ambulances and EMTs littered the parking lot as well, and Jan wanted to scream at all of them to leave. They weren't going to help.

"Owen Aimsworth! Put your hands behind your head!" an officer yelled in a deep voice.

"They're a bit full right now," he said calmly, motioning to

Jan with his head.

The tears finally came. Jan scanned the parking lot desperately through blurry eyes for Gabriel, Shelley, and Mr. Waldbauer. Relief flooded through her when she didn't see them.

He got them out. Gabriel got them out.

The presence of Owen's hand on her neck, however, reminded her of those who hadn't escaped, and she began to sob—briny tears slipping down her cheeks as she thought about the people who wouldn't be saved. The broken shard of glass inside her pocket reminded her of its presence, but Jan knew that using it now wouldn't do anything. Owen was quicker and stronger than her.

The officers shouted something else at Owen, but Jan didn't listen. She focused on her feet, watching as her tears fell off her face and onto her shoes.

"Jan?"

Jan looked up. Although shackled by fear, the voice was sweet and quiet—a stark contrast to the roaring orders of the police officers.

Ms. Johnson stood amongst the crowd, clutching a purse that matched her glasses and graying hair. She peered over the yellow tape and huddled officers, her eyes wrought with a motherly concern that made something in Jan break.

"Ms. Johnson," Jan said, her voice cracking. *Why hasn't she left? Oh god, why hasn't she left?*

"Owen, let the girl go now!" another officer demanded, pointing a gun directly toward them.

"I know her!" Ms. Johnson said, running up to the officer, panicked. Then, to Jan, she yelled, "Hold on, honey, you're going to be okay!"

Jan shook her head violently. "No, I'm not..." was all she could manage to say before Owen snapped her neck upward.

"That's the smartest thing you've said all night," he said.

The childish delight Owen found in taunting her made Jan sick. As much as she dug for it, she could not find the fight within her anymore. All she could do was watch the officers and pray their inevitable deaths would be quick.

Owen thrust Jan in front of him, still holding her with one hand by the back of her neck.

"Shoot me and you'll shoot her," he warned the officers.

More indistinct commands flew back and forth, but Owen didn't heed them.

He bent down slightly to reach Jan's ear. "Watch," he said. His voice sounded just the way it had when she first heard it out on the water—firm and unforgiving.

He put his arm out, still bending down near Jan's ear so she could hear his voice.

"Jinx," he whispered.

A loud clap resonated. Jan couldn't tell if it was from the

guns or from Owen himself. Perhaps it was both. She hit the ground hard as Owen's hand left her neck, her heartbeat booming in her ears.

Though her vision was blurred, it was impossible to miss the thick green vapor that catapulted toward the parking lot. When it reached the civilians and officers, it ignited into a thousand flames, each one the color of the sea witch's eyes. Though the flames emitted no heat, they attacked with the same ferocity, consuming their victims with searing, wisped claws.

It was only when Jan saw the flames reach Ms. Johnson that she was able to scream. A mass of officers rushed forward, obscuring Jan's view, but she didn't pray with false hope.

If Ms. Johnson yelled, Jan didn't hear her. Each scream coalesced with the others as the hellish green blaze did Owen's bidding. They were so distorted—so garbled and jumbled—that they hardly sounded human at all. The sound made Owen laugh; even he seemed surprised by what he had done.

Of course Ms. Johnson was targeted. Of course Owen chose her. He wanted Jan to suffer before she died, just like he had said.

Gunfire started up, and Jan covered her head with her arms instinctively, closing her eyes so tightly that they began to burn.

She wasn't sure how long she remained on the ground—a minute, perhaps five—but she didn't dare to look up.

Eventually, though, every bloodcurdling noise—all of the

screams, bullets, and flames—died down to a low, droning hum. They diminished further with every passing moment until there were no sounds at all.

Chapter 34
JINX

JAN CAUTIOUSLY LIFTED HER HEAD AND LOOKED out beyond the yellow tape. Whether the people were dead, unconscious, or just pretending to be, Jan could not tell. Everyone lay motionless on the ground, surrounded by pillars of smoke left behind in the fire's wake. Music drifting from the Fun Zone continued playing while theme park lights flickered on, unencumbered by the devastation below.

Jan shifted her gaze behind her. Owen lay on the ground, breathing heavily. He clutched his shoulder tightly, dark blood seeping through his fingers.

When she realized he had been shot, Jan jumped up, ignoring the pain in her arm. She mustered her strength and raced over to the body of a young policeman, who lay sprawled on the ground with his gun beside him.

Jan plucked the gun off the ground and turned back to

Owen. She approached him carefully, preparing herself in case he jumped up. Though his eyes weren't open, he was clearly still alive.

Despite her better judgment, Jan positioned herself above him, holding the gun in her trembling hand.

She studied Owen's sallow complexion and the blood dribbling down his shoulder. The bullet had pierced through his coat, but it hadn't hit anywhere vital. Still, his breath was short and rapid, like that of a wounded animal.

He hadn't gotten away from this unharmed. A trace of satisfaction coursed through Jan, the feeling of which frightened her. She never imagined that she would revel in another person's pain, but after all Owen had done, she couldn't help but feel justified.

For a moment, Jan stood still, slowing her breath and gathering her thoughts. Despite everything, she wasn't sure she could bring herself to shoot him. She had never been in a situation like this—a situation where she had the power to take another's life.

Shoot him, she begged herself. And yet, she couldn't. It had been easier to silently beg Aiden and the officers to kill Owen, but when the choice was her own, everything became a thousand times more complicated.

Desperately hoping more police officers had arrived, she turned slowly to look back at the parking lot...

...and felt a cold hand seize her ankle.

Jan cried out and fell to her back as Owen sprung up. Without thinking—without taking time to aim—she held the gun out in front of her and pulled the trigger.

A violent tremor of shock and fear coursed through her body as the bullet struck Owen. He stumbled backward and hit the ground again. Jan pulled herself up almost as quickly as she had pulled the trigger, straining to see where it hit.

This time, though Owen held his arm in pain, he was not deterred. He slowly stood up again, the inhuman green glow in his eyes fueling his every movement.

Jan lifted the gun again, but a flick of Owen's hand sent a spindle-like pain up her arm. She dropped the gun and leaped backward.

"You can try to grab it," he said between breaths, "but I'll kill you before you can pull the trigger again."

Jan stumbled back, her shoes scuffing against the wood of the pier.

"There's nobody else who is going to help you," Owen said. "Not now. Not ever."

He started toward her slowly, and for a moment, Jan wondered why he hadn't killed her yet. After taking another look at his face and hearing his labored breaths, however, she began to think that maybe he wasn't as invincible as he made himself out to be. The bullets in his shoulder and arm weighed him down, and his blood was all but drained from his face, making him look gaunt and sickly.

"You're weak," Jan said.

A hint of a grin appeared on his lips. "I'm still stronger than anyone else here."

"Is that what makes you feel better about yourself?" Jan said, anger rising within her. "That's pathetic."

Owen sucked in his breath and winced at the pain in his shoulder. "No, Jan," he said, gesturing to the scattered bodies in the parking lot. "They are. And it's a shame you'll become one of them. I feel like we've gone through so much together regarding this whole ordeal." His voice turned from patronizing to dour. "Out of everyone I've killed so far, I think I'll enjoy killing you the most. Minus my brother, of course. It's fitting that you were both the ones who stole from me."

Jan took a shaking breath. Her fear was either so immense that it defied feeling, or it had abandoned her entirely. Her memory, however, did not fail her; she did not forget what Owen had said about the way the sea witch's power worked— how he needed to see his victim to do any damage. The shard of glass in her pocket felt cold against her leg.

Jan did not back away. She did not move. She only lifted her hand slightly so it rested on the pocket of her jeans as Owen approached her.

Whatever his plan had been, he did not have time to enact

it. Once he was a little more than arms-length away, the restraint within Jan snapped.

There were no thoughts—only movements. Jan hardly knew what she was doing until she saw the shard of glass sticking out of Owen's eye.

He stumbled backward, cupping his hands to catch the blood. Point first, the chip of glass jutted outward, splattered in scarlet.

Owen screamed, louder than Jan had ever heard him, but she didn't stay to listen. Instead, she whirled around and bolted. She sprinted past the broken bits of yellow tape, around the bodies of the officers and civilians, and across the parking lot. Though the few guns she saw on the asphalt were tempting, she knew she couldn't risk being this close to Owen. She hadn't destroyed the nightmare within him yet.

"You *bitch*!" he yelled.

He repeated the slur multiple times, but Jan didn't listen. Instead, she continued running, her lungs aching and limbs growing weaker, until she reached the Blue Bomb.

Aiden's body must have been removed, for it was no longer on the ground when Jan returned to her car. His Lamborghini, however, was still stationed haphazardly where he had left it, along with nearby destroyed police cars and burnt officers who lay amongst their own ash.

She wrenched open the Blue Bomb's door and grabbed her

keys from under the dashboard, but she didn't drive away. This needed to be quick; Owen wasn't about to hesitate to find her after what she had done.

She needed to end this all now.

Jan unlocked the trunk and pushed it open. Her hands shook as she pulled out a matchbox and stuffed it into the front pocket of her sweatshirt. She fumbled through her junk and pulled out a firecracker, then stuffed it into her back pocket and glanced toward the Fun Zone to ensure that Owen wasn't on her trail.

He wasn't, much to her relief. But even at his pace, it wouldn't take long before he reached her. Shoving aside the old jeans that she and Shelley had used to tie down the hood only a few days earlier, Jan took out the two clear hoses her dad had put in the trunk.

Think, Jan. Think.

Mind racing and hands shaking, Jan rushed over to the side of the Blue Bomb and unscrewed the gas cap. Steadying her hands, she stuffed the larger tube deep into the tank until it stopped, then crammed the shorter tube next to it. It took her much longer than expected, especially since she could only use one hand.

Now what? A harrowing, empty feeling churned in her gut. *Shit. Now what?* Jan closed her eyes and inhaled. *Remember every step. One by one. What would Dad say to do?* Blocking out the fear as best she could, she focused all her strength inward.

The jeans!

Jan dashed back toward the trunk, seizing the old jeans in her hand and getting to work immediately. She used one leg of the jeans to pack around the tubes as tightly as possible. It wasn't the most optimal option, but it would have to do.

The next part Jan had never done herself, but she had seen her dad do it. She took a deep breath, then put her lips on the shorter tube and blew outward.

Nothing.

Panic began to set in, but Jan steadied herself and blew again—this time, a little harder. After a few sputters, gasoline began to flow out of the hose and onto the asphalt.

It worked! Oh my god, it worked!

Though the victory she felt was weak, it was victory nonetheless. Jan slammed the trunk shut and watched as the gasoline poured out of the tube onto the ground. It formed a puddle around the Blue Bomb, growing with each passing moment.

"JINX!"

Jan's heart stopped as she whirled around. The surrounding area was dark, so she strained to listen. All she could hear was the trickling gasoline and Owen's dragging feet.

This needed to work.

Aiden's Lamborghini was too obvious and far too close to

the Blue Bomb to be a good hiding spot. Though the idea evoked overwhelming nausea, Jan pushed the feeling away and ran on nimble feet to the mass of burnt police cars and the bodies that were scattered around them.

Don't look at them. It was the only thing she could do to keep herself from getting sick.

She crouched in a narrow crevice that two of the cars had made in their slapdash attempt to park, concealed even further by the surrounding darkness. A few small, persistent flames burned on in patches—too small to produce noticeable light but large enough to be useful. Jan's stomach churned as she peered at the leg of an officer slumped over a car door. The coiled hem of his pants housed a small flame that, despite its size, flickered stubbornly.

"Jinx!" Owen shouted again, his voice slurred. He repeated himself as he came closer, and Jan pressed her lips together, forcing herself to stop breathing.

"I still have one good eye!" Owen must've been fifteen feet away at most. He laughed loudly, delirious with pain. Then, he repeated, "I still have one good eye."

Silence lingered in the parking lot.

"I know you're here. I see your car. Why don't you come out and we can talk?" Owen said jokingly, more to himself than to Jan. "After all, out of everyone here, we're the ones most connected to the locket. Even if you did only wear it for a few days.”

Jan slowly took the firecracker out of her pocket.

“Maybe if you had worn it a bit longer, you’d see things the way I see them,” Owen said. “It does that, you know. It has a funny way of making you want what you used to think was impossible.” He paused for a moment, exhaling shakily through his pain. “Only, we know it’s possible, don’t we, Jinx? We know what it’s capable of, more so than any of them ever will.” He sighed. “Tanya knew too,” he said. Then again, he echoed, “Tanya knew too.”

Jan wondered if he was really talking to her at all, or if he had grown so disoriented that a one-sided conversation was all he could manage.

“Nothing?” Owen said after a while. “Fine. Why don’t we take a look inside your car? I hope you’re not hiding in there.”

Jan’s lungs ached, but she refused to take a breath.

Owen’s footsteps turned to soft splashes as he stepped into the puddle of gasoline. Painful silence descended upon the parking lot, and Jan could have sworn she felt a change in the air as he noticed the gasoline beneath his feet.

Now was as good a time as any.

Grasping the firecracker in her trembling hand, she disregarded her matches, placing it instead against the stubborn flame on the officer’s trousers. She thought about how the firecracker was supposed to be used on the Fourth of July, how

everything had gone to Hell and back, and how none of this was supposed to have happened.

Her mind swirled with a thousand numb thoughts, and her body moved of its own accord. She stepped out from the mass of demolished cars and chucked the firecracker into the gasoline.

It was short-fused, to Jan's relief, and Owen barely had time to register what was going on. He looked at her, his remaining eye illuminated by the light of the burning firecracker. For a split second, Jan saw the raw and exceedingly human fear in his face.

"Jinx," she said, imitating Owen's jeering tone.

The firecracker went off.

A loud pop was followed by a gasp—Owen's gasp—and the gasoline caught fire.

A salvo of explosions ripped through the air, and a violent shockwave sent Jan flying back with the rubble.

The very spot Owen was standing immediately erupted into angry flames that roared and jutted outward, encasing everything—including the Blue Bomb—in searing feathers.

Jan hit the pavement on her back and shielded her face from the scattered debris. The plumed flames died down as quickly as they had sprung to life, leaving behind crackling remnants that sputtered in satisfaction.

Owen's body lay in a motionless ball by what once used to be the Blue Bomb's trunk. The flames ravaged on, devouring his arms and legs.

Jan did not need to watch the rest. She knew he was gone.

She rested her head on the pavement, looking up at the clear sky and its glittering stars as her world closed in on her.

And for a brief moment, she felt at peace.

Chapter 35
PINK STARS

JAN AWOKE TO THE BEEPING OF A MONITOR AND the overpowering smell of antiseptics. She blinked in the incoming sunlight, which filtered through a window at the side of the room. The rays dispersed through the blinds and projected lines of white onto the tile. Those were the first things she saw.

Then, she looked down at her left arm, which no longer hurt as badly and had been wrapped in a cast the color of honeydew, dotted with lopsided pink stars that had been drawn on with a marker. As she shifted her position, the cheap mattress on the hospital bed crinkled. Warmth washed over her as she glanced toward the corner of the room.

Shelley lay sleeping, curled up in a leather chair. She wore a little cross-body purse, which she clutched tightly in her hands and held close to her body.

"Shelley," Jan whispered.

Shelley stirred, but did not wake up.

"Shelley," she said again, this time a little louder.

Shelley shifted and sat up slowly, her expression brightening upon seeing Jan awake.

"Jinx!" she said, immediately standing up and rushing over to Jan's side. Her purse thwacked against her leg. "How are you feeling? Are you okay?"

Jan nodded slowly, but she wasn't so sure.

"You were out for like thirteen hours," Shelley said, sitting by Jan's feet. "I guess you needed the sleep. My dad had to go to the station for a bit because of..." she cut herself off and shook her head. "He said he'd bring us bagels once he's finished. Do you like your cast? I told them you liked green, and I drew those stars on with a marker I stole from the front desk." Realizing she was rambling, she clamped her lips shut and glanced at Jan for her reaction.

Jan lowered her eyes to her cast. If anyone paid attention to the little details that made her feel better, it was Shelley. Though she tried to hold them back, hot tears rolled down her cheeks.

"I love it," she said. It was all she could manage.

Shelley's face shriveled as she began to cry, and the two embraced, finding what little comfort they could in each other's presence.

When they managed to compose themselves, Jan wiped her tears away with her free hand and dared to ask, "What happened?"

Shelley fiddled nervously with the corner of the mattress before speaking.

"Gabriel found Mr. Parri," she said in less than a whisper. "He got my dad and me out as well. My dad was going to go in after you, but Gabriel lied and said that you'd run out the back."

"And he believed that?"

Shelley shrugged. "I dunno. I didn't. But I knew you must've talked to Gabriel and..." her voice trailed off, but she quickly regained it. "I trusted you. So I told my dad if he went in to find you, I'd go too. That freaked him out. Gabriel didn't need to do much more convincing to get him out of the parking lot. My dad pulled me out of there real quick. Gabriel got his dad out too." She tried to blink back tears, but to no avail. "I really didn't know what was going to happen to you," she said, wiping her face. "But my dad came back with some officers and...he found you. I...God, I was so relieved you were alive. You have no idea."

Jan felt as though a stone was lodged in her throat. She sat very still for a few minutes. Shelley didn't make a sound.

"I killed him, Shell," Jan finally whispered.

Shelley looked up at her, her face awash with apathy. "Good."

Jan shook her head. "I threw a firecracker into gasoline I'd siphoned out of the Blue Bomb," she said as she began to cry once again, "and it went off." She clutched her head with her hand. "I...I murdered him. I murdered Owen."

Shelley pulled Jan's arm away from her face. "Nobody knows

that," she said. "The police are saying Owen killed himself. They found you close to where your car used to be parked, absolutely out of it. Everyone thinks you were just in the wrong place at the wrong time, like so many others were."

"But I wasn't," Jan said between heaving sobs. "And I can't explain that to them."

"Then don't. Nobody's going to believe what happened anyway. Everyone's already making up stories about how he did what he did. I don't think anyone wants to acknowledge the truth."

Jan uttered a shaky breath. "I don't know if I'll ever be able to forget this."

"It will be difficult," Shelley replied, "but I'll be there to help you."

More silence ensued.

"Shelley?" Jan whispered once she had steadied her voice.

"Yeah?"

"How many people died?" She hated herself for asking, but felt she needed to.

Shelley pushed her tongue against her cheek and looked down at her shoes. "I'm not sure. Last I heard, seventeen, not including Owen." After a pause, she added, "More people would've died if you hadn't stopped him."

Jan wallowed in her choice of words. *Stopped,* not *killed.* After a moment's thought, she decided that perhaps killing him had been the only way to stop him. She looked up at Shelley, her lips pursed, barely holding herself together.

"Less would've died if I'd trusted Aiden," she said.

"Well, it was pretty cool how you managed to hide the locket in your jacket until you thought you knew who we could trust," Shelley said gently. "Even I didn't expect that."

Jan didn't respond. She didn't think it was cool at all—not since she had given it to the wrong person.

Shelley put her purse on the bed and unzipped it slowly.

"Speaking of the locket," she said, "look."

With tender hands, Shelley pulled the mermaid box out of her purse. The sea witch's emerald eyes glinted in the sunlight just as Owen's had at the Fun Zone.

"I hid it during all the chaos so I could smuggle it back to you." She grinned weakly, and a lone tear trickled down her cheek. "I guess Owen's story wasn't all a lie."

She opened the box, and Jan craned her neck to look inside. Coiled neatly in the center of the box was the locket, no longer in two parts, but together as a whole—just the way they had found it that day at the cove. Jan's heart skipped a beat and the hairs on the back of her neck stood up.

"I guess so," she whispered.

"That means..."

Shelley didn't have to say it. Owen might have been blown to bits, but the power once inside of him hadn't been destroyed. It had returned to the locket, piecing itself back together just like Owen's great-grandfather had said, waiting for the next person to come along and claim it.

"So what now?" Jan asked.

Shelley put the box back into her purse, then bit her lip. "We try to move on, I guess."

Half an hour passed—maybe more—while Shelley and Jan sat quietly, facing the window at the side of the room, lost in thoughts of their own. A sudden quiet knock made Shelley jump.

"Bagels?" she said hopefully, clearly yearning for an end to the agonizing silence.

Both girls turned to face the door, only to find that the person standing outside the hospital bedroom wasn't Mr. Waldbauer at all.

Chapter 36

A MOTHER'S LOVE

THE WOMAN STANDING ON THE THRESHOLD WAS well-dressed with remarkably refined posture. She was tall and thin, with hair the color of salt and pepper and exaggerated, drawn-on eyebrows. When Jan looked into her eyes, she realized who it was.

Like her sons, Mrs. Aimsworth had deep brown eyes that held a sort of mystery to them. With age, they had turned watery and fatigued, but they still retained a little glint of determination that reminded Jan of Aiden.

"Mind if I come in?" the woman asked softly. Her voice shook.

"Are you allowed to?" Shelley asked, not bothering to mind her tone.

Jan shifted her feet, rustling the starchy hospital sheets—a silent command for Shelley to back down.

"You can come in," she said meekly.

"Thank you." Mrs. Aimsworth gently stepped into the room, her high heels clicking on the linoleum.

Shelley and Jan exchanged nervous glances.

"I have always hated the smell of hospitals," Mrs. Aimsworth said gently. "Something about the mixture of contagion and medicine is enough to make anyone sick."

Shelley didn't react, but Jan managed a smile.

"May I sit?" asked Mrs. Aimsworth. Jan nodded as Mrs. Aimsworth pulled the leather chair in the corner of the room closer to the bed.

"You must be Jan Jenkins," she said. "And you must be Michelle Waldbauer."

Jan nodded. Shelley, on the other hand, didn't react; she was determined to maintain her icy demeanor.

"I'm not quite sure where to start," Mrs. Aimsworth said. Her sad smile waned as the grief in her eyes grew stronger.

Sitting there before them, all the prestige Jan had once associated with the matriarch of the Aimsworth family faded away. She was no longer the wealthy, mysterious woman everyone marveled at—she was a mother who had lost both of her sons only hours ago. No matter how terrible one of them may have been, Jan could not imagine the sorrow.

And they're both dead because of me. The thought evoked an ache so deep in her chest that Jan had to hold back a wince.

"I am so sorry about what you girls had to go through," Mrs.

Aimsworth said. "There are, quite frankly, no words to express how truly sorry I am."

"How do you know what we went through?" Shelley asked, her eyes narrowed and cold.

"Aiden left me a message on the answering machine last night." Her voice broke when she said his name, but she quickly regained composure. "He didn't say much, but he told me what I needed to know."

Jan's heart sank. Aiden must have known—or at least had a very strong feeling—that he was not going to make it. And he had been right, all because of her gullibility.

Jan wished she could sink into the bed and disappear.

"There aren't any words to set a situation like this right," Mrs. Aimsworth continued. "Nobody out there will ever believe—or even entertain the thought—that this had to do with something otherworldly and outside the bounds of logic." She sighed softly and leaned back into the chair, staring off to the side of the room. "But I suppose all three of us are burdened with the truth of the matter."

"I thought you didn't believe in the power," Jan said. She almost added something about how that was what Owen had told her, but quickly decided against it.

"I didn't want to," Mrs. Aimsworth said, "but that doesn't mean I didn't." She shifted uncomfortably. Her movements were slow and pained. "I've made a lot of mistakes," she continued, "and

I won't deny that I played a role in everything that happened. Had I acted sooner, my boys might still be around, along with all of those innocent people."

A tear rolled down her cheek. No matter how hard she tried, she could not hold in her sorrow.

"I miss them both," she said, "and I mourn them just the same. Even Owen, although you might not believe it. He was a deranged and troubled man, and I know that does not justify his actions. Still, I mourn him just as much as I mourn his brother. I suppose it's got something to do with a mother's love." She wiped the tears running down her face with a shaking hand. "I'm sorry. I came to apologize to you both, and here I am, wallowing in my own pity."

"It's okay," Shelley said, more gently now.

Mrs. Aimsworth steadied herself and looked down at her feet.

"Did you...did you happen to see how he died?" she asked. "Nobody seems to know for certain and I...I just can't bear not knowing."

She didn't have to specify who she was talking about. She must have already seen Owen's burnt body, but she had no idea it was Jan's doing.

Shelley glanced at her, but Jan only shook her head. She couldn't. Not now. Perhaps not ever.

Mrs. Aimsworth looked back up, but her gaze rested far beyond the girls.

"Again, I'm sorry," she said, her voice faltering. "That's a terrible thing to ask. I shouldn't be bringing this all up after what you've gone through. I really am sorry."

"It isn't your fault, Mrs. Aimsworth," Jan said.

Mrs. Aimsworth smiled, and Jan could tell that she did not agree. She stood up and said in a quiet, broken voice, "I only have one more question before I leave."

Shelley and Jan stiffened.

"Did you girls ever see what happened to the box and the necklace?"

Jan could see Shelley's grip tighten on her purse.

"No, Mrs. Aimsworth," Jan said quickly. "It must've gotten lost in all the chaos."

Mrs. Aimsworth didn't respond. She only looked at the girls and smiled softly.

Before anyone could say anything else, Mr. Waldbauer strode into the room in his usual lofty way, two brown bags in his hand. The smell of toasted bagels wafted into the room. As hungry as Jan was, it didn't make her feel any better.

Mr. Waldbauer stopped in his tracks. "Mrs. Aimsworth," he said. It was an odd and discomforting sight to see Mr. Waldbauer caught off guard, but Jan supposed if she were ever to experience the rare, it would be now.

"Captain Waldbauer," Mrs. Aimsworth greeted gently. "My apologies for barging in without notice. These girls are simply wonderful, and they are so courageous. I greatly admire them."

Mr. Waldbauer's skeptical expression softened. "I do as well," he said, setting the paper bag down by Jan's feet. Shelley reached for it eagerly. "I'm incredibly sorry for your loss," he continued. He was really searching for words. "Aiden was a hardworking young man who truly made a difference in our department."

Mrs. Aimsworth nodded, teary-eyed. "Well," she said, "it's probably best if I get going now. I just wanted to meet these girls and apologize after everything they've gone through."

Mr. Waldbauer responded with a tight-lipped smile. Shelley brought the bag of bagels over to a side table, and while she and Mr. Waldbauer busied themselves with the food, Mrs. Aimsworth leaned toward Jan, taking her hand warmly. It took Jan by surprise, but she closed her hand around Mrs. Aimsworth's.

"Hide it," Mrs. Aimsworth whispered. "As best you can."

For a moment, Jan only stared at her. Then, as subtly as possible, she nodded. Mrs. Aimsworth smiled sadly, then turned on her heel and clicked out of the room.

Jan sat motionless, blinking back her shock. It was only when Mr. Waldbauer handed her a bagel that she shook the confusion away.

"Your parents are flying back from Scotland," he said gently. "I told them what happened and that you're safe. They should be back here late tonight."

Jan and Shelley looked at each other, their lips clamped.

Whatever Mr. Waldbauer had told her parents wasn't the truth, but Jan didn't have the energy to question him.

The bagel felt heavy in Jan's hands, but she forced herself to take a bite. She wasn't sure they would ever be able to explain what had happened to anyone. How could they? Even if Mrs. Aimsworth decided to make the truth public, which Jan knew would never happen, she doubted anyone would believe it.

The entire ordeal felt like a far-off nightmare, one that played on repeat in Jan's head. Dark eyes glinting with emerald blinked back at her when she closed her eyes, and it was with resignation that she decided not to fight it.

Chapter 37
LITTLE TREASURE

PEOPLE OFTEN HAVE A HARD TIME ACCEPTING what they fail to understand. This, above all, was what Jan realized in the days following the fatal attack at the Fun Zone and the deaths of the Aimsworth brothers. The police issued a statement about how Owen had come into possession of explosives and targeted the Fun Zone, only to commit suicide hours later. The newspaper printed the names of those who died, with only a brief statement about Owen and his unstable past. A mass funeral was held for Aiden—the Chief of Police, murdered by his own brother—and people issued prayers here and there, lighting candles for those who had lost their lives. Nobody dared to question what had truly happened.

Perhaps they knew, somewhere deep down, that the youngest Aimsworth son hadn't used bombs or guns or some unknown type of explosive. Perhaps they forced themselves to believe that nothing out of the ordinary had been involved, just as Mrs. Aimsworth had done for all those years.

It was sickening to bear the weight of a reality that no one else was aware of. Jan wished she could scream the truth out to the world, but she and Shelley kept quiet. Soon the days rolled into weeks, and the weeks into months, and people tried to forget.

Though she decided to move back home for the rest of the summer, the churning guilt in Jan's stomach didn't go away. Her parents helped where they could, but the despondency in their eyes was impossible to ignore. How could they help when they knew so little—when the truth was beyond them?

While some days were easier than others, nights were all the same. When the world was dark, those amber-emerald eyes filled the void, greeting Jan like an old friend—reminding her that they were part of her, and that they would be for years to come.

As June turned to July, and then into August, nothing much changed. Jan and Shelley tried to return to the Fun Zone, which spent its days under construction to repair the damage. While Shelley seemed fine with returning, when Jan saw the "CLOSED" sign on Ms. Johnson's gift shop, blood pounded in her ears, and she began to sob so hard that Shelley took her back home.

The time they managed to spend together was the only solace Jan could find in the months that followed. They spent their days visiting the beach and watching movies—the only things Jan could bring herself to do. Shelley didn't mind; in fact, she seemed quite relieved that they were spending a quiet summer.

It was late August when Jan and Shelley finally decided to get rid of the box and its contents, which had spent the summer collecting dust in Shelley's closet. Though they racked their brains about what to do with it, the abilities of the box and the locket left them with only one option.

The day they reached their consensus, the girls drove the Jenkins' old Nova down to the docks. Jan desperately missed the musty smell of the Blue Bomb, how it wheezed and stalled stubbornly, and how it backfired at the most inconvenient times. During some sleepless nights, she would quell her mind by remembering the uneven purrs it made or how the tires screeched around every turn. And when those memories did not dull the pain, she would remember the way it saved her.

~

The ocean sparkled cheerfully that morning, lapping against the wharf and the boats lined alongside it. Mr. Brown sat in his chair, as he always did, his head lowered and his eyes closed. When he heard the girls approaching, he looked up and smiled.

"Beautiful day for a sail," he said in greeting.

"If you don't mind us going out," Shelley said. "I promise we won't destroy your boat this time."

Mr. Brown shook his head. "Let bygones be bygones," he

chuckled heartily.

Shelley giggled and handed him the cash as he led them to a quaint little boat painted in green and blue.

"How are you girls doin'?" he asked as he helped them onto the boat. "Okay, I hope? I know it's been a rough coupla' months."

"We're doing okay, Mr. Brown," Jan said as she took his hand.

"Glad to hear it. If you ever need some ocean time, feel free to come by. It really does wonders when you need to clear your mind."

"We'll take you up on that," Shelley said, the corners of her lips stretching into a smile.

Mr. Brown nodded. "You girls have fun, m'kay? Stay out as long as you like, no extra fee."

"Really?" Shelley asked. When Mr. Brown nodded, she smiled and took Jan's hand in her own, giving it a reassuring squeeze. "Thank you, Mr. Brown. That means a lot."

"Lord knows our world needs a little extra kindness," Mr. Brown said. "If I'm not here when you return, it's 'cause I'm off finding my treasure."

Jan raised an eyebrow and glanced at Shelley.

Mr. Brown laughed and rested his hands on his hips. "Schätzli," he said. "Means *Little Treasure*. He wanders off every night and has to be discovered in the morning."

"That's a good kind of treasure," Jan said through a grin.

"Sure is," Mr. Brown replied, beaming. "Now go on, you two.

The ocean's waiting."

He gave the boat a push, and within minutes, the girls were out on the glittering water. They sailed silently until the world became completely blue and the wharf was no longer in sight. It was quiet this far away from land, but it was a quiet Jan enjoyed. The only sounds came from the gentle buck of the boat and the little swells of water.

Shelley settled down next to Jan once they reached a calm stretch.

"We're pretty far out," she said, "and the water is deep. I think this is a good place."

Jan nodded as Shelley unzipped her purse. She pulled out the mermaid box, opening it to peer at the locket one last time. It lay amongst little rocks they had placed inside to weigh it down, just as Owen and Nolan had done when they dropped it in the cove that fateful morning. Jan prayed that this spot, however, would ensure that both the box and its contents would never be found again.

"This little thing sure caused a whole lot of trouble," Shelley whispered. "Who'd have thought?"

Jan studied the silver mermaid on the lid, watching the emerald eyes closely.

"After all of this crap, the thought of finally asking Gabriel out doesn't seem scary at all," Shelley said wryly.

Jan laughed. "I think you're definitely brave enough."

Shelley smiled, but her face quickly turned grim. "My dad's

putting me in therapy," she said, shaking her head. "He told me a week ago, and he totally refuses to argue with me about it. I'm pretty sure he's convinced himself that the magic we were raving about at the Fun Zone was our way of trying to suppress what was really going on, and honestly, I'm just not going to argue with him about it." She smiled again, this time sadly. "I think he's worried that watching people die is going to screw me up in the long run. I don't blame him." Then, in only a whisper, she added, "You know the real screwed up part? I don't even really remember it. I think my brain tried to block everything out." She leaned against the side of the boat. "How've your parents been?" she asked. "I know you said your mom was stressed lately."

Jan shrugged. "She's okay. Confused, I guess. They wanted to send me to therapy too, but I turned them down. I'm not ready yet. I mean, God, Shell, what would I tell a therapist? I would be lying my way out of every conversation."

"Do you think you're ever going to tell your parents?"

Jan pressed her fingers against her lips and exhaled. "About which part?"

"About..." Shelley lowered her voice. "About the firecrackers. About how you had to defend yourself against Owen."

She didn't say the word, but Jan knew what she meant.

"I don't know," Jan said. "It gets painful to keep in sometimes, but..." she bit down on her lip. "But I think the reactions I'd get would be worse."

"You wouldn't get in trouble, if that's what you mean," Shelley said. "And you wouldn't go to jail. It's called justifiable homicide." When Jan didn't respond, Shelley reached out and squeezed her shoulder. "He killed seventeen people and he was going to kill you. Can you imagine how many lives you saved?"

"If it weren't for me being so gullible, those seventeen people wouldn't have died at all...Aiden and Ms. Johnson would still be here." She sniffled to curb the burning in her nose. "I was such an idiot, and it got people killed."

"Hey," Shelley said gently. "We've had this conversation a thousand times. I believed Owen too, but I don't hear you calling me an idiot. You're being too hard on yourself...none of this was your fault. There's no way you could've known."

"I *should* have known. I should've realized how stupid it was to blindly trust someone I just met."

"Owen was creepy good at manipulating people. He even got Nolan to think he was on his side. How in the world were you supposed to have realized? That's not fair to expect of yourself, Jinx. You know that."

Jan shook her head and bit her quivering lip.

"If you never forgive yourself, you're not going to be able to move on," Shelley said. A sad smile spread across her face and she put her hand on Jan's arm. "We're going to get through this. One day at a time."

Even though Jan knew Shelley was acting more confident

than she felt, the attempt made her smile.

Shelley snapped the lid of the mermaid box closed and waved it in front of her.

"The first step is getting rid of this nightmare," she said firmly.

The girls pulled themselves to a stand and looked down at the boundless waters before them. Jan had absolutely no idea how far down it went. Perhaps hundreds, maybe thousands of feet.

"How are you feeling, Jinx?" Shelley asked.

"A little scared."

"Me too." Shelley sucked in the salty air through her nostrils. "Want to do the honors?" she asked as she held the box out to Jan, who took it tightly in her hands.

"I'd love to."

She held it out above the water, taking one last look at the silver box and envisioning the little locket inside, coiled around the rocks.

Jan thought about all the trouble it had caused and how many people it had hurt. Whether the legend itself was real or not, the power that resided within the necklace definitely was.

She thought about Aiden and Ms. Johnson and that little girl under the Ferris wheel and all the innocent lives that had been lost. When she glanced back at Shelley, she knew it was the right thing to do.

"You better hide this well," she said to the ocean. The plinking of the waves responded gently as Jan let go.

The box hit the water with a resounding splash. For a moment, it floated, lapping up and down with the waves in metronomic swells. Then, slowly, it began to descend as the sea engulfed it, claiming it once again.

Jan and Shelley rested against each other, linking hands as they watched the box disappear. The emerald eyes of the sea witch gleamed up at them as they faded into blue.

AUTHOR'S NOTE

My grandmother, Patricia M. Kaspar, was born on August 2, 1932, in Santa Monica, California. She spent her childhood and teenage years growing up close to the beaches and boardwalks with her older sister, mother, and father. Much like her father, Earl, who she described as both her "favorite poet" and "The Stalwart Marine," Patricia always had a passion for writing. I imagine that, in some way, her love for and talent with words brought her closer to her father. In a short memoir about Earl, she wrote:

In retirement at his ranch, Earl can be found amid his notebooks, papers, and typewriter, when he is not out working his land. His deep concentration and his inner quiet are reflected in the contentment on his face. The lines that form across his forehead as he raises his eyebrows to receive a new idea have never been marred by frown lines or distorted by worry.

There is a certain joy in writing that I know my grandmother possessed. However, I didn't realize the extent to which she loved writing until she passed away in November 2012. When I was a kid, she would always edit my short stories or mini-novels, but I never got the chance to read anything she wrote. But later that winter, when my family was sorting through her belongings, I came across a file cabinet with all sorts of poems, short stories, letters, and novels—all written by her. As for *Jinx*, I'm not sure exactly when it was started. My best guess would be sometime during the 1970s or 80s. I read the original short draft of *Jinx* in 2016 during my first year of college and decided to use it to write an entirely new story. Taking characters like Jan, Shelley, and Mr. Waldbauer, I sculpted a new plot so as to fully merge the world my grandmother had started with a world of my own. Throughout the process, Owen, Aiden, Nolan, Gabriel, and Tanya (as well as the entirety of the police department) came into being, along with the sea witch's curse. From there, the story majorly changed and unfolded, but bits of my grandmother's ideas remained.

At the end of the day, this book was not a solo effort. If my grandmother had not started *Jinx* decades ago (and kept it around), I would not have been able to write a new novel based on what she began. If she had not been so encouraging all those times I placed simple, two-page stories in front of her to edit, I would not love writing the way I do now.

Though there were many people who made this book possible (including my family, friends, editors, and illustrator), it would not exist at all if it weren't for my grandmother. And for that, I am forever thankful.

Much like her father, Patricia had a way of writing quietly while still inspiring everyone around her. She rarely spoke about her writing, despite the fact that it was such a big part of her life.

I am told, however, that she might have mentioned owning (or knowing someone who owned) a "Blue Bomb."